The Prophecy of Sky

James Todd Cochrane

Special thanks to all my family and friends for their help and support. Thanks to all my fans. You inspire me to keep writing.

Published January 11, 2015

www.darkmoonpublishing.com

Library of Congress Control Number: 2015900834
ISBN 978-0-9915234-3-6

Edited by Janet Michelson
Cover by Kalen O'Donnell
Illustrations by Beth Peluso

Prologue

"I gave you very specific orders to protect my *palace*!" Gree shouted at the top of his lungs, turning his normally green skin almost black. His heavy fat body hovered over a blond woman dressed in black garb, bowing before him on the floor. "And now, I've found there have been intruders in my kingdom. Within these walls. How is this happening?" His voice echoed off the stone walls of the high chamber, vibrating the massive crystal chandelier hanging over his throne.

"Magic," the woman stated, her face still on the ground. "Powerful magic. Unlike anything I have ever sensed before." She chanced a glance at Gree to see he was visibly shaken by this bit of information. "They must be after something."

Gree paced around the circular chamber, muttering to himself. "I found it. It's mine. How did they find out? How did they find…" He climbed the steps to his throne and plopped himself down. A scowl spread across his fat round wrinkled face.

"Do you know what they are after, Master?" the woman rose slightly, revealing a beautiful pale white face with dark red lips and blue eyes that sparkled. Even with her striking features, her face wore a slight expression of distain for Gree.

"Perhaps, but it isn't something you need to concern yourself about, Slave One. You need to stop these intruders from entering my palace," Gree ordered.

"It isn't my…" Her body started trembling as an uncontrollable fear crept over her.

"No," Gree barked. "They are not after your dar. You need not fear. You will be mine…*forever*." A wicked fire burned in his circular eyes.

"Somehow that doesn't make me feel better," she mumbled under her breath.

"What was that?" Gree shot her an angry look.

"Nothing. May I at least see it… please? It has been so long," she pleaded, as an uncontrollable urge crawled up the back of her spine. She couldn't remember ever wanting something so much in her entire life. Her heart rate increased and she took a few tentative steps forward. Standing below the raised platform, she barely reached to Gree's knees.

"You bring me these intruders and I will let you see it again, Slave One," Gree commanded.

The woman's heart dropped, followed by a sinking sensation, and she stepped back and lowered her head. "Will you at least tell me what they are after? It may aid me in thwarting the thieves."

"You need only know it is kept within the vault and they will try to steal it." Gree leaned back and glanced at a door to the right of his throne.

"What if I'm not powerful enough to protect it? The creature or creatures are very strong," Slave One commented.

"Indeed, they are powerful. They are obviously not from this world, slave," Gree snarled.

"Not from this world?" The slave took another step back. She glanced toward the ceiling as if doing so would help her see beyond heavens. "I've always wondered."

"Wondered about what?"

"If there was life in other parts of the universe," the slave answered.

"You may yet find out. I may need answers," Gree said.

"You know…how to travel to other worlds?" The slave's face shone with curiosity.

"No, but you do. I just haven't allowed you to do it yet." Gree rested on his elbows with his hand clasped in front of him, eyeing her. "You are unaware of your full potential. I will show you in time. I will need your powers to achieve my place in history. For now, stop wondering and do as you're told," Gree barked, his voice growing in strength once more. "I don't want any more intruders. Do you understand me?"

"Yes." The slave bowed low and turned to leave.

Gree clapped his hands and several servants of varying species rushed into the room, carrying trays of food and drink for Gree. They wore what looked like burlap sacks for clothing and had loose brown skin hanging from their thin frames.

The slave girl marched out of the chamber at a brisk pace. When she reached the hall beyond, she walked to a large window overlooking a lush green valley. *There is life elsewhere in the universe. A place we could have escaped to.*

"What did he want?" enquired a handsome pale man with short blond hair, standing only a few inches taller than she.

"Tighter security, Slave Two." She continued to stare out the window. "Did you know we have the power to travel to other worlds?"

"We what?" The man's eyebrows knitted together in confusion.

"Gree told me himself. You, I, and the others have the power to leave this place." She glanced up at the partly cloudy sky. "He said these intruders came from another world and I'm assuming they used magic to do so."

"If that's true, we could have escaped this fate." The man waved at the castle around them.

"I know." She frowned and patted the man on the shoulder. "We may never have fallen under the power of the dar."

"So what are we going to do?"

"Send out scouts. I don't know how these beings are coming and going. We need to catch them when they are unaware, to avoid a fight. If they are strong enough to get here, they must have a greater mastery of magic than we do," the slave girl stated.

The man swallowed nervously. "What are you going to do?"

"I want to find out what they are after," the slave girl responded.

"You know you can't disobey him. The dar won't let you," the man stated.

"I know, but he told me to watch his vault. If there have been intruders, I'm sure he will want to check on his possessions." The slave girl smiled a dazzling expression.

"Don't let him catch you spying. Otherwise, he may get more specific in his orders and make our world smaller than it already is."

"Send out the scouts," she ordered.

She waited for the man to exit the door at the end of the hall. "This looks like a job for my little snitch," she muttered to herself as the formation of a plan began to work in the corners of her mind.

Slave One went to the kitchen and grabbed a loaf of bread then headed out onto the grounds. It took a half-hour hike to reach her destination. She sent out a wave of magic to test the area and verify that she and her target were the only ones in the area. Entering a dense forest on the border of the master's kingdom, she walked until she could no longer see the valley behind her.

"I knew it was you. I felt your magic." A small young blond girl with pale skin emerged from behind a tree.

The slave girl squatted to be eye level with the girl and held out the bread. "I have a job for you, youngling."

The girl stepped forward and accepted the bread, then began devouring it. "What do you need me to do?" Her voice was muffled by the mouthful of food.

"I want you to follow someone for me." The slave girl rose to her feet. "And you can't be seen."

The girl twisted her face up into a that-doesn't-sound-too-exciting look. "Is that all? That's easy."

"It's not and it will be very dangerous. I wouldn't even ask, but it could help you to avoid my fate and the fate of our people. But…if you are discovered, I may be ordered to kill you." A flood of guilt rushed through the slave girl's body at what she was asking of this youngling, a girl whose life was just beginning. *I can't do this to her. I can't ask her to do this.*

"Now, that sounds more fun." The youngling's eyes shone with excitement.

"I…" the slave girl stepped back. The horrible image of her slaughtering the youngling flashed through her mind, causing her to feel sick. "I shouldn't have asked. I was greedy. Forget about it." She hung her head and turned to leave.

"Wait?" the youngling shouted.

"I can't ask you this favor," the slave girl said, not looking at the young girl.

"If it will really help us, I accept the possible outcomes," the youngling stated.

"Even if the outcome is *death*?"

"Is a lifetime of slavery really living?"

"No," the slave girl muttered so quietly the young girl didn't hear her. "What?"

"You have to promise me. If you are discovered you will run and never come back. You will never make friends or set up regular patterns," the slave girl stated.

"I promise. Now, who do you want me to follow?"

"My master. I want you to tail him wherever he goes and remember everything he does. You must remember what he looks at or holds, every possible detail," the slave girl stated.

"I can do that. When would you like me to start?" The youngling licked her lips with excitement.

"Immediately. Now comes the hard part. You will need to do it without me or anyone else knowing about it. I have been ordered to stop any intruders from entering his kingdom. You fall under that category. I *cannot* know you are there or I will be forced to catch you. Do you understand?" the slave girl questioned.

"You're right. It sounds too risky. I don't think I want to take that challenge," the young girl said and frowned.

"Smart choice." The slave girl marched back to the castle.

A couple hours later the slave girl bowed before her master. "As part of the new security measures, I am going to put a spell around your vault that will alert me whenever anyone enters."

"And why are you telling me this? I gave you permission to protect my property."

"This spell won't distinguish between you or an intruder. Do you want me to enter into your vault when it is you who are inside it?" the slave girl asked.

"You know you aren't allowed in my vault when I *am* in there."

"I know, sir. But, if I can put a spell on the vault I can protect it more effectively."

"How easy is it to remove this magic when I want to enter?" Gree seemed to be mulling over the option.

"Just as quickly as you can snap your fingers." The slave girl performed the action.

"Leave me. I will call for you when I am ready for this extra measure."

The slave girl sat in her favorite window in a tower overlooking the entire valley. The sun moved closer to sunset. Although dark clouds threatened to hide its descent, it remained visible through a large gap in the storm. Her mind wandered with thoughts of freedom and exploring the universe. *How do I travel to other worlds? Not while you're a slave you won't.*

"Hey, we have visitors and I don't think they are from this planet." The slave boy from earlier snapped her out of her thoughts as he appeared behind her.

"I didn't sense anything." She hopped out of the raised window.

"They're not in our territory. Or at least not yet. And I don't think they used magic like we've ever encountered," the slave boy reported and spun around to lead the way.

"What do you mean?" She found herself almost running to keep up with the taller man's gait.

"I don't know how to explain it. They just dropped out of nowhere. Or at least a few of them did. I spotted two of them on our border and then three more appeared. Like I said, they aren't from here and they appear to be different life forms."

"Really?"

"You'll know what I mean when you see them."

They proceeded out of the palace and turned towards the setting sun. Slave Two led her down the hill and through an orchard toward a hill at the edge of their master's kingdom. They climbed to the top of the hill where more slaves lay in the tall grass, observing the valley beyond. The slave girl and boy lowered themselves to lying positions as they reached the others.

"So where did they first appear?" she asked, spotting the small group huddled in the shade of a tree, conversing about something.

"About twenty minutes ago, close to that small opening by the tree," said another slave girl, who was a little shorter and older.

Slave One peered down and noticed the differences Slave Two hinted at. Three of the strangers, males, appeared to be a taller darker version of her race. One had short brown hair, while another had wavy gray hair with a mustache, and the third kept his hood up, making it difficult to see his face. There was a woman, shorter than Sky, with golden tan skin, and the last resembled something she had never seen. She didn't know if it was male or female. It had grayish greenish skin with large round black eyes.

"What do you think they want?" the other slave girl asked. "Do you think it has to do with whatever's in the master's vault?"

Slave One shot Slave Two a dirty look.

"You didn't tell me not to tell anyone," Slave Two responded.

"They don't look like that big of a threat. Although the one with the hood looks like he knows how to handle himself," she stated.

"You didn't see them arrive. They have some serious magical talent to get here. Don't forget that," Slave Two responded.

"Maybe one of us should go down there and just ask them?" the other slave girl asked.

"Be my guest." Slave One motioned with her hand toward the visitors.

"All right then." The other slave girl sprang to her feet and bounded down the hill.

They all watched her march across the field towards the strangers. When she was within fifty yards she hailed them and waved her arm in the air.

Before they got a chance to watch the encounter, Slave One sat up with a bolt. "Oh no!"

The others around her rose up as well. "What?"

She shot a glance back at the castle. "My spell. Something just entered the master's vault. Come!" She sprinted back towards the castle with the others on her tail. Her speed created a wide gap between her and the other slaves. It was her special skills and magical talents that made her the master's #1.

Most slaves took years to reach her status, but the master chose her only a few months after her capture. It was an event that only caused her pain and regret. The master forced her to fight the old #1 to the death. In the end, she killed him at the master's command. All the others avoided her for several years, but in the end she managed to develop something close to what could be called friendships.

She arrived at the entrance to the throne room to an all-out battle raging inside. Gree cowered behind the side of the door, roaring in his deep guttural voice about something stealing his property. Several slaves from Slave One's race battled an unknown assailant just inside the vault. Fire, sparks, and rays of intense heat flashed through the room—exploding against walls, furniture, and slaves.

She noticed several of her people had fallen and lay motionless on the floor, their clothes and flesh bloodied and burned. The remaining resistance fought from positions of relative safety, the throne and other furniture.

Slave One became a blur, zipping from the door to join another slave behind the throne. The sight that met her eyes caused her to gasp. A creature unlike any other she had witnessed rummaged through her master's possessions, tossing things everywhere with one arm and sending out spells with the other. A tall muscular creature with a black skull-like head and red-rat eyes blocked and attacked as if he didn't face a serious threat out of the vault.

"Where is it, Gree," the stranger barked in a deep voice. "I know you found it in the ancient ruins. The dark ones left it behind and you recovered it."

"Send a volley so I can get closer," slave girl one ordered the slave crouching in front of her.

The slave behind the throne sent a powerful shockwave into the vault. Before the spell reached its target, the slave girl zipped to the wall beside the vault door. She barely ducked out of the way as the intruder deflected

the spell and returned it to the sender. The force cracked the throne free of its bindings and dropped it onto the slave, who let out a cry of pain.

She drew her sword strapped across her back and rushed the attacker. She managed to get only a few feet into the vault when an invisible vice-like force lifted her off the floor. It pressed her from all sides and held her suspended in the open doorway.

"You must be Gree's #1," the intruder mocked. "Not really all that dangerous are you?" He held out his hand and made a fist. The force squeezing the slave girl tightened like a coiling python.

She gasped and the force strengthened making it difficult for her to breathe. Her vision darkened and little lights popped in front of her face. Just when she thought she was about to die, she was free. She fell to the floor and strange flashes of light zipped over her head, forcing the dark creature to turn his attention towards the open doors.

She heard strange voices calling through the doors and a name. Hudich.

The thief roared with rage and swung his arms in a wide circle over his head, creating a tornado which pulled in all of her master's possessions. Things began to spin faster and faster in a rush of loud wind.

"Ahhhhh." The stranger's voice seemed to take delight, and while continuing to control the circling objects with one hand, he snatched an old scroll out of the funnel. Then with one final thrust, he threw his hands forward and everything flew out of the vault.

Slave One covered her head as the deadly speeding projectiles flew over her. She managed one last glimpse of the stranger standing in the center of the vault with an evil smile, before he vanished in a bright light.

She hurt and struggled to move. Everything seemed like she watched it from a great distance. The other intruders were there. Two of them, the woman and the one with the greenish skin and black eyes, examined her and gave her something she assumed would help her. *Why would they be here unless the master allowed it?*

As soon as they left, a warming calm crept over her and she felt a strong desire to sleep. It was as if there was nothing as important in the world as sleep. She struggled to keep her eyes open but gradually drifted off to sleep.

She awoke with a jolt.

Gree was shouting for her and he seemed angry. "#1!"

She winced as she sat up. She hurt everywhere but everything still worked. "That was one powerful creature," she muttered to herself.

She hurried to the restored throne room where two slaves held the youngling between them. Her blond hair was disheveled and there were cuts and bruises on her face. The sight hit the slave girl one with enough force to expel all the air from her lungs and almost doubling her over. Her heart dropped and more fear than she could ever remember feeling spread through her limbs, causing her to tremble and her pace to slow.

"They caught this youngling snooping around my thrown room. I ordered you to keep *all* intruders out. We have had more unwanted guest than necessary today. I will not tolerate this. I want this one made an example of."

"Has she stolen anything?" the slave girl asked, her voice cracking slightly with fear, hoping that was the case in order to plead for leniency.

"She denied taking anything at first but we were able to get it out of her. So, not only has she trespassed, but she thought she could take *my* property," Gree screamed, his green face growing darker.

"What's more, she claims to be operating under your orders," Slave Girl Two stated with a smile.

Slave One felt like she was back in the grip of the powerful intruder. Her world grew small and dark, while her insides contracted in an uncomfortable knot.

"Is that true?" Gree's sheer volume shook the chandelier above him.

Slave One's eyes dropped and she nodded slowly. She felt ill, her head spun with a dizzying nauseating sensation and beads of cold sweat formed along her brow.

"As your reward for this betrayal, you will retrieve what's been stolen from me and then you will kill her. You thought my rules were strict before. You haven't seen anything yet," Gree spat. "I gave you some freedoms, but no more."

Tears formed in Slave One's eyes and she drew a dagger from her belt. Her feet felt like they had sprouted roots as she struggled to take the steps towards her small friend. "What did you take?" Her voice shook.

A smile spread across the youngling's bruised face. "Your dar."

The statement rolled through the throne room like a giant hand had slapped everyone and they gasped.

"Impossible," Gree stammered, almost stumbling backwards before dashing into the vault. A single word issued loudly from the vault. "*No!*"

Slave One struck quickly. Spinning the dagger around she hammered the hilt downward onto the forehead of one of the youngling's captors and blasted the other with a spell that sent him flying. Then, blowing out the window with another spell, she snatched up the youngling and sprang out the window.

They finally rested when they were deep inside the forest. Slave One's heart raced with the thought of holding her dar or possessing it, so no one would have power over her ever again. *To go by my real name again instead of the insult Gree had forced me to accept.*

"Will they come after us?" the youngling questioned between mouthfuls of air, glancing back in the direction of the castle.

"Where's *my* dar?" The slave girl could think of nothing else. She had to have it. To hold it. Nothing in the universe mattered but her dar. It took all her restraint to not start frisking the youngling for it.

The youngling's expression changed to a look of suspicion and the color drained from her already pale face. "Do you need it that bad?" she stammered, taking a step away and glancing around.

"Why are you keeping it *from* me?" The slave girl stepped closer, blood starting to pound inside her ears, causing them to ring. "I *must* have it."

"I don't have it." The youngling shook her head nervously retreating a little more.

"WHAT? YOU SAID YOU TOOK IT?" The slave girl snatched her off the ground by the arms and rattled her back and forth.

"I did. I did," the youngling responded, with tears leaking from her eyes.

"Then where is it?" The slave girl growled with venom.

"I didn't want to be caught with it so I hid it in the pack of that man," she cried. "Please, you're hurting my arms."

It felt like being doused with ice water. The intense uncontrollable desire and rage dissipated as quickly as it had come on. Her fingers snapped away from the youngling almost as if she had received a nasty shock.

"I'm sorry. I'm so sorry." The slave girl stepped back, her own tears starting to flow. "I am grateful but..."

"Is that what it's like? Is it that uncontrollable?" The youngling's eyes grew wide with fear.

"Yes. It is all you can think of once it takes hold of you." The slave girl wiped her eyes and glanced at the darkening evening sky.

"But you're free now, aren't you? That man took it far away," the youngling questioned with curiosity.

"No!" The slave girl shook her head. "Even still I can feel my dar's pull. I belong to him now. In whose pack did you place it?"

"The older one with the graying hair. He seemed like such a nice life form. I figured it would be safe with him. How will you find him? He could be anywhere out there in the universe."

"Magic. My attachment to my dar is already pulling me. Somehow, I know where it is and how to get there."

"Do you have to go?"

The slave girl put her hands on the shorter girl's shoulders and bent so they were eye to eye. "I must and you need to go into hiding. Don't ever go back to the castle. If I can come back and help you, I will." She pulled the youngling into a tight hug. "I appreciate what you did for me. I only hope my situation has improved." She rose and in a flash of light disappeared.

The slave girl landed on shaking knees in front of a strange home. It resembled cottages from her world but was much larger. It was white and appeared to have three levels and an iron barred fence surrounded it. *That fence can't...* She started to ponder the weakness of the fence when she sensed an extremely powerful magic surrounding the premises. *How did I get in?*

She felt exhausted but didn't know how to proceed. She climbed the steps and took a seat on the strange bench hanging from some chains. The device swayed, giving a relaxing sensation when she plopped down into it.

She snapped to attention, feeling a gentle nudge which had awoken her. The seat started to sway again and her eyes grew wide as she noticed the older man with wavy gray hair, mustache, and slight beard was staring at her. She didn't know how long she had slept but she didn't feel rested. Her body was sluggish and sore, which she attributed to yesterday's battle.

"If you don't mind my asking, who are you?" he asked with a kindly smile.

"I belong to you." She sprang out of the bench and assumed a kneeling position with her head bowed.

"You what?" He chuckled putting a hand behind her upper arm, lifting her gently to her feet and setting her back on the bench, where he sat beside her.

"I belong to you, keeper of my dar." Her head remained bent slightly to indicate his superiority.

"Hold it for a second. What? Why do you think you belong to me? I don't understand."

"You are in possession of my dar. A youngling put it in your backpack in my world. I belong to whoever controls it. I belong to whoever owns it. I must do your bidding." Her eyes finally met his but there was something strange in the way he looked at her. There was not the usual greed she noticed in most master's eyes, but pity and kindness.

"I see." He rubbed his scruffy chin as if in thought. "I wondered what that was in my pack and where it came from." He smiled, patted her leg and rose to his feet. "Wait here."

Her heart beat faster inside her chest at the thought of at least seeing her dar again. Somehow she felt better about this new master. He didn't seem cruel or domineering. He actually seemed kind.

He returned with a small wooden box and sat next to her. "I don't think anyone anywhere should belong to another." He held out the box for her to take.

"Y—you're...giving it to...me?" Tears stung her eyes and her hands shook as she accepted the box. For the first time, something odd had happened. She no longer had the irresistible desire to see or hold it. Now that it was hers and in her hand, it had no power over her. She wept for joy.

"Freedom is a grand thing," the old man said, and patted her back.

She could never remember feeling so happy. "Thank you. Thank you." Tears continued to roll down her cheeks.

"You are most welcome, Ms.?"

"Ms.?" she questioned through sobs.

"Let me be more specific." He chuckled. "I am Joseph, Joseph Rigdon. And you are?" He raised his eyebrows.

"I am..."

"Your name?" He smiled.

"My name is Slave...Sk—Sky."

1

"Shh, *quiet* or they'll hear *you*," Masha whispered out of the shadows, motioning with her hand for her sister to stay put.

"I'm not afraid," Sky replied, lying on her stomach under some dense jungle foliage. She was almost an exact replica of her older sister, minus several inches in stature.

"It's not a question of being afraid. It's a matter of freedom and life," Masha pointed out, peering around a group of trees, trying to spot the Roowks behind the guttural voices floating in the air.

Through the thick leafy trees, flashes of gray bulky bodies with dark maroon garb appeared across a twenty-yard span. Screams from their victims echoed through the canopy, making birds take flight. The fear-inducing commotion wasn't as bad as the sudden silence that fell afterwards.

Sky's heart pounded in her chest and her mouth grew dry. She tried to wet her red lips but her tongue stuck in her mouth. The thudding of footsteps indicated the Roowks' approach.

"Is this all of 'em?" a rough voice questioned.

"Yeah, they're gettin' harder an' harder teh find," a different voice answered. "What wit mos' of 'em dyin' in the wars."

"But wit their help we'll win in the end," the first commented. "An' there is younglins out there hidin'. Not yet drawn by the skusnjave, so we have tah keep lookin'."

"Why ain' we breed 'em?" the second questioned.

"We tried. But we can' control them kids until they's old enough and they's still magical. If we left 'em with da parents, they'd help 'em. So, we put 'em in camps away from their folks," the first said.

"So, where this lot come from?"

"Some of dem parents kept 'em hidden and then turned 'em loose."

Sky listened to their conversation with mild interest. Her sister had told her the story before. Sky never knew her parents. They gave her to her older sister to raise when she was only one and one-half years old. Her sister was her senior by almost ten years and was quickly approaching the transformation. Then she wouldn't be safe from these raids but, for now it seemed, she could still hide and stay out of sight. They didn't know the exact age this took place but had seen other friends fall victim to skusnjave.

"Open the box lad, and let's catch us some more Dijinnies," the second said.

An overpowering curiosity rose inside Sky's chest, driving her to press the limits of her concealment. Using a soft whisper, she influenced the men to hear a noise in the distance, drawing their attention long enough for her to move. From her new position, she could see the Roowk out front holding a small wooden box with a lid held on by leather straps. He flipped open the lid and a dazzling light radiated from the contents. The jungle seemed to be alive with a spine-tingling power that affected everything in the area.

A gasp from Masha's hiding spot alerted the Roowks.

"Oh, I think we stuck a nerve," said the one holding the box, chuckling in delight. "Does someone wanna come an' touch the pretty object?"

Sky's attention jumped from the alluring item to the place where Masha waited.

"You don't have ta come out if you don wanna. Maybe you can jus' look at it from where you are," the Roowks voice tempted. "Jus' a peek." He rotated so as to show the contents of the box in all directions.

Don't look, Masha. Don't look! Sky imagined if she thought hard enough her sister could hear her. A cold sensation like sinking in ice water spread over Sky. A great fear ate away at the edge of her mind, squeezing her airways. She knew if Masha so much as glanced at whatever was in the box, she would become a slave like the rest of her race when they passed the age of skusnjave.

A stick cracked, and Sky's heart threw itself against her ribcage. She could hear herself screaming but no sound broke her lips. *Run, Masha! Run!*

"Tha's right, pretty. We won' hurt you. Just come to the shiny dar," the Roowk spoke. "You only need ta touch it."

Do something Sky, or your sister is going to be lost forever. She begged herself to move, to take action, but she was so scared. *Don't let her touch that thing. Move.* She struggled against the invisible bands holding her fast, choking her will. Tears filled her eyes and the world grew darker.

"Jus' a little farther, deary."

Through her limited line of sight, Sky spotted the thick vegetation moving beyond the legs of the Roowk. *You're going to lose her!* Panic rose up inside her mind, growing in power with each passing second, threatening to break out. "NO!" she screamed, springing to her feet. With all the power she could muster, she sent the box sailing into the jungle. "Run, Masha, run!"

"Why ya little brat." The Roowk backhanded her hard across the face.

Pain erupted on the side of Sky's face, and lights swam before her eyes as she fell backward into the tall forest grass. A trickle of blood rolled down her chin and she cupped her face in her hand. A hard boot slammed down on her midsection, pinning her to the ground. Sky gasped at the shock of the force.

"After her!" he ordered his companion. "Your friend is ours and there's nothen ya can do 'bout it. As you will be, in time." The Roowk spit on her and then released her with his foot. He kicked her hard in the knee, causing her to cry out, and then chased after his companion.

Tears spilled down her face as she struggled to get to her feet. Her whole body shook with the effort. She was in agony but fear propelled her forward. How could anyone treat her so harshly? *I'm only a little girl.* A flame flickered in the back of her mind. It fluttered a few times but then took hold. *And these are the people who will control my sister and maybe someday me!* The flame grew with her anger and drove out all her other thoughts.

She sent out her magic to locate her sister, a trick her sister had taught her so they could always find each other. The signal came back telling her to head to her left. She tried to run, but her knee almost buckled with the strain. A rush of pain, like being hit with a hot iron, spread through her leg every time her foot hit the ground.

Gritting her teeth, she forced herself to push through the injury. Normally she was very light on her feet, but her injured leg caused her to limp, which allowed the thick vegetation to snag and impede her progress. She pushed her way to the edge of a clearing where cattle-drawn wagons with cages, formed a long chain. The Roowks placed captured males and females from Sky's species into the small prisons.

She sent out her spell again and it located Masha. Three Roowks were escorting her across the clearing toward the wagon train. *How can I help her?* Her rage drove her forward. She blasted the Roowk out front with a spell that hammered him in the stomach. He doubled over and dropped to a knee.

She launched another, but to her complete shock, Masha blocked it. "Masha, what are you doing?" she cried.

A blast like a stone wall smacked into Sky, throwing her backward. She barely had time to register the tears streaming down Masha's face, when Masha's hands shot forward and a second spell hammered Sky down into the grass as if a giant stone had fallen out of the air and landed on her.

All the air escaped Sky's lungs with the blow, and the force continued to press down on her, holding her fast. The spell crushed her, until she couldn't draw a breath. Fear and panic overwhelmed her as she struggled to free herself to get the air she so desperately needed. Blackness crept around the edges of her vision and began to block her sight until everything disappeared into darkness.

###

Sky's eyes snapped open when she heard a strange animal call. She looked up at a star-filled sky, not knowing where she was. *I'm out at night!* That realization kicked her heart into another gear and fine-tuned her senses. *How did I get...* She tried to move, but her entire body protested with sharp stabbing sensations. All the pain triggered the memory of the day's horrible events, which played in front of her mind like a nightmare.

"Masha," she whispered, experiencing the loss again. She felt empty and cold and she started to shiver. "What am I going to do?" Her arm hurt when she used it to wipe the tears from her eyes.

A strange animal call caught her attention, momentarily snapping her out of her grief. *You shouldn't be out here after dark. You need to find cover.* She strained her ears in an attempt to hear anything above the noisy night insects filling the air with their array of chirps and buzzes.

She attempted to crouch to see above the tall grasses in which she lay, but her entire body screamed in objection. She hurt everywhere and moving forced her to gasp and wince with each shot of pain. She lay back down to catch her breath when the creaking of wagon wheels and thudding of hoofs on the road reached her ears. As the sound grew nearer, the pounding of her pulse in her ears increased as well.

"Keep an eye on him," a male voice called. "We're about to enter the forest. He could get lost in there very easily. In fact, why don't you put him in the wagon until we pass through it. There are dark things in there at night. I don't want him to attract any unwanted attention."

"Dek. Dek, come here boy." What sounded like a boy responded, moving closer to Sky's position. "Look, Dad, I think he smells something. Look at him go."

Panic and fear crawled over Sky once more as a rustling in the grass, mingled with a loud sniffing, seemed to be heading toward her.

"That he does," the man replied.

Using all her concentration, Sky used her magic to create a loud thump thirty yards away from her. The energy to cast the spell cost her wounded body as a searing sensation ignited almost every cell, and she groaned.

"What was that?" the boy questioned in a frightened tone. The sniffing, which had paused for a moment, resumed. "Dek, *come* here," the boy ordered with emphasis.

Before Sky could react, a pes emerged through the grass with his nose pressed to the ground. He let out an excited yelp and then began sniffing Sky up and down. When he reached her head, he licked her face. He inadvertently stepped on Sky's leg, and she cried out from the pain. The noise startled the pes, which bolted back through the grass.

"There's someone in the grass," the boy's voice whispered.

"Stay still," the man ordered.

Sky attempted to rise once more but the pain grew to an excruciating level. *I cannot flee!* she thought with despair, dropping back to the ground.

"It's a girl. I saw her. Just there." The boy pointed.

Soon a light appeared and grew brighter and brighter until a man and a boy hovered over her. The man carried a lantern, making it difficult for Sky to see anything but their shadows.

"I think she's hurt," the boy said.

"I believe you're right." The man set the lantern on the ground next to Sky and then knelt over her. "Can you understand me?" he asked.

"Yes," Sky replied, fighting back more tears. The man had a kind face with black hair and a neatly trimmed beard. The boy joined the man at her side. He had the same features as the man, and Sky assumed they were father and son.

"Is she a Dijinni?" the boy questioned in a disgusted tone.

"Yes," the man responded.

"Are we safe?" The boy's eyes grew wide and he leaned back. "I thought they were deadly. Shouldn't we leave her?" His voice full of disdain. "Or better yet…"

"Mika." Loov shot him a silencing look.

"We shouldn't help her. We should go. It's getting dark. This isn't right, she *will* bring a curse upon us," the boy said.

"No, she won't. You need to stop listening to your friends and certain trainers. Remember, what you send out comes back to you. Send out mercy and kindness and you will receive the same. Send out hate and brutality and you will receive destruction."

"But they are dangerous. They kill our people."

"They can be, but this one won't harm us at the moment," the man said. "Do you have a name?"

"Sky."

"I'm Loov and this is Mika. How bad is it?"

"I hurt everywhere." Her scrutiny continued to shift from the man to the boy. *What is a Dijinni? Why would they be afraid of me?*

"What happened to you? Someone got lazy in their work?" the boy asked, still keeping a little distance.

"A Roowk and… and…" Before she could continue, the tears began to flow.

"Our *enemy*." The boy glanced at his father.

"They must have been hunting for Dijinnis. She's not yet of age," he answered his son. "Tried to help someone did you?"

"Yes." Sky's breathing came in large labored gulps. "My…my…sister."

"I'm sorry." He frowned. "Let's see if we can get you out of here. I'm going to check for any broken bones. This may hurt. I will try to be gentle."

Before he could start, the pes returned and began licking Sky's face excitedly once more.

"Dek, no!" The boy struggled to pull the pes off her. "I thought he was supposed to hunt Dijinni, not lick them to death." He managed to get the animal under control and hold him several feet away.

Loov chuckled and then began carefully inspecting her arms and legs, softly squeezing and checking her joints. Sky winced and gritted her teeth the entire time, but when he tried to bend her leg the Roowk had kicked, she cried out.

"Your leg is broken. Mika, run to the wagon and get me a board and some rope and put Dek in the wagon," he ordered, and the boy pulled the pes out of sight. "And bring some water," he called.

"Helping her, a Dijinni. You better hope the village council doesn't find out," Mika grumbled to himself as he went to the wagon.

Sky watched the man, who seemed to be avoiding direct eye contact with her. He continued to survey their surroundings while checking on the boy's return every few seconds. He wore loose clothing with an assortment of daggers and a sword around his waist.

The thudding of footsteps indicated the boy's return. He handed the items to his father and then knelt on her opposite side.

"How about a drink first?" Loov said more than asked as he opened the top of a water skin. He placed a hand gently behind her head and tilted it off the ground.

Sky's face twisted in a knot at the shot of pain the movement created. The cool water felt better than she'd expected. It seemed to send a jolt of life through her body as it worked its way down her throat.

"Better?" He smiled, still not looking her in the eyes as he lowered her head back onto the grass.

"Yes." She raised her hand and put it on his forearm. "Thank you."

He glanced into her eyes and couldn't seem to pull away from her gaze. "You're welcome."

"Dad." The boy grabbed his attention. "It's getting darker. We should just leave her."

"We need to hurry. This is going to hurt. I'm sorry. Mika, take her hand."

"What?"

"Just do it. And I warn you, she is going to squeeze super hard." He chuckled.

Mika placed his rough hand inside Sky's. The small boy, about her age, had lines of worry and disgust on his face. Sky wasn't sure if he was afraid she would hurt him when she squeezed or if touching her would give him some unknown disease. She closed her eyes and very slowly nodded her head. She took a deep breath and clenched her teeth. The pain was so intense, she struggled to remain conscious. A loud deep crack reverberated through her body, along with a blinding shot of pain. She fought the urge to scream by breathing heavily through her teeth and clamping down on Mika's hand.

Mika's hand went limp and then there was a jerk that moved her sideways.

"What happened?" she asked.

"I think he fainted. Let me bind your leg to the board and then I'll wake him so we can get out of here."

Her leg ached while he applied the splint but not like it did before he reset the bone. After he finished tying the leg, he quickly woke Mika. He handed Mika the lantern and then lifted Sky off the ground. "It will be over in a second."

They scurried through the grass back toward the wagon. Every time Loov's feet hit the ground they bounced slightly, sending a shockwave through her body. She closed her eyes and tried to concentrate on how grateful she was to not be left in the grass, vulnerable and unable to defend herself.

He set her in the back of the wagon where the excited Dek tried to lick her face again.

"Down, boy. Down," Mika said and tried to control the pes. "Stupid animal doesn't even recognize his prey."

Sky put a hand on the animal and thought, *Lie down.*

The effect was immediate. The large hairy animal sat on its stomach next to her.

"Did you see that, Dad?" There was a hint of fear in Mika's voice.

"Don't worry about that now. We need to hurry. We're late already. Let's get out of here." He helped Mika onto the bench at the front of the wagon and then climbed aboard.

There was a snap of the reins and the wagon started to roll down the road. Sky desperately wanted to close her eyes and go to sleep, but the bumpy ride continued to jar her battered body. The darkness of the night grew deeper as they followed the road under the canopy of the thick jungle trees. The sound of insects lessened and the calls of strange beasts took control.

Sky kept her hand on the pes, feeling comfort in his touch. The animal curled into a ball at her side. Every now and then he would raise his head in response to a strange sound, and shadows of his large ears twitched back and forth, trying to determine the origin of the disturbance. The air felt still and muggy, adding to the thick oppressive blackness of the jungle at night.

A familiar call in the distance caught Sky's attention as well as the others. Sky's neck hurt as she careened it in the direction of the cry. She strained her ears when the noise came again. *Closer! Does it know we are here? They can't stop it. They don't have the power. They don't know its weakness.*

Dek's fur bristled under her hand when the call happened once more, louder and closer. Sky used a little magic to keep the pes under control. She had to be careful or the creature would detect her. She would need the element of surprise to get them out of this.

Loov tugged on the reins, bringing the wagon to a stop. The horses fidgeted in their harnesses nervously. Another ominous growl only a short distance down the road made the wagon jerk as the horses tried to back up.

In front of them, two very large red eyes with black slits for pupils glowed in the darkness. They rose slightly skyward and two large sniffs followed.

There was a soft snap and the gentle sound of a sword sliding out of its sheath.

"What should we do?" the boy whispered, and the creature responded with an immediate roar of delight.

"Get in the back," his father ordered and almost lifted his son into the back of the wagon.

"We shouldn't have helped her," Mika muttered under his breath. "We lingered too long."

Another roar and the red eyes charged. They bounced up and down several feet as the monster closed the distance between them in a hurry.

2

The wagon creaked as Loov leaped from the driver's seat down to the forest floor to meet the charging beast.

"Hold, Dek," Sky ordered, snagging Mika's hand out of the air and pulling him down on the pes.

Fighting back the pain and the dizzying blackness threatening to overwhelm her conscious mind, Sky hauled herself to a standing position. Her stomach lurched from the pain, but she maintained focus and straightened to the best of her ability.

The creature was so close. Any moment it would spring and its momentum would put it on top of them.

"Close your eyes," Sky yelled and used every last bit of energy she possessed to use the only mode of protection she knew. A brilliant, blinding light enveloped her body and shot outward, filling the forest with an intense white light.

The monster with its black scales and massive teeth recoiled from the light. It let out a high-pitched shriek as the beast skidded to a stop. The beast flipped dirt and rocks while clawing the earth to escape the light.

Sky managed to maintain the light until the beast disappeared into the trees. Then the darkness returned. Sky could feel herself falling but she was at peace.

###

Sky awoke to the grumbling of her stomach. Opening her eyes, she didn't know where she was as she stared up at a thatch ceiling. Her body felt tired and sore as she discovered she lay in a soft bed covered with warm blankets. It gave her a strange sensation of comfort as if it touched a long forgotten memory of home. She could barely remember the last time she'd slept in a bed. It was so long ago, it seemed she'd dreamed it.

The cabin door opened and Loov, Mika, and Dek entered the small one-room wooden structure. Dek bounded up to her with great excitement and began lapping her face once more. Mika struggled to pull the pes off her.

"It's nice to see you awake," Loov said.

"What happened?" Sky questioned.

"You saved us, that's what happened," Loov said and smiled.

"I thought I would return the favor." Sky slowly pushed herself into a sitting position, noticing the aches and pains with the effort.

"Are you hungry?" Loov questioned.

"Yes. Where are we?" Sky asked.

"We can't tell you that." Mika eyed her suspiciously.

"This is our home." Loov started taking items off a shelf and quickly prepared her a plate with meats, cheese, and berries.

Sky couldn't remember ever eating anything so different, but tasty, in all her life. Her diet had consisted mainly of wild fruits found in the forest where her sister had taken care of her. The thought of her sister gave her pause halfway between a bite.

"Is everything okay?" Loov looked concerned. "Is the food not to your liking?"

"Um...yes. It's very good. I just thought about my...sister." She fought the tears swelling along the bottom of her eyes.

"I'm sorry." Loov passed a plate to Mika and then put a comforting hand on Sky's shoulder.

"When will you be strong enough to walk?" Mika kept his eyes on her as he shoveled the food in his face.

The way Mika looked at her gave her the impression something was wrong. She couldn't tell if he didn't like her, was afraid of her, or both. *Is it my magic?*

She took another bite of the salty sweet meat and then gave a portion to Dek, who gulped it down.

"You're going to ruin that pes." Loov chuckled, helping himself to a serving of lunch.

"Yeah," Mika grumbled. He dropped his plate on a small table and then hauled the struggling pes outside.

"Did I do something wrong?" Sky inquired when Mika slammed the door behind him and the animal.

"Pay no attention to him. He has been influenced by the younger generation. There is a new movement among our youth and it isn't a positive one. Our people used to believe that everyone deserved to live free to do with their lives as they chose as long as it didn't interfere with others. Then the Roowks discovered they could control your people if they used dars. I don't know if it is your natural magical powers that make you lose your freedom to whoever possesses your dar. The Roowks use your race to hunt and slaughter my people and others. You have given them a great advantage over everyone else. While others can learn magic, your race is born with the talent and develops it much faster and stronger. So there is a movement, a very popular one, to hunt you and destroy you while you are young. They think by wiping you out, they can break the Roowks domination. Another idea is to capture you and use you as the Roowks do, but we don't have access to the dars."

"They don't understand my people are slaves?" Sky questioned with curiosity.

"They do, but the Roowks have decimated our older generation, which has left the young to be raised by the young. Many have become hardened and have grown up not knowing the older ways of my people. They are angry and afraid. A dangerous combination."

"I'm sorry." The pain of losing her sister rose to the surface while feeling this man and his people's troubles.

"It's not your fault." He smiled and patted her shoulder. "You will have to stay here until you are healed. Then I don't know what we will do. If others knew you were here it would be very dangerous for both of us."

"What if I agreed to help your people?" Sky questioned, finishing the last of her meal and handing him the plate. "I have magic and I want to defeat the Roowks too."

Loov had a sad look in his eyes. "I'm sure you do but they could eventually use a dar to turn you against us. That could be very dangerous. The longer you stay here, the more you learn about us. That would be information that could be used against us."

"Then I…must leave?" Sky swallowed the lump pushing its way up into her throat. She liked Loov and felt safe with him. She still hadn't accepted the loss of her sister. *Where will I go? Will I be alone?*

"Not yet. Get better and then we can decide what to do."

Sky recovered from her injures quickly. With the aid of a crutch, she moved about the cabin two days after her arrival. Mika continued to avoid her and mutter things under his breath while Loov let her help him with chores inside the cabin.

Although Loov wouldn't let her outside, he allowed her to watch through the window as he trained his son in hand-to-hand combat. When they left her alone, he warned her to stay out of sight of the windows. The lessons he taught his son transfixed her. The grace of his movements and how he rendered his opponents off-balance to overpower them held her attention in every precise detail. She observed he didn't go full speed in order to teach Mika the exact place to put his hands and feet before shifting his weight. Once Mika understood the maneuver, Loov went a lot harder.

Sky slid a hand across her face where the Roowk had struck her, remembering how powerless she had been. She hated that feeling and never wanted to experience it again. *Maybe if I had known some of those moves I could have helped my sister.*

By the fourth day, Sky no longer required the aid of the crutch Loov had made for her. She started mimicking the maneuvers Loov taught Mika every day. She took in all his instructions and played them over and over in her mind. She started practicing them whenever they left her alone in the cabin.

She was in the middle of working on a particular defensive move when the door to the cabin swung open, and Mika and Loov stepped across the threshold. She jumped at the surprise and felt her face redden while her heart kicked into high gear.

"What are *you* doing?" Mika demanded with a hint of sarcasm. "As if a Dijinni or a girl could learn to fight."

Loov wore a curious expression, as if he had seen something unexpected.

Sky's embarrassment quickly turned to anger at Mika's derogatory comments. "I could whip you," she blurted out before she'd had a chance to think things through.

Mika burst out laughing. "Wanna bet?" He taunted.

"Yes, I will beat you senseless, you haughty little brat." Sky couldn't believe the words coming out of her mouth. She had never stood up to anyone in her life like she was doing right now. Somehow, the taunting of this angry boy had gotten under her skin and she wanted to put him in his place. *He is probably going to kick your butt! He has been training all of his life and you have only watched for a few days.*

Loov jumped between them with a big smile painted on his kind face. "This is not going to happen. Mika, you've been training for a long time and she's still injured."

"If she thinks she can take me, let her *try* it!" Mika blustered, struggling to push his way around his father's outstretched arms.

"He's not protecting me. He's saving you the embarrassment of being whooped by a girl." Sky teased.

"Hey," Loov shouted, "settle down." It took him several moments to get them under control. "We can't do anything today. It will be dark soon."

All through dinner, Mika and Sky shot each other dark looks. Mika often wore a smirk that really made Sky's blood boil. She imagined herself throwing him to the ground and him growing angrier with each attempt to subdue her. *What will you do if you really have to fight him? He seems a lot more confident than you feel.*

These thoughts continued after she had climbed into bed. She listened to the two of them breathing, wondering if Mika was sleeping or just pretending. *Why can't I get to sleep? He will be fresh tomorrow and I won't.* It was early in the morning when she finally dropped off.

Morning came too quickly. Sky's head throbbed from the lack of sleep and she felt sluggish. Not only was she tired, the soreness from her injuries was stronger than the previous day. *How am I going to get out of this one? I can't back out now.*

"Good morning, Sky." Mika wore an exceptionally large wicked smile. "Ready for what's coming to you?" He smacked his palm with his fist, making a loud crack. "This is going to be a great day."

"For me," Sky retorted, but not feeling the enthusiasm from the previous night.

"Who says I'm going to let you fight her?" Loov shot a worried glance at Sky, as if he could sense what she was feeling.

"But she was talking big. You can't stop it now!" Mika complained.

"Why don't you take Dek out for a walk? I'll think about it while I prepare breakfast."

"Come on, Dek. Let's let them think of an excuse to save the Dijinni a throttling," Dek grumbled while escorting the pes to the door.

Loov watched Mika and Dek through the window for a moment before turning to Sky. "Now, I know Mika hasn't shown you much kindness and it's always tough to swallow one's pride when someone has treated us badly, but I don't want you to get in over your head. Granted, your leg healed in an unnatural amount of time. I'm guessing it has to do with your magic, but you probably still aren't at one hundred percent. So, tell me honestly, do you want to have a go with Mika?"

"Yes." *What are you saying? Are you crazy?*

"Are you sure?" Loov raised one eyebrow.

"Yes. I might not be that confident. In fact, I'm scared to death, but..."

"But what?" Loov smiled.

"I remember how helpless I was when they took my sister. I wish I had been trained so I could have fought back. Then you brought me here and I've watched you and Mika. I want to learn those things. I never want to feel helpless again. The way I figure it, I will probably lose today, but I might learn something. I don't think I will really master the skills just performing the moves by myself. I need someone to push me."

"I admire your line of thinking but Mika isn't going to take it easy on you. If you've noticed, I don't give him my best," Loov commented.

"I know. That's what I want. His *best*!"

"Well, I don't want you to take a beating. Do you mind if I give you a few pointers?" Loov asked.

"No, not at all," Sky said and gave Loov her complete attention.

"You are smoother than Mika and you have better balance. I can tell how you moved with your broken leg. Mika likes to overextend himself. You need to take advantage of this."

"How do I do that?"

"You need to anticipate his strikes. Avoid and counter."

"Again, how do I do that?" The little excitement she had felt at Loov offering to help her started to disappear.

"I recommend you use your magic. I'm not claiming I know how you should do this, but from what I know, magic puts you in tune with things around you. If you can use it to read Mika's intentions, do it."

"What if it helps me beat him? Wouldn't that be cheating?" Sky questioned, wanting to beat Mika at his own game.

"Oh, I'll let you slide this time since this will be your first time at hand-to-hand combat. So…" Loov checked the window for any sign of Mika. "Okay, I don't see him. Hurry, before he returns. Let me go through a few things with you."

Sky joined him in the center of the cabin where he demonstrated a few moves that used one's opponent's weight against them. He showed her where to put her hands and feet and how to shift her body to finish the job. Sky didn't know if it was because she practiced the moves by herself, but the maneuver felt like an old routine.

"Okay, that's enough. I better get breakfast started before he returns." Loov began getting items out for their morning meal. He continued to check the window, as if he might have missed Mika watching him help Sky.

They were in the middle of breakfast when Mika and Dek finally returned. He appeared flushed and breathing heavily.

"What took you so long?" Loov questioned.

"Dek got away from me. Stupid pes," he grumbled, snatching up the plate meant for him.

"I don't want you blaming Dek. I don't want to hear how tired you were from chasing him," Sky said and smirked.

"You're going to let us spar?" Mika eyes widened with excitement.

"Yes, but we are going to set some ground rules," Loov said.

"Like?" Mika asked.

"When I say stop, you stop. If either of you wants to stop, you stop. Once someone is down, you stop," Loov said, looking at the ceiling as if he were trying to see whether there was anything else he should set down as a rule. "Ah…no cheap shots."

"Anything else?" Mika asked.

"You don't start until you both agree you're ready," Loov added.

"So, after breakfast." Mika smiled eagerly.

"Sky?" Loov turned to her.

"The sooner, the better." She flashed the prettiest smile she could, her eyes sparkling in the low light.

"Well, we better pack some supplies. I don't want anyone from our village spotting you. We'll have to go on a short hike and find a good clearing where we can avoid any unwanted attention," Loov suggested.

An hour later the three of them, with Dek in tow, took off in a direction that Sky assumed was away from their village. Dek bounded around them in a wide circle, sniffing at every new thing he discovered. To annoy Mika, Sky sent out silent waves of magic to influence Dek to disobey Mika every chance she got. She observed how quick he was to anger, and whenever he got to that state he became reckless. Often yelling at the pes when silence was required or chasing after him when he should have stayed close.

Loov constantly corrected Mika, telling him that to lose one's head would lead to trouble. Sky sensed Mika's feelings in his facial expressions and body language. The influence of his friends was evident in his reactions to being told what to do and how to behave.

They had traveled for about two hours when they found a small clearing with tall grass at the base of a massive cliff face which stretched almost a thousand feet into the air. While Mika and Sky rested and drank water, Loov checked the surrounding area. He then returned and marked out a small section of grass where Sky and Mika would engage in combat.

Sky struggled to keep her hands from shaking, taking deep breaths to steady her nerves. Her stomach twisted itself into uncomfortable knots and there was ringing in her ears.

Mika began to stretch and practice his fighting techniques, often slapping his fist to his hand or elbow to indicate a strike. "I hope you're ready for a beat down. I've been storing up a lot of energy for just such an occasion."

Sky stood and stretched lazily. She yawned, patting her hand over her mouth. "I'm just sad there isn't anyone out here to witness this."

Mika's face reddened with anger. "Yeah, it would be a shame to see you cry. Oh, wait. I have seen that. T—they...they...t—took my sister." He pretended to rub his eyes with balled up fists.

A spark ignited behind Sky's eyes. *Control your emotions. Don't let them control you.* She could hear Loov's voice inside her head as the counsel he had given Mika played in her mind.

"Are you ready?" Loov asked.

"YES!" Mika almost shouted.

Sky gave a quick nod.

"Okay, final rule. I've marked out a ring." He showed them the area where he had trampled the grass flat by walking over it. "If you leave the ring, the fighting stops until you re-enter. Got it?"

Sky followed Loov and Mika into the designated area. Mika moved to the opposite side and continued his stretching. Loov signaled Sky to wait where she was.

Sky noticed Mika was taller than she by several inches, and his training had given him a slight muscular build. He wore a twisted grin, as if beating her or hurting her would give him great pleasure. Finally, after his stretching, he assumed a ready position with his fists clenched in front of him. He bounced lightly on the balls of his feet with his knees bent slightly.

"Okay, remember. Follow my instructions and no dirty tactics." Loov shot Mika a quick glance. "Are you ready?"

"YES," Mika responded.

"Yes," Sky answered, mimicking Mika's stance. Her heart raced inside her chest and her palms began to sweat.

Loov held a hand out between them. "Ready. Go!" His swung his hand up out of their paths and backed out of the way.

Mika launched himself across the distance between them with outstretched hands. Sky spun out of the way as Mika dove past her. She danced to the opposite side of the ring when Mika advanced again. This time he didn't try to run through her but fired several strikes with his fists and knee. Sky managed to duck and weave away from his flying punches, but his knee caught her right in the stomach.

All the air rushed out of her body and the surge of pain dropped her to her knees, coughing and struggling for air.

Loov hurried between them waving his hands. "Point, Mika."

"*Points*? I thought this was until they were submitted," Mika complained.

"We're doing points until she gets the hang of things. Then we'll move to a full-blown match."

"You're just *trying* to protect her. Well, at least now she knows how the rest of her morning is going to be."

Loov squatted in front of her and put a hand on her shoulder. "Are you all right? You can stop any time you want."

"I'm okay." Sky inhaled deeply and rose to her feet. She blinked her eyes several times to regain her focus.

"Are you okay? Do you want to continue?" Loov eyed her curiously. She gave a sharp nod.

"Point Mika," Loov said and placed his hand between them again.

"The first of many. Unless you give up," Mika taunted in a babyish voice.

"Fight." Loov jumped out of the way.

This time Mika and Sky circled each other. Mika made several threatening gestures as if he were about to throw a punch or a kick, and Sky reacted. He wore a wicked grin, moving with confidence. Sky watched how he placed his feet, observing how he shifted his weight with each threat. The more he danced, the easier it was for her to see him move.

He fired off several combinations of punches and kicks, forcing Sky to scramble all the way out of the ring to avoid being hit. A disgusted expression twisted across Mika's face as Loov ordered him back to the other side of the ring to allow Sky to reenter the area.

Loov motioned for them to start once more and Mika changed tactics. He came straight at her. He feinted like he was going to kick her with his left leg and she stepped right into a hard right hook. Little lights popped before her eyes and everything went black for a second. She managed to catch herself on her hands and knees. Before Loov could jump in and stop the action, Mika kneed her in the face.

Blood shot out of both nostrils and her eyes filled with tears, blurring her vision. She cupped her nose in her hands and swallowed a mouthful of blood.

Loov berated a laughing Mika, who didn't seem fazed by his father's threats of punishment. Loov lectured him on honor and cheating in a fair match.

You saw his move. He wasn't leaning with the fake. He didn't commit his weight to the kick. Trust your instincts dummy! she cursed herself. After making sure her nose wasn't broken, she used her magic to stop the bleeding.

"I raised you better than *that*," Loov continued his lecture.

"I'm ready," Sky interrupted.

"What?" they both questioned. Their expressions reflected shock.

"I'm ready. Maybe if he had any power behind his punches, I might be hurt." She flashed a brilliant smile.

Mika's jaw dropped and a grin spread across Loov's face.

Loov stepped closer to her and whispered so only she could hear. "Are you sure? Sometimes pride rewards us more punishment than we normally should have taken."

"Don't worry. He won't touch me again. I see him moving as if he is in slow motion. And I have an idea that should keep him off my back." Sky winked.

"Okay, but one more cheap shot and you're going to fight me at full speed." Loov raised his voice, turning to Mika.

The grin Mika wore faded and he clenched his teeth before nodding his agreement. When Loov raised his hand to continue the match, Mika's smirk returned.

"Fight," Loov shouted.

Mika sprang forward as fast as he could with outstretched arms. He dove when he was within a few feet. Sky leaped as high as she could, letting him go flying underneath her to land face first in the tall grass. She whirled around to face him as she landed.

Mika rolled onto his back and hopped to his feet. He wasted no time in attacking again. He unleashed a flurry of punches and kicks.

With each new tactic Mika threw at her, it seemed easier for Sky to see a pattern. She blocked, ducked, and spun out of the way of each strike, to Mika's frustration. She observed his breathing as he seemed to be losing speed and strength with each failed attempt.

The words she'd heard Loov speak through the window played in her mind. She remembered the pressure points Loov pointed out in his lessons and how they were the desired locations to land a blow.

Mika threw a hard right hook. Sky was ready. She leaned back hard, then swung her left arm in a circle, catching Mika off balance in an overextended position. She snagged his arm just behind the elbow and yanked him forward. Mika fell forward easily. Sky summoned all her anger at

Mika's taunts and testy looks, and landed a powerful punch at the base of Mika's neck, knocking him unconscious.

3

"I didn't mean to hit him that hard," Sky said franticly, seeing Mika unmoving and out cold at her feet.

Loov rushed forward and checked his son. He ran his hands lightly over his neck.

"I'm so sorry." Sky began to hyperventilate with fear. She wanted to beat Mika, not kill him. *What have you done? You let your emotions control you.*

Loov began to laugh. "Oh, he's all right. You just rang his bell. That was a nice punch and perfectly placed. Did you use magic?"

"Ah, no." Sky's wits started to return with the realization she hadn't seriously injured Mika.

Loov rolled Mika onto his back and then patted his face lightly. "Mika. Mika, wake up."

Mika's eyes opened slowly and he acted groggy while trying to move and focus. "Wha...what happened? Where are we?"

"You just had it handed to you by Sky." Loov glanced at Sky and gave her a quick wink.

"What? No way?" His voice took on a slight edge as he pushed his father's hands out of the way and attempted to stand.

Loov caught Mika as he tipped forward, almost falling. "You're done for the day. She knocked you senseless." He sat Mika back on the ground and handed him a water skin.

Mika shot a hateful look at Sky and rubbed the back of his neck. "She must have cheated," he spat.

"She did no such thing. *You* overextended yourself and she caught you off balance. Then she placed a beautiful punch to the back of your neck. It was like she had been training for months."

Mika's mood grew darker at his father's words.

Sky struggled to contain a smile as it seemed to her Loov was enjoying playing with his son's ego. She wiped the beads of sweat from her brow. For some reason, she didn't feel like rubbing it in Mika's face. He was very angry and she didn't want to inflame the situation any further.

"I want to have another go," Mika demanded. "She got lucky. I want to prove it."

"Well, maybe I'll let you train together. But I don't want you getting all ornery if she hands you a new beating every other day," Loov said and chuckled.

"That's not going to happen," Mika growled.

"Well, it will be getting dark in a few hours. I think we better wait until nightfall to return to the village. I don't want anyone to see us. Let's eat and rest a bit before we start heading back," Loov suggested.

Mika was loopier than Sky had first thought. He had trouble regaining his balance. While he rested, Loov taught Sky several things about the world around them. He showed her how to find tracks in the ground and to determine the direction an animal had traveled and how long ago. Sky took in all of Loov's instructions. He knew a lot about survival and how to protect oneself in the wild.

"You're eating this stuff up, aren't you?" Loov looked into her eyes with curiosity.

"What does 'eating it up' mean?"

"You find all of this very interesting, don't you?"

"Very. Before, when I lived with my...sister," Sky swallowed the lump trying to push its way up into her throat and pressed on quickly, "there wasn't anyone to teach us anything. We worried about finding food and avoiding the Roowks. I would love to learn everything you know. How to survive in the wild when I *am* not familiar with my surroundings. How to fight and defend myself. How to find food and water. I know how to do that when I am in my element but not in a strange land."

"I..." Loov shook his head. "It can't be by accident."

"What can't be?"

"Me finding you. It seems like it was meant to be." He smiled at her.

The shadows of late afternoon stretched across the small clearing when they started for home. Loov helped Mika along the trail when he stumbled several times and used trees to maintain his balance. He didn't speak the entire time. Sky couldn't tell if it was the blow to the back of his head or if he was extremely angry.

By the time they had reached the cabin, night had settled in with a clear star-filled sky. They managed to slip in without running into anyone from the village. They ate a quick meal before turning in for the night.

Sky lay in her bed, trying to discern Mika's mood. His deep slow breathing sounded as if he were asleep, but she couldn't be sure. An ever deepening sense she had only caused Mika to resent her even more grew in the back of her mind. She wanted Mika to like her. She didn't want anything to force her to leave her new home. Loov gave her a lot of comfort and she felt like she still had a great deal to learn from him. *But, I don't want to come between a father and son.*

The next day brought about a change in the way Mika acted toward her. He wasn't exactly nice to her, but he no longer grumbled about her under his breath or to Loov. Sky did observe that he continued to give her dark loathing looks when he didn't think she was paying attention. She wasn't sure if she liked this new attitude or not, but at least the constant comments about getting rid of her stopped. This might give her more time to learn from Loov. Still, she had an uneasy feeling Mika was planning something.

Over the next few weeks, Loov tried to find opportunities to train the two of them together. He would take them back to the field whenever possible. There were still days where Sky had to watch through the window. Loov told her they needed to be careful and didn't want to draw attention to themselves by leaving every day.

Sky's fighting skills increased rapidly. Mika tried harder and harder to beat her but could hardly even touch her. Even Loov sparred with her and had difficulty with her ever growing arsenal of moves. They had transitioned from hand-to-hand combat to swords and knives. In addition to combat training, Loov continued to teach her how to find food and water and to track the movements of others. In no time at all, she could track Mika over several different terrains.

The hard work kept Sky's mind off her captured sister. It wasn't until night came that the loss consumed her. She imagined being able to help free her sister with her new capabilities. No more would she feel helpless against the Roowks. *Oh, I will be ready.* She dozed off to this satisfying thought every night.

A loud blaring sound startled her out of a deep slumber. She sprang from bed in complete darkness, groggy and confused. The noise continued to ring out loud and clear and seemed to be coming from several sources.

Loov and Mika were on their feet and immediately began dressing.

"What is it?" Sky questioned as Loov lite a candle.

"A warning. The Roowks are at our border," Loov shouted above the blaring horns, looking concerned. He pulled out all his weapons and started to strap them on.

"What should I do?" Sky questioned, a sense of dread spreading over her. She had looked forward to this kind of event and desired a chance for revenge, but now she wished it hadn't come.

"Nothing. Stay here and keep out of sight. Mika will come back to check on you," Loov said and headed for the door with Mika right on his heels.

Mika called Dek to follow him and waited for the animal to hurry past him. As Mika closed the door, his eyes met Sky's and she could feel his hatred for her. He wore a twisted grin that gave her a sense of dread.

The door seemed to echo in her head when it closed, sealing her inside. The horrible sense of helplessness returned as she blew out the candle. She didn't want to be stuck in this cabin all alone, when her only friend in the world was heading off to a possible battle. She went to the window but it was still pitch black outside, adding to her isolation.

What is Mika going to do? She pondered this question in her mind. She didn't know what he would be doing at the battle or whether he had some other plan. *Maybe something to do with me?*

He had been a lot more tolerable over the last couple weeks, but never friendly. They pretty much ignored each other unless they were practicing against one another.

Sky lay back on the bed with her eyes open in the dark. The horns continued to blow for a short time and then silence reigned. She wanted to know what was going on and wondered if the Roowks were using her people to fight for them. Did they train them as Loov had done with her or did they rely only on the use of their magic? *Look how good you have become at fighting. Why wouldn't they teach them to fight?*

Thoughts of the skirmish, her people, Loov, and Mika played over and over in her mind. She didn't know how long she had been lying on her bed or what time it was when the warning had sounded. The blackness through the window changed to a deep blue, the first hint of morning's approach.

Not knowing what was happening started to eat away at her nerves, and she jumped at any little sound beyond the cabin walls. Soon she was on her feet, pacing the floor. She started to chew on her nails, a habit her sister had discouraged. The sudden thought of her sister prompted her to pause and stare at her nails.

She had just made up her mind to quit biting her nails when a soft knock at the door startled her. She froze. The only part of her body that seemed to be working was her racing heart. *Did I imagine it?*

She waited silently and the soft rapping happened again. As soundlessly and as quickly as she could, she snatched up one of Loov's extra swords and then sprang to a window near the door. Standing at an angle that would keep her out of sight from anyone on the other side of the glass, she circled the window with her head, avoiding exposure as much as possible. The knock repeated.

"Sky." A soft hiss just slightly above a whisper sounded. "Sky, I'm here to warn you."

Holding the sword with the tip pointing toward the door, she stepped closer to it. "Who are you?" she responded.

"I know Mika. I'm here to warn you," the voice said again.

"Warn me about what?" She now stood just behind the door. Mika's face with his malicious expression flashed in her brain. *This could be some sort of trap, payback.*

"Mika and some others are on their way. They want to turn you over to the village counsel. We need to hurry. They are coming for you."

This has to be a trick. "Loov wouldn't allow Mika to do this. Mika would be in so much trouble with Loov when he returns."

"Loov isn't coming back. The Roowks, with the aid of your people, wiped out our armies. Mika was furious and told everyone about you," the voice responded.

The speaker's words hit Sky like a brick. "Loov's...dead?" Tears welled up in her eyes and she felt faint. Her hands trembled and she struggled to remain upright.

"Yes. We have to leave. NOW!"

Sky didn't really know what she was doing. It was like watching her own body respond to someone else's commands. The sword dropped to the ground with a clank and her hand extended, opening the door.

A young boy waited on the other side, smaller than Mika, with messy brown hair and freckles across his nose. He eyed Sky before glancing in all directions. "We have to hurry. They are not far behind me."

The calls of peses in the distance told Sky the boy spoke the truth. Her mind struggled with all this troubling information, making it so her limbs didn't want to obey. The boy took her by the hand and led her off in the opposite direction of the approaching animals. He kept peeking over his shoulder and began to sprint, almost pulling Sky after him.

Sky didn't know how long they had been fleeing. She just kept moving. Her eyes burned from the tears, and the lack of sleep started to catch up with her and she felt ill. The news about Loov ate away at her insides more than the fact Mika was hunting her. The sound of the peses had stopped for a while and then their faint calls returned, adding to the sense of malaise.

"They're tracking us," the boy warned, continuing in the same direction.

"I—I need water," Sky stammered.

"We can take a break. A really short one." The boy released her hand. He retrieved a water skin from his belt and passed it to Sky.

She took a long drink. The water spread through her, reviving her, bringing back their desperate situation. *You need to focus.* "Who are you?"

"They call me Keal." He accepted the water back and tipped the skin to his mouth.

"So, Keal, why are you helping me?" Sky shot a glance back the way they had come as the call of the peses grew in volume.

"You're welcome." Keal turned and started hiking away from their trackers.

Sky hurried after him. "I'm sorry. I am grateful for what you've done. I just don't understand why you're helping me. Aren't you a friend of Mika's?"

"I am. Well, sort of. I don't share his or the other boys' views. We've watched you for weeks. Ever since that day you knocked him silly in the valley, actually," Keal said.

"So, if you and...others knew about me, why didn't they come for me sooner?"

"The others follow Mika. He's the best...second best." Keal chuckled. "Anyway, they've been plotting how to get rid of you without involving Loov. Now that..."

Sky lowered her head momentarily when control of her emotions started to slip away.

"I'm sorry. Loov was a good man." Keal watched her out of the corner of his eye.

"The best. He saved my life. So, why are your views about my kind different from the rest of your people?" Sky questioned.

"I have my reasons. Maybe I'll tell you about them when we aren't on the run." Keal threw a nod in the direction of their pursuers.

"Okay, but where are we heading?"

"I'm not sure. Right now we're just trying to outpace our tails. This is just one of those spur of the moment deals."

"That's no good. We need to come up with a plan." Finally, Sky's mind started working correctly for the first time all day. Even her pace quickened with the new purpose. *Think! Use your magic. Loov's training. Loov?* "Do you know where the Roowks attacked?"

"Yes. What are you thinking?"

"We ditch Mika and the others and then go to the battlefield."

Keal reached out and snagged her arm. "No good can come from going there. Loov is gone, like the others. I'm actually surprised Mika and his gang are still following us. They were supposed to prepare defenses for the village in case the Roowks marched against it."

"I realize he may be gone but I need to make sure. He saved my life. I must check." Sky's eyes met Keal's. "Besides, if they realize where we are heading and they think there is a chance they might run into a Roowk army, they may give up."

Keal looked back in the direction of their pursuers. "Good point but what if *we* run into the Roowks?"

"I will watch out for you. I promise. Remember, I have magic."

Keal inhaled a deep breath and then exhaled slowly. "Okay. We need to move quickly as we will give up some of our lead to change direction." He pointed to his left at an angle behind them. "Are you ready for a little exercise?"

Sky gave a sharp nod.

Keal started jogging and Sky matched his pace. The sound of the peses increased as they zigzagged through the trees and bushes, trying to create enough space to the left of Mika and his group to avoid detection. At one point, they hid behind a large group of rocks to let their stalkers pass.

For the first time, Sky got a glimpse of those tracking them. There were about a dozen men and five peses. Mika appeared to be one of the youngest in the group. Most were armed with swords, while several others carried long bows. They flashed through the sparse trees on the side of a hill a couple hundred yards away.

"Dek," Sky whispered.

"What?" Keal questioned.

"Get ready to move. I have a way to lead them off track for a bit." She sent a pulse of magic out through the forest air. Sky aimed for a tree ahead of Dek and to the right. The young pes detected the familiar touch and immediately grew excited. He bounded up and down, yelping with enthusiasm.

The group responded immediately. Mika gave a loud whistle and waved his hand at the pes. The group tightened together, having a short discussion before increasing the speed of their march away from Sky and Keal.

"What was that all about?" Keal whispered.

"Dek loves me. He just responded to something familiar. Now let's create more separation before they realize they've lost our trail."

They traveled for almost two hours without seeing another living thing. The forest grew thinner and turned into rolling hills with green lush grasses reaching all the way to Sky's elbows. The sun was about to descend below a distant mountain range when the sight of scavenger birds circling an area a half mile away indicated they had reached their destination.

Without realizing it, they'd stopped and lowered themselves deeper into the grass. They watched the area for several minutes, trying to spot any hidden dangers. Keal attempted to proceed when Sky's arm shot out and grabbed his shirt to stop him.

"What?" he whispered, whirling around to face her.

"There's something out there." Her eyes scanned the hills, but only the grass swaying in the breeze and the large black birds moved.

Keal lowered himself even deeper than before into the sea of green. "Where is it?" He tried to spot whatever Sky was talking about.

"I'm not sure." Sky shook her head. "I feel it though. It's like nothing I have ever felt before. It is very dark. I'm afraid." She shivered.

"Is that a gift?"

"What?"

"That you can sense things, magic?"

"This is the first time I have ever noticed any other creature's magic. That's what scares me. It isn't trying to conceal itself. It is more like announcing its presence," Sky said.

"Why would it do that?" Keal's voice grew hoarse with fear.

"It's like a warning, telling others to stay away. I better not use any magic or it might detect us."

"What do we do now? How are we going to search for Loov with that thing prowling around?" Keal motioned to the hills out in front of them.

"Let me lead." Sky rose slightly and started down the hill.

They crept along, with Sky stopping them several times to feel more than listen. With each step forward, the warning grew stronger. It started to create images inside her mind. Horrific pictures of dismemberment and pain but also of hunger and satisfaction. *What are these? Desires? Predictions?*

They turned right to follow a small creek at the bottom of the hill. As they circled a rise to their left, Sky observed a direction to the strange magic. She paused until Keal stepped even with her. She motioned with her left hand. "It's that way," she whispered.

The air around them seemed to change. The fresh breeze they had experienced at the top of the hill vanished. The air was still, almost suffocating. It grew hot and their breathing was louder than they would have liked.

When they reached a fork in the stream Sky led them to the right, as the power of the creature to the left almost knocked her backward. It wasn't long before the shadows of the mountain range stretched over them, indicating sundown approached.

"We don't have much time. I don't want to be caught out here with a monster." Keal constantly shot uneasy glances to his left.

"Me either. But look." Sky pointed to the first signs of a battle.

The hills ahead appeared to be littered with the dead or dying and the grasses had been matted down. The carnivorous fowls chattered and fought over several of the carcasses.

Sky swallowed the acid the disturbing scene pushed into her mouth. She wanted to escape these horrible images but knew she must press on in order to find Loov. *Where am I to look? What would he do? Think!*

They worked their way slowly through the dead, looking for Loov. The majority of the bodies were men, with the occasional Dijinni amongst them. Sky struggled with the work. Not only did she see the physical mangled bodies of the deceased, but the images the magic of the beast put into her mind were even more horrific. She struggled to maintain her composure and contain the desire to run as fast as she could from this terrible place. She hoped they would be able to avoid a confrontation with the beast, realizing she had left the extra sword on the floor of Loov's cabin. *Weapons!*

"Gather weapons," Sky whispered, motioning to the swords, spears, bows and arrows lying with the dead.

Keal nodded and picked up a sword lying by his feet.

They started searching on opposite sides of the hill from each other. Sky's stomach sank lower with each passing face. Blood soon covered her hands after she had to roll several bodies over to verify that they didn't belong to Loov. She and Keal exchanged a glance and a quick shake of the head after checking each body.

The fact that she hadn't found Loov among the dead was comforting and worrying at the same time. She received a little relief as the creature appeared to have moved farther away from them, and its influence diminished slightly.

A sharp cry escaped Keal's lips and echoed over the hills, giving away their presence. Sky spotted the cause of his alarm as a pale, bloody hand had grabbed his pant leg.

A deep, ominous roar followed Keal's outburst.

4

A sense of dread spread through Sky's body, raising all the hairs on her arms and neck. Her eyes met Keal's, which were as wide as saucers, and all the blood seemed to have drained out of his face. In a state of panic, Keal tugged his leg several times to release the hand's grip.

Sky flew across the hill to where Keal stood staring down at an injured Dijinni. It was a woman about a foot taller than Sky with the same blond hair, blue eyes, and pale skin. One of her legs was missing below the knee and her face had a large gash across her right cheek. Her shirt had a dark red stain in the abdomen.

Another roar from the creature, a little closer, momentarily grabbed their attention.

"Help me." A weak voice brought them back to the Dijinni.

Sky looked down into the frightened woman's eyes. *Had she been forced to do the will of the Roowks and then left for dead?*

"We need to go. That thing sounds like it's heading our way," Keal whispered, reaching out to take Sky by the arm.

"We have to help her." Sky motioned to the woman. She wanted to run but couldn't leave the woman to be devoured by some hideous beast.

"We don't have time," Keal stressed, his face full of fear. "I can feel it. Like it's in my mind, telling me…no showing me horrible things."

"I know. You go then." Sky hurried to another dead soldier and stripped off his shirt.

"What do you want me to do?" Keal asked reluctantly, constantly looking to the nearest hill.

"Find a couple of bows and all the arrows you can carry," Sky ordered as she started to tie off the woman's leg. *We have to hurry. It will kill us!*

Another hair-raising call echoed over the hills. A thick sense of dread and despair descended upon the battlefield. Sky could feel it. She struggled with the urge to flee from it but felt trapped as if there were no possible escape.

"He's close," Keal hissed with a shaky voice as he gathered up weapons.

"It is the Smirt," the injured woman said and swallowed through gritted teeth. "The Roowks release him after a battle to destroy all the dying. It feasts on the fear and emotions of those it kills."

"Lovely." Sky lifted the woman's shirt with shaking hands to see a stab wound in her lower left abdomen. "How do we stop it from killing us?"

"I don't know."

Keal returned with a couple of bows and four sheaths full of arrows. Sky took one of the bows and two of the sheaths and swung them over her shoulder.

"Grab her under the arm. Let's see if we can pull her out of here."

They each looped an arm under the woman's armpits and began to drag her away from the approaching creature. The woman moaned and tears streamed down her face as she did her best to endure the pain. Moving her was hard work and they had to stop several times to catch their breath.

"We're not going to make it," Keal mumbled.

Sky glanced around for a solution, realizing Keal was right. She scanned the weapons scattered among the dead. "Spears." She sprang to a spot where several long spears lay among a group of fallen soldiers. She snatched up two and tossed one to Keal.

Before she could return to his side, a massive hideous beast, about seven feet tall, appeared at the top of the hill in the direction of the main battle. It had a bat-like head with huge nostrils, tiny black marble eyes, and fangs for teeth. Two muscular longer legs out front supported a barrel-like chest with two short legs in the rear. It pawed the earth with sharp claws as it sniffed the air. A coat of short brown hair covered its body.

Sky chanced a peek at Keal, who appeared frozen with fear. She stepped sideways slowly in an effort to rejoin Keal and the woman. The beast didn't appear to notice her movements. It continued to sniff the air, even tasting it with a long black tongue. It took a tentative step forward as if it were uncertain how to proceed.

Pointing the spear toward the beast, Sky continued to move toward Keal and the woman. She had just about reached their side when the monster started forward with its nose to the ground, sniffing the grass.

Keal assumed Sky's defensive position, aiming the spear at the thing heading down the hill.

Sky tried to keep her hands from trembling. They felt like they were full of water while her mouth was dry. *Loov never taught me how to deal with anything like this. Think! Keep your head.*

The beast paused at every dead body it found, sniffing and licking the corpse. Then a horrible scream filled the air as it found a man who wasn't dead. The terrified man tried to fend off the creature by swinging a knife. The man managed to stab the monster in the mouth but this only seemed to excite the creature. It snapped its sharp teeth nearer and nearer the man, who cried out louder and louder until finally—snap! A sickening crunch silenced the man.

After holding the lifeless body in its teeth for a few moments, the beast released the man and continued searching the fallen.

"Move farther down the hill," Sky whispered out of the side of her mouth.

"What?" Keal replied, exchanging a quick worried look with her.

"We need to be able to retreat a little without giving her up to the creature." Sky nodded toward the injured Dijinni.

The beast paused to sniff the air again, holding Sky and Keal in their current position. When it put its head down to start sniffing the ground again they crept forward, cautiously putting one foot lower down the hill than the other. Keal accidentally stepped in a hole and gasped loudly trying to regain his balance.

The creature's head turned toward them and sniffed the air.

"I don't think it can see," Sky whispered, holding the spear at the ready. "Or if it can, its vision is very poor."

The monster gave a high-pitched call that caused Sky's knees to tremble. It took one tentative stride in their direction and then it charged down the slope, heading right for them. The ground vibrated every time its massive front legs hit the hill.

Sky sprang forward, keeping the spear tip between her and the charging beast. *Place it well.*

The thing roared again as it reached the bottom of the hill and started up toward Sky and the others. It raced recklessly forward, not worrying about the possibility of injury.

It's not going to slow down! A surge of panic flooded through Sky as she pictured the heavy beast running over the top of her and trampling her to death.

She braced herself for impact. The creature opened its massive jaws as it drew near and Sky struck. She stabbed the spear deep into the beast's open mouth. The creature put on the brakes but its momentum knocked Sky several yards backward. She collided with the hill and all the air escaped her body.

As she struggled for breath the beast thrashed about, swinging its head back and forth, digging in its mouth in an effort to dislodge the painful spear. Keal leaped forward, stabbing at the creature's face. With a powerful swing of its head, the pole of the spear still sticking out of its mouth, it caught Keal and threw him through the air.

Sky sprang back to her feet with bow in hand. She loaded arrow after arrow, finding her mark with each release. In a matter of seconds, the beast had a half dozen arrows sticking out of its face.

Finally, the thing managed to extract the spear from its mouth and spit it on the ground. It swiped its face several times with its powerful forearm, scrapping the arrows out of its flesh. Sky continued to send arrow after arrow, keeping it busy so it couldn't advance up the hill. She shot her entire quiver and then withdrew a sword Keal had found.

Once the beast realized the pesky darts had stopped, it refocused on Sky. A cry of madness escaped its lips but it proceeded cautiously up the hill. Sky held the sword at the ready as she realized the beast's massive arms were longer than her weapon. *You will have to be quick.*

Before it could reach Sky, Keal returned with spear in hand. The longer weapon and the creature's fresh memory of what had happened seemed to keep it at bay. It swatted at the spear with its sharp claws, but Keal managed to retain his grip. He actually advanced on the beast a couple times, and it reared up on its weaker hind legs to avoid the sharp end of the spear.

They played a game of retreating and advancing to keep the thing away. Slowly, it pushed them closer and closer to the wounded woman.

"I'm getting tired," Keal called. "We need a plan."

"I wish I had a spear." Sky spotted hers lying in the grass behind the beast. "We might be able to flip him over if we had two. It's kind of wobbly on its hind legs."

"Too bad we couldn't get it to fall on a sword or something," Keal commented quickly, wiping the sweat off his forehead with his sleeve.

"What?"

"Too bad..."

"Are you up for something?" Sky questioned.

"Yes, if we do it quickly."

"When he rears up again, get in closer and keep him up a little longer," Sky ordered.

"What are..." Before Keal could finish the beast reared up angrily again, screaming with rage.

Sky launched herself forward and then kicked her leg out in front of her, going into a slide. Momentum carried her down the hill. Lying back on the grass, she zipped between the beast's legs and snatched up her spear. She quickly rolled to her feet with the spear in one hand and the sword in the other.

Keal charged the creature, forcing it to step backward a couple of paces on its shorter hind legs.

She got up right behind the beast and stabbed the back end of the spear into the ground and then cut a gash across the back of the monster's left leg. The thing spun around, losing its balance, and fell onto the spear. Sky barely cleared the thing's immense body as the spear impaled the beast through the chest, killing it.

"That…that was amazing," Keal stammered with open mouth, motioning to the lifeless creature. "How? I mean, why? What were you thinking?"

"It was Loov's training. I observed and found its weakness." Mentioning Loov's name, created a sense of urgency.

"Yes, but to slide through its legs like that. That was crazy." Keal panted.

Sky stared at the beast for a moment and then hurried to the injured woman, wanting to continue her search for Loov. She removed a cloak from one of the dead men nearby and propped the woman's head on it.

Keal continued to gaze at the dead monster.

The woman peered at Sky with a look of curious wonder. "Where did you learn to fight like that? You are a Dijinni, are you not? You fight like a man."

"I am a Dijinni, yes, and a man trained me. A man somewhere out on this battlefield." She lifted the woman's shirt to see the wound again. "It doesn't appear to be bleeding. We should probably clean it. Keal, gather as much water as you can from the fallen soldiers."

The woman reached out and took Sky's hand. "Thank you."

"You're welcome." Sky squeezed her hand gently.

"Are you the Odreshinik?"

"What's an Odreshinik?" Sky said.

"You've never heard of the prophecy?"

"No."

Keal returned with an armful of water skins and set them on the ground next to Sky. "Do you think I should start looking for Loov?"

The woman's grip on Sky's hand tightened like iron. "We should move. The Roowks will wonder what happened to their pet and come to investigate."

"The Roowks turned that thing loose?" Keal questioned.

"Yes, after every battle, to destroy the survivors. They have more of them."

At this remark, Sky and Keal checked the surrounding hills. "Has anyone killed one before?" Sky questioned.

"Occasionally, but not very often."

"We should make something to carry her," Keal suggested. "I'll tie some spears together to make some poles, then we can stretch some cloaks between them to make a cot."

"Good idea. Get busy. We need to hurry. The sun has set. It's going to be dark soon. I will clean her up a bit."

While Sky took care of the Dijinni, she learned that her name was Sanya.

"So, are you still under their control? And what is this Odreshinik?" Sky held a water skin to Sanya's lips so she could drink.

"When they, the Roowks, leave you for dead, they destroy your dar. I am free for the moment. That doesn't mean they can't lure me into service with another." Sanya frowned. "There is a prophecy among the Dijinnis in captivity, that a deliverer, an Odreshinik, will free them from the Roowks."

"Well, I'm not this Odreshinik," Sky said. "This is the first I'm hearing about it."

"That doesn't mean it isn't you. You are different and you are currently free. I'm guessing you are still several years away from coming of age. The prophecy says it will be a Dijinni not controlled by a dar. Everyone always believed it would be a Dijinni who had managed to avoid falling under a dar's influence. But a youngling, that makes sense."

"It's as ready as it's going to be." Keal returned with the make-shift stretcher.

Even with the use of the stretcher, it was slow going. To Sky and Keal, Sanya was heavy. They had to take a break every twenty or thirty yards. The sun had set behind the hills by the time they reached a forested edge to the east of the rolling hills. They found a tight group of high shrubs and cut out several branches to make a hiding spot for the three of them.

After stowing Sanya in their makeshift shelter, Sky and Keal made one last trip out to gather weapons, water, and what little food they could find. They retrieved plenty of water and weapons but food was scarce.

Sky found one small pouch of jerky, which the three of them shared. The meager meal only increased Sky's hunger pangs.

"I wish I had thought to pack some food," Keal said after his stomach grumbled.

"We'll find more food in the morning."

A half-moon under a cloudless sky gave them enough light to see in case anything passed by their immediate surroundings. The calls of nighttime predators and insects filled the air with chirps and howls. An occasional flash of torchlight winked at them from the battlefield.

"What are those?" Sky questioned.

"Thieves," Sanya said. "Looking for anything of value among the dead.

"Don't they worry about things like that creature we fought?" Keal asked.

"Possibly. But they are willing to risk it."

"We should probably take turns keeping watch," Sky suggested, while they watched a torch disappear.

"I'll go first. I'm useless in the early morning. You should try to get some sleep. I'll wake you when the moon is heading toward the west," Keal offered.

"Okay. Don't fall asleep. We can't afford to be caught off guard."

Sky used a rolled up cloak she had taken from a dead soldier for a pillow and closed her eyes. She tried to clear her head so she could sleep, but the day's events and the mystery about Loov's condition played over and over in her mind. She tried concentrating on the steady chirping of some unknown insect, but then she noticed noises which she associated with larger predatory animals.

"Sky. Sky."

A gentle nudge woke her from her slumber. Her head swam with a dizzying affect after being awoken without enough sleep. It took her a couple minutes to remember where she was.

"Are you up?"

She noticed Keal only a few feet away, observing her closely.

"Yes." She nodded. "Anything out there I should be aware of?"

"Some large animal passed by earlier, but I think it could smell the dead and didn't slow or act as if it detected us."

"Get some sleep. We should probably leave as early as we can."

"What about Loov?"

"We can look for him when it gets light," Sky said, as a sudden feeling of dread overcame her. *Do you really think he is alive?*

"What do you want to do with her?"

"We'll have to take her with us," Sky said.

"What if Mika and the others are still out there. We won't be able to outrun them carrying her."

"Get some sleep," Sky suggested.

Sky found a spot where she could look out through the branches of the shrubs, toward the rolling hills. Several times she spotted dark figures on all fours moving over the hills, but nothing moved around their immediate area. She yawned widely and shook her head from side to side in an effort to rouse her mind from the desire to go back to sleep.

The moon had descended below the horizon and the sky began to change color as dawn approached. Her desire to stand and stretch her sore muscles grew to an almost unbearable level.

"Where are you going?" Sanya asked, making Sky jump slightly.

"I'm not sure. The man who took me in and saved my life is out there somewhere. And even if he is alive, I can't go back with him," Sky said.

"Why not?"

"They do not trust our kind. There is a group who wants to wipe the rising generation out so we don't grow up to fight for the Roowks. His son is one of them. Once his son heard his father didn't return, he informed them of my existence. They came for me and if it wasn't for Keal, they might have caught me and killed me."

"I'm sorry."

"So, how do you feel?"

"Besides sore and hungry, a little better," Sanya answered.

"I have a sister who fights for the Roowks now," Sky said.

"What's her name?"

"Masha. Do you know her?" Sky's hunger for news about her sister increased her anticipation.

"How long ago was she taken?"

"Several months ago."

"I'm sorry, I don't know her. But new slaves aren't put into combat. They are trained first," Sanya said.

"Trained? In combat?"

"Magic combat. We aren't taught to fight with weapons or hand-to-hand."

"I thought Roowks didn't know how to use magic?"

"Most know a little. A few know a lot and are very powerful. All life can learn magic. Some come by it more naturally than others. Powerful Roowks teach us new spells and how to control our magic better," Sanya said.

Maybe if you know how to fight with magic and weapons you can avoid being captured by the Roowks one day. "Do you think you can teach me what they taught you?"

"That depends."

"On what?"

"Whether you're the Odreshinik," Sanya whispered.

"I doubt I'm this Odreshinik. I hadn't even heard of it until yesterday," Sky said.

"Why do you want to know how to use combative spells?" Sanya questioned.

"So I can fight the Roowks. Rescue my sister," Sky said with a determined voice.

"You may very well be the Odreshinik."

"How are we to ever know that?" Sky asked.

"There is a way but it is very dangerous because if you aren't the Odreshinik, you will very likely be killed."

"Why would I want to do that?" Sky raised her voice a little louder than she'd liked and shot a glance out her little spy window through the shrubs.

"It is the only way to help your sister."

"If I agree to go do whatever it is to see if I'm this Odreshinik, which I don't think I am, will you start teaching me how to use combative spells?" Sky questioned.

"I will."

"So, what do I have to do to find out?"

"You have to pay a little visit to the Black Fairy."

5

"The Black Fairy? Who's that?" Sky asked.

"The Black Fairy is an evil sorceress. No one who goes in search of her ever returns," Keal surprised them both.

"How long have you been awake?" Sky questioned.

"Since you started speaking loud enough to attract any Roowk within ten miles," Keal said, exaggerating.

"Yeah right," Sky scoffed.

"We should probably leave soon. I would hate for Mika and the others to catch up with us," Keal whispered.

"We still need to hunt for Loov." Sky nodded in the direction of the battlefield.

"And find some food. Do you think it's light enough to venture out?" Keal motioned to the early morning light.

"I'm willing to chance it. Are you?"

"What about her?"

"I can wait here. I have recovered enough strength to protect myself magically. Go, search for your friend," Sanya urged.

"Let's make this quick," Sky said, as she checked the immediate area before venturing out from their hiding place.

"Let's also collect more arrows and all the water and any food we can," Keal said.

"Do you want to stick together or take opposite sides?"

"Well, we're probably safer if we stay together but we can do the job a lot quicker if we split up. I'll chance it alone. We need to get moving," Keal said.

Sky nodded. "I'll take the south."

They spent over an hour probing the battlefield for Loov without so much as a trace. They managed to find enough food and water to keep them going for several days and more arrows than they could actually carry. They stopped to discuss their options when their paths crossed.

"Any luck?" Keal frowned indicating his lack of success.

"No. I'm starting to wonder if they took him prisoner or he got away. I can't find any sign of him."

"I did collect a bag full of gold." Keal jingled the bag.

"We're not thieves." Sky knitted her eyebrows while cocking her head to the side.

"No, but they can't use it anymore and we may need to purchase supplies somewhere along the road," Keal pointed out.

"You're right. Smart thinking."

"I think we should get out of here. We aren't going to be able to move very quickly while carrying her," Keal said.

"I thought about that. Maybe this will help once her wounds have healed." Sky showed him a peg-leg complete with straps. "It's going to be too big for her but maybe we can adjust it."

"That belonged to old Varg. He lost his leg years ago and usually only served behind the lines. They finally got to him." Keal glanced over the battlefield, as if he could see the old man standing several hills away.

"I'm sorry. Maybe by helping her, we can help your people." Sky motioned for them to head back toward Sanya.

"That's if you are this Odreshinik she's been talking about. Otherwise, you may end up...our enemy." Keal raised his eyebrows slightly.

"Yeah." Sky felt a surge of guilt after viewing so many dead men scattered all over the battlefield. The numbers of deceased were far greater than those of the Dijinnis, by more than nine to one. "Saving me could be a costly mistake."

"I don't think so."

"So why did you do it?"

"What?"

"Save me. Why didn't you let Mika and the others get me?" Sky questioned as they headed back toward Sanya.

"I've watched you fight since that first day you knocked Mika out cold. Who says I was saving *you*." Keal smirked at her.

For the first time in a long time, Sky felt the tug of a smile at the corners of her mouth. She shook her head. "Wait, you saw that first fight? That would mean..."

"Mika told us about you right from the start," Keal finished. "He was actually confident he was going to wipe you out."

"Wow, I could tell he wasn't happy I beat him. How did he face you again after the loss?"

"Oh, he was ticked. There was no being around him. All he talked about was turning you in to the council and watching them deal with you.

If it wasn't for his dad, he would have left you to die where they found you," Keal continued. "Anyway, with each passing week, he grew more and more hostile toward you. The battle gave him what he needed to turn you in, when Loov…didn't return."

They grew silent for a moment and walked with their heads down.

"You still haven't told me why you saved me," Sky said as they drew near the tree line.

"Well, I, like Loov, think it is wrong to hunt a species just to wipe them out. Your people are slaves, they have no control over their actions. You aren't our enemy. The Roowks are. I think working together will be the only way to defeat them. And, after hearing Sanya's tale, I'm thinking it is a real possibility."

"What if I'm not the one? Again, saving me could be a huge mistake." Sky frowned.

"I'm willing to take my chances. Look how you risked your life to help this woman you didn't know. That says a lot about you."

They found Sanya safe where they had left her. After helping her out of their make-shift shelter, they ate a quick breakfast and discussed their options. They decided to try to carry her as far as they could. They rigged straps from rope they had collected from the battlefield so they could haul the homemade cot, hanging its weight from their shoulders. In addition to Sanya, they loaded the supplies they had collected onto the cot.

"Where are we going?" Keal looked around.

"It seems like the only idea we have on the table is Sanya's, so where do we go from here?" Sky looked at Sanya.

"We head west." Sanya pointed across the battlefield away from the early morning sun.

"At least we are heading away from Mika and the others as well." Keal whistled in relief.

They positioned themselves on opposite ends of Sanya's cot. Sky inhaled a deep breath and then squatted to secure the straps over her shoulders. Gritting her teeth, she lifted Sanya and the supplies off the ground.

"You ready?" Keal questioned, already breathing heavily against the strain.

"Yes. Ready? Go!" They started walking together. The extra weight forced Sky to make sure her footing was secure before shifting her weight. She began sweating in a matter of minutes. When they went uphill, her hamstrings screamed in protest due to the extra load, while her knees took over going downhill.

They worked their way straight across the battlefield before skirting the rolling hills to the south in an effort to avoid being spotted easily by any Roowks that might be hiding just inside the forest along the north side of the grasslands. They hoped Mika and the others would avoid traveling out into the battlefield until they'd exhausted all other options. In an effort to keep ahead of Mika and his group, they agreed to endure the strain of carrying Sanya and the supplies without stopping until they were at least a ways to the west of the battlefield.

By the time they took their first break, sweat had completely soaked through her shirt and pants. Her heart pounded against her chest and her breathing echoed in her ears. They found a cool shady patch of trees to set down the cot.

Keal and Sky emptied several water skins and rubbed their aching shoulders.

"We're going to have to hold on to these skins and fill them whenever we can." Keal gulped air and wiped his brow on his sleeve.

"Well, the cot should be lighter without that extra water," Sky said and managed a weak smile.

"Keep your eyes open for a strong sturdy stick I can use for a crutch," Sanya suggested. "I might be able to do small jaunts with a crutch over easy terrain."

"How about I double back and see if anyone's following us? If there isn't any sign of pursuit, we might be able to slow down and take more breaks," Keal offered.

"Good thinking. Just be careful. This isn't your neck of the woods. There are probably things out here we don't want to run into," Sky cautioned.

Keal glanced about uneasily. "Point taken. I'll hurry." He picked up one of the food packs and then headed back toward the battlefield at a good pace.

Sky shared some food with Sanya while they waited.

"I'm sorry to be such a burden," Sanya commented between mouthfuls.

Sky patted her good leg. "You're not a burden. You've given me a purpose. Without Loov, I don't know what I would have done. Now, at least we have a direction."

"He sounds like a decent man."

"He was. He helped me like we are helping you. He set a good example," Sky said and smiled sadly.

"Well, judging by the other skills you've acquired, you're a quick learner."

"Speaking of learning, how about you teach me something while we wait?" Sky peered into Sanya's face. She noticed how the deep gash had already started to heal.

"Okay. How about a defensive spell? Watching you fight the beast back there, I think one would help your other fighting skills."

They worked on a blocking spell for about twenty minutes. Toward the end of the short session, Sanya could send projectiles at Sky and she was able to deflect them.

"Very good," Sanya said and eyed her curiously. "Your magic is already ahead of your years. Tell me, how did you feel when I sent objects toward you?"

"What do you mean?"

"Did you notice anything about your surroundings or did you rely on sight alone?"

"Um…sight. I think. But, it was like I could see them coming before I tracked them with my eyes." Sky tried to remember what had happened during her lesson, what images had passed through her mind. "Why?"

"True defense is to interpret the magic around you and read what it tells you. Your sight can deceive you but magic will not. You want to picture it before it happens," Sanya said.

"Someone's coming," Sky whispered.

"How do you know?" Sanya questioned. "Magic?"

"No, I can hear the warning calls from the birds. Something is moving among them." Sky picked up her bow and placed an arrow to the string. She pulled back and waited for whatever it was to show itself.

Finally Keal appeared, jogging through the trees. He hurried toward them, breathing heavily. When he reached them he hunched over, resting with his hands on his knees and gulping air. His face was blotchy and his brow sweaty.

"Mika…and the others…are still following." Keal gasped.

"How far?" Sky glanced over the top of Keal as if she might see Mika and the others moving through the trees behind him.

"They're in the battlefield. I don't think they know which way we went, so we better create a larger gap between us." Keal straightened up and downed another water skin.

"I think we should carry her a little differently," Sky commented.

"How's that?" Keal questioned.

"I think if one or both of us drag her by the upper end of the harnesses, it will be easier and faster. Plus, we will be able to take turns and go farther without resting," Sky pointed out, moving to the end with Sanya's head.

"How did you figure that?" Keal raised his eyebrows.

"Actually, Loov's training about weight distribution. When we both carry her, we have to hold her and the weight of the supplies. If we drag her, the ground will hold the majority of it. If you would be so kind as to haul some of the water and weapons for our protection, it will make it even more tolerable."

"Are you sure?"

"Let's give it a try. We'll know in a few minutes." Sky squatted down and pulled the straps over her shoulders. She rose to her feet, noticing the effort to do so was definitely less than before. This new method of transporting Sanya didn't require as much effort, but she did have to walk at a different angle.

"Well?" Keal asked after they had traveled a hundred yards.

"It's still a lot of work, but it *is* easier." Sky's heart had already started to beat harder with the strain.

"Yes, but we are going to leave an excellent trail for Mika and the others to follow." Keal pointed to the deep cuts in the dirt created by the ends of the spears.

"On the contrary, I think this might play to our advantage." Sky flashed him a satisfied smile.

"How's that?"

"When we were carrying her, we were leaving a trail even Mika could follow. Now I admit these grooves are going to stand out, but they will have no idea what created them. This could cause them to worry. Worry can make you hesitant."

A smile spread across Keal's face. "Brilliant. You're right. If I didn't know what was making these marks, I wouldn't be able to figure it out."

Sky managed to drag Sanya another mile before she changed places with Keal. Sky walked alongside the cot and constantly glanced back over her shoulder to listen. As of yet, no sounds of the peses reached her ears.

"So, how do we find this Black Fairy?" Sky asked.

Keal's pace slowed and he cocked his head to better hear the answer to this question.

"I will be honest with you. I'm not entirely sure. Like Keal said before, none of our people have ever returned from seeing her," Sanya said.

"Then why do they go in search of her?" Keal asked.

"We want the same thing you want, freedom. Freedom from the Roowks. Many go in an effort to find out more about the prophecy. I only know she lives in the west. The prophecy also speaks about how the Odreshinik will find answers in the west. I must confess, there are other stories about her that indicate she lives there and should make it easy to find," Sanya said.

"What are those?" Sky spoke this time.

"They aren't very pleasant stories," Sanya said and frowned while looking away. "But they aren't important."

Keal stopped. "What aren't you telling us?"

"What?" Sanya attempted to recompose her expression.

"You can't say they are pleasant stories and they are not important. Usually, those are the most important ones. They will tell us what we are getting ourselves into," Keal said, staring back at Sanya.

Sky squatted to eye level with Sanya lying on the cot. "Tell us. I give you my word. I'm determined to see this through but I need to know everything."

"Okay. This Black Fairy is evil and cruel and vicious. There are stories of her wiping out entire villages of people who tried to settle too close to her kingdom. Her land is extremely dangerous. She uses her magic to defile and transfigure life forms into monsters to do her bidding," Sanya said.

"Then, how is she supposed to help us destroy the Roowks?" Keal rolled his eyes. "If no Dijinni has survived entering her kingdom and she wipes out villages, how are we supposed to approach her? And what does she have to do with this prophecy specifically?"

"I'm not one hundred percent sure." Sanya shook her head. "I've actually never heard the entire prophecy. The Roowks have the dars. They control us. We are forbidden to repeat it."

"Then how do you know anything about it?" Sky questioned. She retrieved a water skin and took a swallow before passing it to the others.

"Isn't it obvious? They found some loophole in their masters' orders," Keal said and chuckled.

"Yes, we're forbidden to even talk about it, but they never said anything about writing pieces of it in notes. It was decided a long time ago never to put it all out in one messages in case it fell into the hands of the Roowks. We share what we can to keep up hope but parts have been forgotten. Without hope, our lives would seem pointless. Slavery isn't a life," Sanya said.

"Well, what can you tell us about the prophecy?" Sky asked.

"That the Odreshinik will deliver us from the Roowks. The Odreshinik will go into the west and find the answers from the lips of the Black Fairy, Sarvina," Sanya said.

Sky glanced at Keal, who shrugged his shoulders.

"Do you have any idea where we can find the actual prophecy?" Keal asked.

Peses' howls in the distance behind them, drew their attention.

"We have to move." Keal started forward once more.

"We need to disguise our trail." Sky bent over and slid into the straps at the foot of Sanya's cot. She grunted as she lifted it off the ground.

"What are you doing?" Keal questioned slowing with the sudden increase of weight.

"It's only for a short distance. Try to step on rocks wherever possible," Sky ordered.

After they had created a good-sized gap without any ruts, Sky lowered Sanya's feet back down to the ground. "Are you okay for a bit?" Sky questioned Keal.

"Yes."

Sky drew her sword and wacked off two thick branches. "I'm going to create a diversion trail. Plus, I might be able to send Dek in the wrong direction again."

"Okay, but hurry," Keal said.

Sky dropped back and hustled through the trees along the path they had used. Before she reached where the ruts started, she used her two sticks to create a false trail. She faced back toward the original direction for about five feet and erased the original trail before slowly veering to her right.

While continuing to angle farther away from the direction Keal and Sanya were traveling, Sky left little magic markers for Dek to recognize. She moved quickly, trying to lay down a sizeable section of false trail. She made sure to break branches and trample down grasses and plants. *I hope they don't notice only one set of footprints.*

Sweat began to stream down her face and back due to the amount of energy spent pushing the sticks down into the ground as hard as she could, while marching at a brisk pace. The call of the peses continued to grow as she worked to build a convincing decoy. *I just need to get them several hundred paces away from the real trail.*

After a good half hour of making a new trail, she picked up the sticks and started to head back toward the others. She used Loov's training to carefully conceal her passing. *We need time. I'd rather not run blindly into the Black Fairy's domain. Plus, I'd also like to hear the prophecy before I try to meet her. If the answer is going to come from her lips, I will have to meet her.*

Once she figured she had reached a safe distance from where she'd left the false trail, she tossed the branches and started to jog. She weaved her way through the trees and bushes quickly. *Keal will need a break soon.*

She slowed to a brisk walk when she reached the general area where she estimated Keal and Sanya should be. Her head rotated in all directions, trying to capture any sign of them through the trees. *Where are they?*

She paused to listen. *Keal should be breathing so loud it should give them away.* Nothing. *Did I get that far ahead of them? Or turn at a sharper angle than I thought?*

"What should I do?" she asked herself. "I don't want to backtrack. Where could they be?"

Panic began to eat away at her nerves as she rushed back and forth trying to spot them. Her pulse pounded in her ears and her breathing turned into short quick gasps. The slightest movement of a bird or the breeze in the trees caused her to take notice, hoping to find her companions.

Stop! You're not going to find them this way. She inhaled deeply. Even though she didn't want to, she started to back track. When she found the sticks she had tossed aside, she chose a steeper angle back the direction Keal should have taken. The sounds of the peses closing the gap between her and Mika grew louder with each new stride she took.

She struggled with the urge to go frantically running through the forest calling their names, as panic threatened to overtake her once more. The noise created by the peses couldn't drown out the voice inside her head screaming that something was wrong. Biting her lip, she paused. She was just about to start forward once more when she spotted what she had been looking for, the ruts.

Finally!

She followed the marks like a beacon pointing the direction she should go. The grooves in the dirt stood out so well, she started to jog in an effort to rejoin her friends as soon as possible. *They're probably just as worried about me.*

She tracked the ruts, thinking she would overtake a tired Keal at any moment, when the trail disappeared completely. "What!" she said so loudly she glanced around, thinking she might have given away her position.

Where did they go? An uneasy feeling crawled up her spine. *If they didn't wait for me, something had to happen.*

Examining the location thoroughly showed multiple tracks made by extremely large feet. These footprints led her to a road created by years of constant wagon wheels and horse traffic.

"They're gone!"

6

Sky struggled to understand what had happened to Keal and Sanya. No matter how hard she tried to spin it into something positive, the obvious destroyed her feeble hope. *Something bad has happened. They would have waited for me if they had just hitched a ride. Why didn't Sanya use her magic to defend them?*

The only bright spot she could make out of her friends' disappearance was the fact the wagons were heading west. She wanted to run as fast as she could to catch up with them, but she realized she didn't have any food or water. She had not planned on losing her friends, and now thirst began to gnaw at her, making the situation seem more desperate. Her mouth was dry from her frantic search for their trail.

The road turned southwest, away from the forest and out onto open plains with sparse plant life. The lack of cover increased Sky's uneasiness. Off into the distance, a slow steady column of dust rose into the air, giving her a sense of how far she was behind the wagons.

The need to rejoin her companions outweighed her desire for water. She changed pace from a brisk walk to a slow jog. She continued to check behind her for anything or anyone sneaking up the rear.

After thirty minutes of continued jogging the increased body heat, combined with the sun beating down from a cloudless sky, started to zap her energy. She couldn't remember ever feeling so thirsty. The gradual decrease in plant life told the story of very little water in the immediate area.

She had closed the distance between her and the wagons. Instead of only billows of dust, the small shapes of several wagons driven by large pinkish skinned creatures appeared. Tall bulky horse-like beasts, with gray scales instead of hair, pulled the heavy wooden wagons.

The realization she was catching up with her friends and her only possible source of water drove her exhausted body forward. She tried to lick her parched lips while continuing to push her tired legs toward the wagons. The closer she drew to her target, the lower to the ground she ran.

It took her half an hour to get within a hundred yards of the wagon train. The creaking of wheels mingled with moans of uncomfortable prisoners in cages and the deep voices of their jailers. Sky continued to check behind her because she had dropped back a little to avoid being detected by anyone on the wagons.

When the sun moved closer to the horizon, the wagons turned off the road and formed a wide circle. The large pinkish creatures busied themselves setting up camp. Soon they had fires going and several tents erected. A couple of the strange life forms walked the perimeter wearing armor and carrying spears the length of medium-sized tree branches.

Sky settled herself down among the sparse vegetation to wait for nightfall. She tried to lick her cracked lips with her dry tongue, without much relief. Thirst dominated her thoughts to the point where rescuing her friends was secondary. *You can't help them if you aren't at your best and you need water to be your best.*

After the sun had set and the stars began to spread across the darkened sky, Sky snuck out from her hiding spot among the weeds. She hurried from one small grouping of plant life to another, zigzagging her way closer to the campsite of what she assumed were slave traders. She managed to find a small rocky formation about twenty yards away from the camp from which to spy on the happenings inside the perimeter.

Most of the wagons held large cages made of metal bars, containing several occupants. She watched the sentries make their rounds for a long time, learning their routines. They were lazy in their patrols. Their lackadaisical actions indicated they didn't expect anyone or anything to challenge them out on the plains.

From her vantage point, Sky spotted Sanya's cage in a wagon. An extremely withered old man with long gray hair and a beard was sitting in a chair, leaning back against the wagon. The way the man sat there made her wonder if he was with these strange creatures. No matter how hard she tried, she couldn't figure out where Keal's cell was located. Finally, she found what she so desperately needed—water. One of the wagons was loaded with barrels and crates, with a cook nearby who busied himself preparing a meal over a fire. One of the barrels was sure to hold water. She decided to keep away from Sanya until she figured out what the old man was about.

She waited for one of the sentries to pass her position as he circled the camp, before leaving the shelter to tail him. She followed slightly behind him and twenty yards away from the camp. The guard kept his eyes forward, feeling so secure in his patrol that nothing new had approached the camp since his last ten trips around their position. When they reached the food wagon, Sky found a small bush to lie behind.

She paused there long enough for the guards to reach positions where they wouldn't be able to see her enter the camp. She raced forward and ducked under the food wagon. Huddling behind a wheel, she observed her surroundings. The cook continued to prepare a meal at the fire with his back to her. A couple yards to his left, a water barrel stood with its lid open. One of the strange pink skinned people strode to the barrel and, using a large metal cup, got a drink.

The firelight exposed the man's features to Sky for the first time. He had no hair and a large bulbous nose. His eyes were positioned so far apart on his face that they were almost on the sides of his head, giving unfettered peripheral sight. His mouth also stretched farther around each side of his face. This allowed him a very large mouth which gulped down an entire scoop of water in one large gulp.

How am I going to get a drink without being spotted? Think! I wish I had one of our...water...skins. We had water skins. They must have taken them. She hoped these strange people hadn't taken the time to empty the skins into their own water supply. They would need water if they were going to get away from these creatures.

She slipped behind the other wheel facing the plains and waited for the guards to pass once more. After the sentry moved around the corner, Sky climbed out from under the wagon to take a peek at the supplies in the back of the wooden structure. To her great joy, she discovered their full water skins, the fake leg she had found for Sanya, and food items.

Grabbing one of the water skins, she ducked back under the wagon to take a drink. The water refreshed her tired body. It spread through her, reviving muscles and senses. Without constant thirst dominating her thoughts, she was able to focus on the job before her. *Now, how do I help my friends? First, find Keal.*

Once more she huddled behind the wheel in an effort to find which wagon held Keal. To her disappointment, she still couldn't locate him. She weighed her options and decided to wait until the camp settled down for the night before she would venture out to find Keal. *Still, you need to find out how the cages are sealed*, she thought.

When things began to quiet down, she snuck from the food wagon to the first wagon with a cage in the back, in between the movements of the guards. Risking the possibility she might startle the occupants of the cell when she checked the cage, she popped her head over the back of the wagon for a quick glimpse.

The occupants of the cage sprang to the opposite side of the bars in surprise but made no sound. A woman and two small children glanced back at the camp before returning their attention to Sky. They wore filthy ratty clothing.

Sky worked her away around the bars until she reached the back of the wagon. The woman and the two children eyed her suspiciously the entire time. When Sky reached the back of the wagon, she spotted a chain secured by a lock keeping the door shut. *A lock! Where am I to find the keys?*

After waiting for the guards to reach opposite ends of the camp and confident that no one had noticed her, Sky climbed into the back of the wagon for a better look at the lock. When she grabbed the bar of the door to help haul herself up, there was a soft click and the door swung open, throwing her off balance. She had to hang on to the open door to keep from falling backward out of the wagon. Her heart jumped into her throat and adrenaline created goose pimples all over her body as she lowered her feet to the ground to stop the door from slamming into the wagon.

Sky checked once more to make sure she hadn't alerted anyone to her presence, including the old man. Her eyes met the woman's and they exchanged an unspoken word of utter bewilderment. As Sky slowly swung the door back around, the woman, with her children right behind, moved toward the opening. Everyone's eyes fell on the lock and chain still hanging in the same place just as before the door popped open.

Sky closed the door and the outside bar passed right through the lock and chain. She felt a soft click as some mechanism held the door shut. Sky had to tug hard to reopen the door again with the same result, leaving the chain and lock in the exact location as before.

The woman reached out her hand to grasp the lock and her fingers passed right through it. She waved her hand all over the chain with the identical result. Again, Sky's eyes met the woman's. The woman pointed to herself, then the children, and then outside the cage.

Sky glanced around to see one of the guards heading around the corner. She motioned for the woman to back up as she quickly shut the door and ducked under the wagon. The sentry strolled on by, totally oblivious to what was transpiring around it.

Once the guard was about to move out of sight, Sky sprang back up to meet the woman at the door of the cell with the palms of her hand waving the woman to stay put. The woman shook her head to object. Sky motioned for the woman to come closer.

Sky cupped her mouth up to the woman's ear. "I will help you, but we need to figure out what else is an illusion here and who or what's creating it. Understand?"

The woman nodded and looked around the camp if somehow whatever or whoever was creating the visions of the chain might appear.

"Any ideas?"

The woman shook her head.

"Watch. See if you spot anything strange."

The woman nodded and then whispered to her children. They then took up positions where they could observe the camp.

Sky climbed back under the wagon, looking for anything out of the ordinary. The occupants of the camp huddled in small groups around several small fires while eating their dinner. The cook had started cleaning up the pots and pans. The strange beasts that pulled the wagons nibbled on the sparse vegetation in a small area just outside the wagons, but still inside the guards' perimeter. *The guards?*

Leaving the protection of the wagon, Sky snuck up to the rear of a sentry circling the camp. She kept herself low to the ground, so she wouldn't be spotted easily from anyone inside the camp. She edged her way closer and closer to the creature in front of her, observing his movements. His gait was constant. His head did not move, but remained focused straight ahead.

With all her attention focused on the creature a few yards ahead of her, Sky tripped over a small shrub and landed hard on the ground, creating a small dust cloud. Her head snapped up so quickly, knowing the noise should have alerted the guard, that she almost kinked her neck. To her utter astonishment, the thing continued his patrol as if nothing had happened at all.

Sky watched him walk away for a moment when her mind locked on Loov's training. She started searching for prints left by the two guards. *Nothing! They're not real!* She sprinted forward until she caught up with the sentry and then ran right through him. *What's going on here? The cages are real! The woman and the two children are real! Sanya is real! Keal, where ever he is, is real! So, some of these creatures have to be real? Don't they?*

She headed back toward the woman and children when peses' calls in the distance caught her attention. She paused to listen to make sure she had really heard it when they came again. *Mika.*

To Sky's amazement, the whole camp transformed in front of her. There were more of those strange creatures than before, materializing out of nowhere. These extra life forms were fully armed and hustled in the direction of the approaching peses' cries. A handful of the others hurried about the camp, loading the wagons and yoking up the beasts to the wagons.

"They are going to pull out or at least preparing to run if they have to," Sky muttered to herself.

Sky had to wait outside the camp while the creatures finished hooking up the beasts to the wagons. She tried to spot Keal without success. The commotion in the camp aroused most of the prisoners, including Sanya. *Did Keal get away? Was he killed?* She decided to have a quick word with the woman and her children before heading toward Sanya to get a closer look at the old man. Something told her he was creating the illusions. He was no longer leaning his chair back against Sanya's wagon, but was sitting up straight, staring in the direction of the peses.

After the creatures hooked up the beasts to tow the wagons, they picked up their weapons and went to the other side of the camp. The calls of the peses grew ever nearer with each passing moment. With the peses' noises from Mika and his group distracting the creatures, Sky went to the woman.

Sky had to tap the bars of the cell lightly to draw her attention. "I think there are a lot more illusions in this camp than we know," Sky whispered and the woman nodded.

"Have you noticed anything out of the ordinary, especially involving the old man, that might let me know who or what is creating them?"

"Did you see the way the camp transformed?" the woman asked. "I've never seen anything like it. Until you opened the door, I thought everything was real."

"Do you know where they are taking you?" Sky questioned.

"I don't know. But I want to get out of here. I think they are going to sell us." The woman shot a nervous look around the camp.

"Not if I can do anything about it. I will help you, but I need a little time to figure out who is causing the visions. If I can control or stop them, it will be easier to get us out of here. I'll be back soon." Sky swung around the back of the camp heading toward Sanya's wagon.

The old man rose to his feet as the calls from the peses continued to draw closer. Sky kept her eyes on him while she slowed her pace to avoid detection when approaching Sanya's cage. Sanya was sitting up, peering in the same direction as the others in the camp.

Sky picked up a pebble when she was within a few yards. She tossed it at Sanya, hitting her in the back and catching her attention.

Sanya waved a hand, signaling Sky to stay away, while glancing back and forth between Sky and the old man. Her face reflected concern when it flickered in the firelight.

Sky ignored her warning and tiptoed right up to the back side of the wagon so she could press her face against the bars. Sanya slipped quietly to the back of the cell while watching the old man the entire time, who had taken a few steps toward the other side of the camp to discern what was transpiring on the outside.

"You need to go!" Sanya whispered. "He has a dar. He could force me to hurt you."

"Where's Keal?"

"He didn't find you? He managed to get away when these things jumped us."

"No, he didn't find me." Sky shot a glance in the direction of Mika's group and the calling peses. "I hope they didn't get their hands on him."

"You need to get out of here. They can make me use magic against you. Please, the dar." Sanya nodded toward a small brown box secured with leather straps, sitting just out of her reach in the back of the wagon.

Sky checked the old man, who remained facing the same direction. She eyed the box and then moved over to it.

"Sky! No!"

Sky stared down at the box and then looked back at the lock around the woman's cage. "Are you sure it's a dar? I mean, do you feel it?"

"I *saw* it!"

"Yes, but do you feel it? Do you know it?"

"Does it *feel* like it? But..."

Sky took out a knife and cut the leather straps and opened the box. A bright warm light emanated from the inside of the box, illuminating the area. Sky found herself so mesmerized by the object that it held her fast. She had no desire to do anything else but stare at the dar.

The rays were so intense, it attracted the old man. He spun on his heels with outstretched hands. "NO." The old man's shout alerted the strange creatures to Sky's presence. He sprang forward, reaching for the box.

The old man's protest snapped Sky out of her trance. She reached with her hand to snatch the dar when her hand hit the bottom of the box. She grabbed once, twice. The box was empty. She flipped the box upside down and shook it for Sanya to see. "It's an illusion."

"WHAT?" Sanya shouted in disbelief.

The old man stopped so quickly, he almost fell backward. His face reflected fear as several of the creatures arrived on the scene, holding their weapons at the ready.

"It's not my fault. It's not my fault." The old man was almost crying and dropped to the ground covering his head with his hands. A chain appeared as if from nowhere, running from the wagon to a shackle around the old man's neck. "The girl figured it out. I don't know how," he wailed.

"There is NO dar," Sanya screamed.

Sky drew her sword and sprang forward to place herself between Sanya and the oncoming creatures. She struggled to keep her hands from shaking as she pointed the tip of the sword back and forth between the creatures.

The pink skinned life-forms halted just a yard behind the old man, fidgeting nervously.

"Sky, get out of the way," Sanya commanded.

"What?" Sky called over her shoulder.

"I need you to get in the driver's seat. We're leaving." Sanya sent out a shockwave that flattened all of the creatures, knocking them backward off their feet.

The old man looked up to see the creatures on the ground, not wanting to challenge Sanya's power. "Please, take me with you. I'm a prisoner...just like you," he pleaded, clasping his hands out in front of him like he was praying.

"Get *in*." Sanya snapped Sky to attention.

Sky hurried to the front of the wagon and climbed on board. Her gaze met the tear filled eyes of the old man. "What about the old man? If he was creating the illusions, he could come in handy."

"Come on," Sanya ordered, and the man scrambled to his feet and into the back of the wagon.

Sky cracked the reins on the backs of the beasts hitched up to the wagon and they moved forward. When she reached the wagon with the woman and her two children, she pulled the beasts to a halt. "Let's go." She swung her head, telling them to get into the wagon.

The woman hopped out of the wagon and helped her two children down. They hurried over to Sky's escape vehicle. The woman had just assisted her children on board when Mika's group reached the outer edge of the camp.

The sudden arrival of Mika and the others forced the strange pink skinned creatures to defend themselves. Bearing their weapons, the ten real creatures formed a defensive line, while letting Sky and the wagon with its cargo drive away without a fight.

Wanting to put some distance between them and Mika, Sky was just about to push the beasts hard when Keal jumped out in front of the wagon. Waving his arms high over his head he shouted, "SKY, WAIT FOR ME!"

Sky stopped the wagon to allow Keal to climb onto the front seat. His breath came in heavy fast gasps and he wiped the sweat off his forehead on his shirt.

"How did you find us?" Sky urged the beasts on with several cracks of the reins. The large animals pulled the wagon at a pace that surprised Sky. Even though they appeared to be only trotting, their long legs covered a lot of ground, faster than smaller cattle.

"I...trailed...Mika," Keal panted. "When...I saw...the fires, I...ran...around them...to get ahead," Keal informed her. "I figure...I just...barely missed...you back in the...forest."

"How did you escape those creatures?"

A large bump almost dislodged them from the driver's seat.

Keal inhaled a deep breath to calm himself. "I think we better slow down so we don't hit something in the darkness. You've created a good gap. Besides, I've never seen these creatures before. Who knows what kind of endurance they have. I'd hate for you to run them to death."

"Good point." Sky pulled slightly on the reins to bring the beasts back to a slower gait. Without the fires and the fact the moon had not risen yet, they didn't have enough light to see very well.

"Anyway, I took a page out of your book. Those things were so tall and I'm so small, I slipped through their legs and managed to lose them in some thick shrubs. I tried to find you, but by the time I realized I must have missed you, Mika and the others were so close I had to hide to avoid them," Keal said.

"I'm glad they didn't catch you." Sky snapped the reins lightly to keep the beasts moving.

"Do we have any water?" Keal turned to the back of the wagon.

"I'm afraid not," the old man spoke for the first time since their escape. "No water and no food."

"Just keep your eyes open for a stream or something," Sanya said, still sitting in her cage.

"You know you can get out of there, don't you?" Sky questioned over her shoulder.

"Yes, but there's no room outside it at the moment and we need to keep ahead of our friends back there. We may very well have two groups following us now. If you find some water, we can see about getting rid of this cell," Sanya said.

"Do you think someone can get me out of this collar?" the old man pleaded.

"I can help you out when we stop," Sanya offered. "You're not the only one who wants to be set free."

"So, Mr., what's your story?" Sky questioned the old man. "Why were you helping *those* things?"

"They're called Rikits and it wasn't by choice. If you haven't noticed, I'm chained to this wagon...*by my neck*," the old man grumbled.

"Okay, what were they *forcing* you to do?" Keal asked.

"Create illusions," the old man replied.

"What?" Keal asked with confusion.

"Yep!" Sky responded to Keal's question. "You didn't see them but they were all over the camp. So, how do you do it?"

"Magic. Not like yours or your friend's in the cage, which is real. I can cause most life forms to see illusions," the old man said.

"Most?" Sanya joined the conversation.

"Pretty much everyone but the Rikits. They are slave traders and were going to sell me as an ordinary slave. It wasn't until I escaped from one of their best clients, using my magic, that they learned what I could do. So when they captured me the second time, they didn't sell me but forced me to do things for them. If I refused, they would torture me. I found if I did what they wanted, they treated me well enough, so I went along to survive. I have been looking for a way to escape them. I *am* grateful to you, but they will be coming after me. I allowed them to make more gold than they ever had before. They won't give me up that easily," the old man continued.

"I'm Sanya and that is Sky and Keal." Sanya motioned to herself and then the others. "What's your name?" Sanya asked.

"Feeleep," the old man responded.

"And who are you?" Sanya asked the woman and her two children.

"I'm Marga and this is Shi and Nene, my daughters," the woman responded. "There is something you..." The woman glanced around as if unwanted ears might hear what she was about to say. After a long pause, she merely added, "Thank you for rescuing us."

"You're welcome," Sky replied.

"I hope we find some water soon," Keal commented, rubbing his arms as the nighttime air brought on a slight chill.

Sky yawned widely and shook her head to revive her senses. The events of the day, tracking the Rikits and rescuing Sanya and the others, suddenly caught up to her. She was exhausted and wanted more than anything to curl up somewhere and go to sleep. The fact the Rikits or Mika were probably tracking them, forced her to keep going. The farther they traveled, the quieter everyone grew.

They rode on in silence. Sky's eyes grew heavy. The beasts continued to pull the wagon at a steady but slow pace. Sky shivered against the ever increasing chill as Keal's head bobbed up and down with the bumps in the road. She noticed it seemed to be getting slightly lighter out. She glanced around for the source and spotted the moon rising above a hill in the east.

Several terrifying growls and a shriek of terror and pain snapped Sky fully awake.

7

"Help me." At Feeleep's piercing cry, Sky jumped out of the wagon.

She tugged on the reins to bring the beasts to a stop before whirling around and drawing her sword at the same time. She sprang up on the seat to see three black creatures attacking a screaming Feeleep.

Sanya cast a spell that threw the creatures off the helpless man. Then she created a brilliant ball of fire that hung over them, chasing away the darkness in a wide circle around the wagon.

The black twisted shapes, with sharp fangs and claws, shrieked and scrambled out of the light. They moved back so only their yellow eyes reflected the fire Sanya had created.

"Where are Marga and her daughters?" Sky had a sinking feeling in her stomach. "What happened to them? Did those things get them?"

"I think those things are them," Sanya reported.

"*What*?" Sky and Keal both asked, as Keal hurried to Feeleep's aid.

"I think we would have heard them scream if they had been attacked. There was just growls and Feeleep screaming. Help him, I will keep them at bay," Sanya ordered.

Sky went with Keal to help. The wounded Feeleep was breathing very shallow breaths, while gritting his teeth. He had large gashes all over his body, his shredded clothing soaked with blood.

"What do we do?" Keal questioned in a shaky voice.

"I don't know." Sky felt ill at the sight of him. "He's very pale. Do we have anything to tie off his wounds?"

"No." Keal shook his head and met Sky's eyes with a fearful look.

The creatures continued to pace just beyond the light, grunting and growling. The sounds seemed to contain a hint of madness in them. Every now and then, they would charge forward into the light and then jump back, as if it burned their skin.

"I *don't* know how to help him," Sky cried to Sanya.

"Do you think you can keep those things off us?" Sanya asked.

Sky swallowed. "I will have to. If you don't help him, he's going to die."

"Give me a weapon." Keal rose to his feet.

"Take the sword. I can use some magic." Sky held out the sword.

"You keep the sword. I will need Keal to help me. We will need to move him inside the cage once I get his bleeding under control," Sanya said.

Sky took a deep breath and, while holding the sword with both hands, faced the beasts.

"Are you ready?" Sanya asked. "Try not to kill them. They may not know what they are doing."

"What?"

"They might be under some sort of curse. So just try to keep them back."

"Okay." Sky's mouth was dry. *How do I make them want to stay back without killing them?*

"Are you ready?"

"Yes." Sky swallowed against the dryness.

"Go." The light disappeared.

The sudden transition left Sky momentarily blinded, forcing her to use her other senses. She concentrated on the growling of the monsters charging the wagon to block out what Sanya and Keal were doing. Her eyes managed to track the dark shapes the moment the largest of the three sprang to gain the back of the wagon.

Sky swung the sword around, rotating the blade to hit the head of the beast using the flat side of the blade. The blow cracked the creature against the side of its face, spinning it sideways, keeping it from gaining the back of the wagon. The dark monster crashed beneath the back of the wagon. The blow rocked Sky's body, almost ripping the sword from her grip.

The creatures thrashed around angrily under the cart, panicking the harnessed beasts into a stampede. The wagon bounced around the dirt road, lifting Sky's feet off the planks of the bed of the dray.

"Grab the reins," Sanya ordered Keal.

In the moonlight Sky spotted the creatures giving chase. She used the sword like a giant fly swatter, smacking the beasts on the head every time they tried to leap inside the wagon. Each failed attempt only infuriated the creatures more as their howls of rage chased after the out-of-control wagon.

Heavy perspiration formed along Sky's forehead, and with each swing of the sword she could feel her energy drain away. Each blow had less and less force. *You need to find a better way. If only I could hold some light for a long duration. If I create fire, it will zap the rest of my energy and only chase them off for a minute or so. Think! Think!*

Sky swatted as the cart hit a large bump, throwing off her timing. She lost her footing. She put one hand down to break her fall and connected with the beast at the same time as the wagon dropped back to the ground. The force of the impact jarred the sword out of her hand and sent it spinning off into the dark.

"NO!" Sky gasped, feeling like she had been dipped in ice water. Fear spread through her over the loss of the only sizeable weapon that could keep the creatures back.

The largest of the beasts charged again, gaining quickly on the wagon, while the smaller two seemed content just to run along in the larger creature's wake. Its clawed feet tore up the earth as it raced forward with its sleek black body reflecting the moonlight. Its eyes reflected madness seeming to burn with an inner fire. The monster's movements were so smooth and effortless, Sky had trouble detecting when it was about to spring.

Instead of waiting for another attack, Sky went on the offensive. She threw a spell that slammed into the advancing nightmare. The magic caught the creature off guard, driving its head downward into the hard dirt road. The thing's powerful back legs flipped over its shoulders in a summersault. It spun through the air several times in a roar of fur and dirt.

This new tactic gave Sky a little more time to recover as the move created a bigger gap than merely swatting the beast with the sword.

Keal managed to get the team somewhat under control. Instead of sprinting wildly, the animals pulling the cart were running at a good steady pace. The ride, although still bumpy, did not threaten to launch anyone from the wagon.

"I may need your help," Sky screamed over her shoulder, as the creature regained its senses and charged again.

"I'm a little busy at the moment. This constant bouncing around isn't helping much. Try fire," Sanya responded.

Fire, why didn't...

Changing its tactics, the monster leaped toward the wagon ahead of its normal assault. Sky threw up a defensive spell that kept the thing from grasping her with its sharp claws. The impact smashed Sky into Sanya's cage with such force it knocked all the air from her lungs and rocked the cage a foot off the bed of the wagon, tipping it at an angle. The thing bounced backward from the force of the spell, landing a dozen yards behind the wagon.

Sky struggled for breath while trying to regain her focus. *It's a good thing those bars... The cage!*

Inhaling a deep breath, Sky regained her composure and cast several fireballs, one after the other, behind the wagon. The monsters shrieked high-pitched wails of pain at the sudden appearance of light. They scrambled to get away from the light as if any part that touched them would cause great pain.

Sky spun around, stepped to the right of the cell around Feeleep, and then yanked open the door to Sanya's cage.

"What are you doing?"

"Getting you out, so I can put a monster in," Sky shouted, as she hurried into the cell and started to drag Sanya out. Sky walked a tightrope while moving Sanya along the narrow space between the front of the cage and the back of the wagon. A good sized bump forced Sky to temporarily let go of Sanya with one arm and hold on to the cage to keep them all from tumbling out the back of the wagon. Sky managed to set Sanya next to Feeleep as the last fireball went out.

A roar told Sky the monsters were coming again. She sent out another round of fireballs, making the monsters retreat once more. Sky climbed around the cage and pushed against it with all her might. Struggling with all her strength, she started to rock the cage back and forth, inching it closer to the edge.

When the cage reached the edge of the wagon, Sky sat on her butt and wedged herself between the back of the driver's seat and the cage. She placed her feet on the bars and waited for the fireballs to go out.

In a matter of seconds, the moon was the only source of light and the monster gave chase again. Sky could hear the creatures' breath gurgling in their throats as they rushed forward. The large one sprang as the wagon struck another rock, slamming the cage door shut. The creature crashed into the bars of the cage, pinching Sky between the cage and the back of the driver's seat. The creature fell to the ground, dazed, while Sky found herself with her knees wedged up by her head.

Sky had to roll sideways in order to stretch out across the back of the cart to free herself from behind the cage. She swallowed hard as she spotted the monster catching up to the wagon. This time she launched a fire ball right at the creature, striking the big one on the tip of the nose. The monster roared and thrashed about, driving its face into the dirt and whipping it about in an effort to extinguish the flames.

Sky scrambled to move the cage until almost half of it was hanging over the back of the wagon. She then climbed onto the top of the cell so she could hold the door open. She struggled to reach the door without putting too much weight where it would send the cage over the back of the wagon. *Please don't hit a bump.*

"What are you doing?" Sanya asked, catching sight of Sky on top of the cage, balancing it halfway out of the back of the wagon while holding the door open.

"I have an idea, but it's mad!"

The creature recovered and all three charged after them. The biggest beast leaped into the air with outstretched claws. The devil flew into the cage with one clawed paw smashing into a bar on the roof of the cage while the other went through the bars and clamped onto Sky's thigh. Sky screamed from the pain as she swung the door closed and leaned forward. The cage fell out of the back of the wagon and slammed into the ground.

Sky tried to push herself away to keep the cage from rolling on top of her, but the creature's grip held her fast. The cage rolled onto its door, and Sky and the creature dropped to the ground. Sky smashed face first into the hard dirt road and everything went black.

Someone was speaking as if from a great distance. Sky tried to understand them, but she couldn't make out the words. *What are you saying? I can't hear you.* Sky found herself at the beginning of a tunnel with a light shining at the other end. Slowly, she began drifting toward the light, which grew brighter and more intense. Somehow she was flying, but the ride was very bumpy.

"Sky, wake up," Keal pleaded.

Sky's eyes snapped open, but closed again quickly as the noonday sun hurt her eyes. Squinting, Sky could see Keal leaning over her while Marga, Shi, and Nene watched from inside the cage. It took a moment for everything to come into focus. Her head pounded and her face felt sore and swollen. By the rough ride, she could tell she was in the back of the wagon.

"Whew, you gave us a scare back there." Keal breathed a sigh of relief.

"What happened?" Sky asked, closing her eyes and trying to remember how she got there, but she couldn't process the information in her brain. *Where did Marga and her daughters go last night?*

"You did one of the stupidest things I've ever seen, but you saved us by doing it," Keal said.

Sky bolted up but the rush of blood to her head caused her to almost black out again. Keal lowered her to the ground.

"How is Feeleep?" Sky's eyes jumped to Marga, remembering the three monsters.

"Sanya saved him. He's resting."

"What happened last night?" Sky asked and Marga started sobbing, burying her face in her hands.

"Well…apparently, Marga and her daughters have been cursed," Keal started. He explained how, after Sky's cage maneuver, Sanya was able to get the creature to release her leg. The two smaller creatures calmed down and hovered around the cage. When the sun came up, Marga and her daughters returned to their human form.

"I didn't want to believe it, but it's true," Marga wailed. Her daughters huddled behind her, acting very frightened.

"How did it happen?" Sky asked.

"It was…the Black Fairy," she said and moaned. "We strayed into her land and…and…she cursed us for being humans."

Sky forgot about the pain in her head and sat up on her elbows. "So, you've been to her land?"

Marga nodded with a scared look.

"Can you take us there?" Sky questioned.

"You don't want to be going there. She is a horrible creature. Full of hate. She hates Dijinnis most of all. She told us so, before she transformed us," Marga said.

"I don't know for sure, but if you take us to her land, there's a chance we can help you," Sky said and tried to give the woman a reason to lead them to the Black Fairy's land.

"You can't help us. You can only protect others by keeping us in this cage when the moon is out."

"Is that what happened last night?" Sky questioned.

"Yes," Keal answered. "Don't make her explain it again. The Rikits were going to trade them as a weapon. Although, I don't know that anyone could control them. The only thing I could see, is sneaking them into your enemy's land by day and leaving them."

"Did we ever find any water?" Sky asked.

"Not yet, but we should leave the plains within the next hour or so. We are drawing nearer a forest and hope to find water and maybe some food," Keal said. "And no, we haven't seen or heard any hint of the Rikits or Mika's group."

"And we don't have any weapons." Sky remembered her sword bouncing away into the darkness.

"No, we don't have any weapons, except a few knives you had." Keal frowned. "But you and Sanya have magic, Feeleep has a sort of magic, and Marga here turns into a…" Keal shot a look at Marga's tear-streaked face. "A fierce fighting machine."

"Ah…So…if they only transform in the moonlight, why are they…you in the cage now?" Sky questioned.

"We decided it was safer for them to remain with us. Well, more for them than for us, but we need to keep them in the cage at night and since there is only a limited amount of space in the back of the wagon, they are just sitting in there for now. They can open the door, we will only lock it at night," Keal said.

"And, we'll have to keep out of arms reach." Sky looked at her leg.

"Yeah." An uneasy look passed momentarily across Keal's face.

"So, does anyone know where we are heading at the moment?" Sky questioned. She noticed Feeleep riding uneasily with his eyes shut in the seat next to Sanya, who appeared to be the person in the best position health-wise, after Keal.

"I actually know where a stream is not far into the trees. Then we can decide from there. I know the locations of a few trading communities," Feeleep offered in a voice so soft and hoarse that Sky barely heard him.

"How are you doing?" Sky could tell he was in a lot of pain.

"I've had better days, but hey, I'm free." Feeleep flashed a quick smile but then his face went back to a grimace.

Sky slowly lowered back down to the floor of the wagon and closed her eyes. She gently touched her face to feel it was tender and swollen. "Did I break anything?"

"Sanya was surprised you didn't break your nose or any bones in your face, but no. It must be that hard head of yours," Keal said and chuckled at his slight tease.

Despite the pain, Sky smiled. "Now you know why Mika couldn't beat me. I have a rock for a head."

It took them almost an hour to reach the forest. The ride was bumpy and uncomfortable, but Sky was grateful she didn't have to walk on her injured leg. She hoped they would soon find the water Feeleep mentioned, so she could at least quench her thirst. To her relief, there still wasn't any hint they were being followed.

Finally, when Sky's discomfort from her battered body being jolted around on the hard wooden floor of the wagon reached an unbearable level, they arrived at a stream that ran under a small bridge in the road.

If it wasn't for the fact Sky was hurting so badly, she would have laughed out loud at the sight of all the wounded helping each other out of the wagon and down to the creek. Sky's face hurt every time her heart beat, while her leg burned each time the muscles contracted.

"Boy, we're a pathetic group." Sanya smiled before leaning over the water to take a long drink.

"Keal, you better untie the animals and lead them down to the water," Feeleep suggested.

"Good point." Keal busied himself taking care of the tired and thirsty beasts.

Sky cupped water in her hand as leaning over made her face throb. In addition to drinking the refreshing water, she washed her arms and face. The water made her feel better, but putting the liquid into her empty stomach only made it growl harder with hunger.

How are we going to accomplish anything? If we are going to get better we are going to need food. She sighed. She rose slowly to her feet, her body protesting the entire way. *Loov said rivers were a good place to find food.* Sky frowned at the thought of her lost friend. *You don't know he is really gone.* She tried to comfort herself.

She limped along the stream, looking all along the shore for anything that might be edible.

"Don't go too far. There are dangerous things in this forest," Feeleep called.

Her eyes stopped on the clear water. "Hey, Feeleep, do your illusions work on animals?"

"Sometimes yes, sometimes no. Why, do you see something?" Feeleep asked and everyone glanced around where Sky stood, trying to spot some unseen animal.

"Well, if you could hide one of us from these fish, using your magic, we might have something to eat." Sky pointed to a small pool in the stream.

Everyone but Sanya stood to look down at the water.

"It's worth a try. I think Marga or Keal should be the ones to go in the water. While I might be able to get rid of their visible appearance, I can't affect the current or vibrations in the water. They will need to move very slowly," Feeleep suggested.

"I'll *do* it," Keal said, practically licking his chops.

"I can help with the currents," Sanya said.

It took them several tries to get the right combination, but in no time at all they had eaten a sushi breakfast and were back in the wagon. After rehydrating and with food in her stomach, riding in the wagon didn't seem as uncomfortable as it had a couple hours ago. Everyone else seemed to be doing better as well.

"I've decided I can trust you," Feeleep said after they had traveled for a time. "I know where you're heading and I may know someone who can help you get there or maybe understand what you need to do."

"Who would know what we need to do?" Sky questioned.

"Someone who knows the prophecy." Feeleep winked.

"You know someone who *actually* knows the prophecy? How is that possible? I thought we would only hear it from an old Dijinni." Sanya said.

Feeleep patted her on the shoulder and a sad expression flashed across his face. "Not many Dijinnis make it to a very old age. Their masters are not compassionate and dispose of them before most reach the age of fifty. No, I know someone who is older and knows a thing or two about magic, or has a gift, I should say. But you have to agree to take us with you."

"Who?" Keal raised one eyebrow higher up his forehead.

By Keal's expression, Sky could tell he was thinking the same things she was. In her mind's eye she pictured an ancient person with a vast amount of knowledge, but not the strength to go on an adventure. *Especially a dangerous one.*

"Why would you want to go with us? We will gladly use your help, but you need to recover from you injuries," Sanya pointed out.

"You don't understand. I will not help you unless you agree to take us with you. The Rikits are excellent trackers and they will never stop hunting me. If I go to this person, they will eventually go there, and I have been protecting her by staying away."

"Yes, but where we are going could potentially be more dangerous than if the two of you went on the run," Sanya said.

"It is more dangerous," Marga spoke up. "Look what happened to us when we only strayed into those lands in search of food. She has foul creatures patrolling everywhere. They say even the plants and birds spy for her and I believe it. We never saw the danger until…"

"Why do you want to go back then?" Feeleep gave Marga a questioning stare.

"We have no place else to go. And…somehow, I think this could help us."

"Exactly," Feeleep said and smiled at her.

"This woman told me the prophecy and it is supposed to bring to pass a great change. I'd like to take the path of hope instead of living life on the run," Feeleep said.

"So, who is this woman?" Keal asked.

"My wife!"

8

"Do you *really* think the prophecy is true?" Keal whispered to Sky out of the side of his mouth as they sat in the driver's seat of the wagon.

Keal drove the team down the road through the lush forest trees. The wagon no longer created a steady trail of dust, but the going was still rough. Instead of rocks, thick tree roots pushed their way under the road, creating a lumpy path for the wheels to travel over.

"I don't know." Sky shook her head. "It didn't seem possible, but everything that's happened, like finding these people to help us. It can't be coincidence, *can* it?"

"Yeah, that's what I've been thinking," Keal said. "I mean, what are the odds we help an old man whose wife happens to know the prophecy?"

"Maybe we should hear it before we decide how great of an idea this whole thing is," Sky mused.

"Agreed."

"You're going to want to take a right at the fork in the road shortly," Feeleep called feebly from the back.

They rode for another couple hours when Feeleep had them turn down a heavily overgrown road. Tree branches hung down to the top of their heads and the cage in the back of the wagon. Every so many feet they had to duck to avoid being snared in the trees' outstretched limbs. The grasses grew so tall along this path they brushed the underside of the wagon. The only clue for Keal to follow was an almost tunnel-like road with no big obstacles in the way.

The road had a suffocating feeling to it as if the plants were trying to choke off the path. They could only see a half dozen yards in front or behind. The way the branches and grasses snapped back into place after they passed made it appear like no one had driven on the road in a very long time.

"How much…" Keal started when suddenly the road opened up into a small valley.

"Just pull under those trees on the other side." Feeleep pointed toward a section on the opposite side of the valley.

They proceeded across the small valley and found a spot under a massive tree with enough room to park a couple of wagons. The sound of running water nearby caught their immediate attention.

"Where are we?" Sanya inquired.

"About a mile from the village of Pohora. We should be safe here for a while. You should untie the Falaps, let them rest. They won't leave this valley," Feeleep said.

"So that's what these things are called." Keal climbed off the wagon and held out a hand to help Sky down.

As sore as Sky's leg was, it felt good to stretch it out. She was happy to be out of the cart and not have the bumps in the road shoot pain through her injuries. She assisted Keal with unhitching the team as best she could while Marga and her daughters helped Sanya and Feeleep down.

"Is Pohora where we will find your wife?" Sanya asked.

"Yes, but only two of us are going to get her." Feeleep stared at Sky.

"What?" Keal protested after releasing one of the Falaps to graze on the grass in the valley.

"I'm the only one she will let in. And if Sky is the Odreshinik, she may be the only one that will be able to get my wife to help us."

"Yes, but how long is it going to take the two of you, no offense, to travel a mile. You're not exactly in the best of shape," Keal pointed out.

"I agree it's probably not an ideal situation, but that is how it is going to have to be. And, if we want to be back so the Rikits or your friends don't catch up to us, we better leave now," Feeleep said.

Sky put a hand on Keal's arm. "It'll be all right. We'll be back before you know it." She leaned in so only Keal could hear. "You're the only one who doesn't have an injury or a curse on them. You'll need to take care of everybody else." Sky nodded toward the rag-tag group.

Keal glanced at the others and took a deep breath. "Okay, but hurry."

"Which way?" Sky asked.

Feeleep pointed in a southeastward direction. "There is a trail just through the trees on that side of the valley."

"Do you need help?" Sky watched him attempt to walk.

"Not if someone will find me a good stick."

"I'm on it." Keal hustled off into the forest.

"We will bring back whatever supplies we can carry," Feeleep reported.

"Is that river good for drinking?" Sanya referred to the melody of the running water.

"Yes."

"Then just bring empty skins. We can fill them up here and that's less weight you have to haul."

"Good point," Feeleep agreed as Keal returned with a sturdy stick that would support Feeleep's body but still not be too heavy for him to use. "Thank you." He gave a slight bow while waving his hand in the direction he and Sky should go and then started walking.

Even with her limp Sky found she didn't have to go very fast to keep up with Feeleep. He led them across the valley and pushed through a thick tangle of grasses and leafy plants onto what looked like a rather well-used trail. If Feeleep hadn't known where it was, Sky did not think she would have ever found it, but once past the clogged beginning it was wide and appeared well traveled.

"How is it the plants haven't overtaken this part of the trail?" she questioned.

"Poison." Feeleep turned and winked. "We put down a very toxic chemical to keep the plants from growing on it, but left the plants around it because we did want it to be hidden."

"What do you use it for?"

"Oh, we used to do a bit of smuggling. That was in our younger years. We had stowed away enough goods and money to retire on, but that's when the Rikits found me. At first they just wanted to take over the business, but when they discovered they couldn't run it the way we did..."

"Because you used magic?" Sky questioned.

"Yes, and we weren't about to tell them that. In fact, they never knew about my wife and only had dealings with me. Anyway, when I wouldn't help them, they took me to sell for a slave." Feeleep breathed heavily and paused to lean against a tree.

"How are you doing?" Sky felt a little weak and tired herself. Her leg was hurting more with each step.

"I've been better, but we can't rest long. I don't know how far behind us the Rikits are. They still have the rest of their wagons so they will be able to travel as well as we did. We need to be out of here just as fast as we can. From what you already know about the prophecy, it sounds like we might be heading into country which could discourage our pursuers." Feeleep frowned with a look that suggested he wasn't entirely convinced of what he had just said. He pushed away from the tree and started forward once more, leaning heavily on his walking stick.

"If you need to rest though, we can take short breaks. It won't do us any good if we don't even make it to where we are going," Sky pointed out.

"Are you referring to me or yourself?" Feeleep chuckled, his eyes looking her up and down.

"Both." Sky smiled, the effort hurting her face.

They pushed on through their pain and weariness. A few times, Sky thought Feeleep was going to go down and was reaching out to help him when he corrected himself. They had traveled the trail for almost an hour when they reached a large farm.

Feeleep put out a hand and waved her behind a tree. "Wait here, I haven't been home in over a year. Let me go and check things out first. Everything seems in order but we better be cautious." He started heading toward a small farmhouse in the middle of some corrals. A large barn stood beyond the house and what looked like plowed fields.

Sky tried to find a comfortable position at the base of a tree where she could observe the farm but not be spotted easily by unwanted eyes. She watched Feeleep head for the farmhouse, but before reaching it he turned right and followed a trail until disappearing from sight. *Okay, where did he go? Is this just some sort of decoy?*

The day approached midafternoon and the air was warm. Sky eyes grew heavy and her brain turned fuzzy. She struggled to keep her eyes open. *Stay awake. You can't sleep now.*

Why is my face wet? Sky thought as her eyes snapped open to see the head of a large black dog licking her face.

She startled so sharply that she jerked her head back and smacked it against the tree. Little lights swam before her eyes and she bit her tongue to keep from crying out. A wave of blackness replaced the little lights and her reaction scared the dog so it retreated a few paces but didn't flee.

Sky rubbed the back of her head gently to ease the pain. "Hello boy, where did you come from?"

The dog's tail wagged and he stepped close enough for her to rub him behind the ears. He groaned softly at the contact and turned his head so she could better reach where he really liked it.

She glanced around to see if she could spot the dog's owner, but there wasn't a soul in sight. *I wonder how long I was out.* She checked the positon of the sun and determined she hadn't slept very long.

She climbed to her feet and stretched. Her head and leg throbbed from the effort but the end result felt better. From her standing position she still couldn't see the dog's master.

The dog started to make a whining sound and then let out a loud bark.

"Shh." Sky hurried to the animal and began stroking its back. Using her magic she calmed the dog so it wouldn't give away her location. The animal responded instantly to her touch and turned its head to lick her face once more.

She kept a hand on its back while raising to her full height to scan the vicinity some more. After not detecting any sign of unseen danger, she released the dog.

The animal looked back and then started trotting toward the farmhouse. Before it got very far it turned around and stared at her. When Sky didn't move he jogged back to her, but before he got too close he spun and headed back for the farmhouse. Once again he stopped to look at her.

Does he want me to follow?

The dog was almost dancing twenty yards in front of her when it barked again.

Sky took a step toward the dog and it acted even more excited and hurried back a little before spinning around and trotting in the direction of the farm.

Sky glanced around one more time, took a deep breath, and then started forward. The dog stayed within her sight. It periodically verified she was following before continuing down the path. When they reached the point where Feeleep had turned before reaching the farmhouse, the dog turned as well. This gave Sky more confidence she was to follow the animal. *Does it belong to Feeleep?*

To the right of the farmhouse stood a very old shed which actually leaned against a massive tree trunk for support. Sky imagined if a large gust of wind whipped through the area, the entire structure would collapse. The canopy of the tree covered almost forty square yards and the leaves grew so thick that no sunlight passed the foliage.

The dog continued to pace back and forth in front of the rickety door, barking every few seconds.

Sky sent out a little magic to calm the dog, who immediately returned to her side. She patted the dog while eyeing the crumbling structure. Even though it looked as if a good nudge would knock the entire wooden shed to the ground, Sky noticed she couldn't see anything inside. There didn't seem to be any light penetrating any of the cracks or small holes. It was completely dark inside.

Sky approached cautiously. She doubled checked her surroundings to see if anyone was spying on her. She pushed the door open slightly and the dog bolted inside and disappeared. The sound of his paws thumping on a floor slowly diminished before ceasing entirely. *There has to be more to this building.*

After stepping inside the shed, a small light appeared to her right where the tree's base should be. She moved forward and the light increased to reveal a spiral staircase leading up the middle of the enormous trunk. Sky followed the staircase until she reached what appeared to be a small house hidden in the top of the large tree.

"Well, it's about time," Feeleep said, sitting at a table, petting the dog behind the ears as Sky emerged into the room. "I really didn't want to go back and get you myself with my injuries and all."

"I wondered who the dog belonged to. Is this were you live?" Sky admired the elaborate wooden interior. It appeared only the finest wood-workers had created the smooth polished surfaces.

"Is she here?" An old crackly female voice called from a room off to the side of where Feeleep sat.

"Yes," Feeleep answered.

"Well bring her in, don't dawdle."

"In a minute," Feeleep responded.

"Make it quick. It's time for my nap," the old lady snapped.

Feeleep rose slowly to his feet, wincing a little from the effort. "This is for you." Feeleep motioned to an ornate glass which he filled with water, and a plate loaded with fresh fruit and cheese.

Sky accepted the offer and devoured the food and gulped down the water. She wanted to ask for more, but didn't want to leave her friends in danger. "We should probably hurry," she said with a mouthful.

Feeleep led her to the open door and into a comfortable sitting room where a woman with wild stringy gray hair sat in a comfortable chair, wrapped in a blanket up to her hips. Her eyes were wider than normal, and her face contained a lot more wrinkles than Feeleep's, but she was just as thin.

"Sky, this is my wife...Sariah," Feeleep started, but the old woman gave such a loud audible gasp with a hint of a sharp cry that it stopped him.

The woman sprang nimbly out of her chair and scuttled across the room on spider thin legs. Her large eyes looked Sky up and down. "Where did you find this one?"

"She helped rescue me," Feeleep reported.

"It's nice to..."

"Very interesting. Very interesting." Sariah spoke more to herself than Feeleep or Sky. "I was expecting a mature Dijinni. Not a youngling. No, not one who hasn't come of age. This is different, very different." She continued speaking aloud but more to herself.

"She's come to hear the prophecy." Feeleep said.

"Of course she has." The woman peered at Sky as if she could see right inside her. "And she shall."

The woman's gaze snapped off Sky and landed on Feeleep. "This is what we've been waiting for. You know what to do."

"Are you sure?" Feeleep questioned.

"Absolutely."

"I'll hurry." Feeleep exited the room.

Sky felt totally confused. *What were they talking about?* She turned to follow Feeleep but before she could take a step, the old woman wrapped a wiry arm around her shoulder and pulled her into the room. The woman sat her down in a chair beside the one the old woman had occupied, and then she went to a bookshelf on the opposite wall.

"Where did Feeleep go?" Sky questioned, shooting a glance in the direction of the door.

"We are going away with you and your friends, of course." The woman ran her finger over book after book, reading the titles.

"So he told you where we are going?"

"Oh, yes. And I wasn't prepared to go until I had met you." She moved to the next row.

"And how has meeting me changed your mind?"

"You are the one." The woman pulled an old leather-bound book off the shelf and flipped it open.

"The one…what?"

"The Odreshinik. You are the one who can fulfill the prophecy. I'm sure even the wisest didn't see it before, but a youngling. It would have to be. This is very important information. We are moving into new territory. You will be hunted." Sariah stopped on a page and held her finger over a spot before moving to her chair to take a seat.

"Sanya said the same thing about me being a youngling. And I already am hunted." Sky sat a little taller in her chair and leaned over to be able to see the pages of the book.

"I'm not talking small bands of idiots. If this secret gets out, you would bring the entire Roowk army, with all your people under their control, down on you. This information would bring a price beyond measure," Sariah said.

"So, the Roowk's believe in the prophecy too?"

"I don't know if I would call it a belief, but they will do whatever they can to maintain their control. Even squash any hint that some 'so called' prophecy might be true. They don't want their slaves to have any hope of freedom. They want to break their will." The old woman paused and glanced around the room. She set the book down and sprang to her feet. She hurried to two open windows Sky hadn't noticed before, and shut them tightly before returning to her chair.

Sky eyed the windows nervously. "Who do you expect to hear us?"

"One never can tell. It is a dark world out there. All sorts of magical creatures have spies where you least expect them. Sometimes information is more valuable than gold." The old woman used her boney finger to find her spot once again.

"So, you really think...I'm the one?" Sky's voice grew softer with each word.

"*Yes*. Now let's get to the prophecy."

"Who wrote the prophecy?" Sky questioned before Sariah could begin.

"Why, the mother of the Dijinnis of course. When she knew her people had been cursed and would fall under the control of the dar, she knew this would lead them into captivity."

"So there is a way out?"

"I don't remember, but we can try to figure that out together once we read the prophecy. It has been many years since I've read it." Sariah gazed at her for a moment. "It seems to me it wasn't so much a way out as a way through."

"Okay, let's hear it."

Sariah returned to the spot her finger had been holding on the page and began to read.

Through many a century there lived a glorious queen,
Whose children were magical and fair to be seen.
They created a kingdom of beauty, full of great wonders and life.
They helped the races of the ages to live free of pain and strife.
None thought anything but foul evil deeds could bring an end to it all,
But sometimes the worst enemy is an emotion that starts out ever so small.
The queen had a beloved daughter the fairest one by far,
A fairy princess Lepotica, whose glory was lovelier than that of a star.
She fell in love with a human, to her mother's dismay,
And this worked like a poison, eating the mother's kind heart away.
She forbid the daughter to marry someone not of their race,

But the love for the man was firm in its place.
Out of pure anger the queen used her magic to cast a dark spell,
Against the offspring of her daughter for all time, the evil soon fell.
Though magical and fair the daughter's children would be,
Under the control of the dar they could never be free.
What became of the queen whose heart grew hard like stone,
Her emotions transformed her to the Black Fairy on a throne.
Instead of creating beauty full of glory and light,
Her appearance and kingdom became a dark and loathsome sight.
She created monsters and creatures to obey her will,
Throughout the years her daughter's children they did kill.
It was an emotion from which this poison did start,
And only an Odreshinik can penetrate this old queen's black heart.
The Dar caused her daughter's children to become easy prey,
As slaves to the Roowks they will have to obey.
Through decades of suffering they follow the Roowks commands,
As Roowks conquer and spread their evil empire through far distant
lands.
Looking for a deliverer all races will yearn,
One to rescue them from bondage to give freedom a turn.
Return to the Black Fairy the one must proceed,
To destroy the evil queen will be a great deed.
It won't be by sword or weapon the black one will fall,
But with the world's most powerful magic, the Odreshinik will over-
come all.

The old woman paused and appeared to be rereading the prophecy to herself.

Sky tried to be patient and wait but too many questions were building inside her. "So, what does all of that mean?"

"That's what I'm trying to decide." Sariah continued to scan the page. "It appears you have to destroy the Black Fairy."

"I think I got that, but it didn't say how," Sky said and felt overwhelmed, her stress level rising.

"It says with the most powerful magic," Sariah read.

"What is the most powerful magic? I only know a little. Does it say where I am to find this magic? How am I supposed to use it?" Sky had risen out of her chair to stare at the page, hoping to see the answer appear right in front of her.

The old woman spun the book so Sky could view its contents. "It doesn't say. It only says the world's most powerful magic."

"How are we supposed to find the world's most powerful magic if we don't even know what or where it is? All we know is where to find the Black Fairy and what good would it do us to go into her lair without this magic in hand?" Sky felt frustrated and it showed in her raised voice. Everyone had been suggesting she was this Odreshinik and how the prophecy would tell her how to save her people, but it only told her she should defeat the Black Fairy with a powerful magic. She had no clue what it was, where it was, or how to obtain it.

Feeleep returned, catching both Sky and Sariah's attention. He gave a quick sharp nod and then asked, "Is everything all right?"

"Yes. We just finished reading the prophecy. Is everything ready on your end?" Sariah quickly closed the book and jumped up to put it away.

"WAIT! I want to read it again," Sky protested. "Maybe we missed something."

"It did *not* say where you were to find this magic." Sariah slipped the book back on the shelf. "Besides, we mustn't waste any more time. Your friends will be in danger if we wait too long."

"I've gathered up supplies and have them piled on a pack horse for our journey. I also have some first aid supplies to change your bandage before we leave. It should help you with your pain," Feeleep added, motioning for Sky to exit the room with him.

"Why can't we take the book with us?" Sky refused to move.

"What if it fell into the wrong hands? That might give you away as the possible Odreshinik and tell our enemies where we are heading," Sariah said grimly.

"Please, we must hurry," Feeleep urged.

"Are you coming too?" Sky questioned Sariah.

"Absolutely, I wouldn't dream of missing this."

Sky could not remember ever feeling so frustrated. *That Prophecy didn't tell me anything, except I have to go to the Black Fairy. What is the world's most powerful magic?* She limped past Feeleep and headed for the kitchen.

Feeleep quickly changed her bandage with a clean cloth that had a really strong minty odor, which seemed to drive Feeleep's dog wild. Feeleep had to keep pushing the excited animal back in order to finish tying it off. Sariah joined them in the kitchen, dressed in a traveling cloak and carrying a polished wooden cane.

"It's for her, you stupid mutt," Feeleep grumbled at the excited animal.

"What's his name?"

"I've always just called him Mutt. There, you're all ready for your journey."

"Don't you mean our journey?" Sky smiled.

"Of course. Now, let's get out of here."

Sky stood, noticing the pain in her leg had greatly decreased. The smell also seemed to revive her somewhat as if it took away most of her weariness. She wished it would help her know what the world's greatest magic was.

"Let's go get the others before they get into trouble." Sky descended the spiral staircase and exited the crumbling old shack to find herself surrounded by a squad of fully armed Roowks.

9

Sky stopped dead in her tracks, mouth agape, when she spotted the Roowks. They wore greedy expressions with twisted grins on their faces, and acted like they had expected her. Sky moved to retreat but found herself completely immobilized. She couldn't move an inch. Even her voice was unresponsive and she couldn't figure out what was going on.

Then the strangest thing happened—she was suddenly rising off the ground. Something carried her through the air and set her on the ground next to a massive Roowk with a huge scar on his face and an eye patch. She spotted a Dijinni standing a few paces behind him and understood what had immobilized and transported her.

"Now, ya behave yourself deary and nothing bad will happen to ya. At least not right away," the Roowk said and chuckled in a sinister way. He trussed her up with hands behind her back and placed a gag in her mouth.

The magic which had made it impossible to move ended, and she spun around to see what had happened to her friends. The sight caused her to drop to her knees like a tremendous force had punched her in the gut. Instead of them being taken as prisoners or even killed, the Roowks were giving them money, huge bags of gold.

What? What's happening? Sky's stomach heaved and she struggled to maintain control, not wishing to vomit into a gag.

"Looks like you and the missus will finally be able to retire," a Roowk said to Feeleep and his wife.

"We've waited a long time for this haul." Feeleep scooped out a handful of gold coins and slowly dropped them one by one into a bag.

"Like we'd want to change the way things are run. You make us rich, why would we want you to lose power," Sariah said.

"WHAT ARE YOU DOING?" The gag muffled Sky's voice into a jumbled moan. Tears streamed down her face. She attempted to run toward them, but the Roowk snagged her long blond hair and threw her to the ground.

"Where are ya goin?" the Roowk grumbled. "We'll let ya go when we've reached our destination."

"Oh, don't look so surprised. I told you we were smugglers." Feeleep flashed a twisted grin and a conspiratorial wink. "You should have realized we had dealings with all sorts of people in low places."

"The dreams of a child, how easy they are to use against them." Sariah chuckled and all the Roowks laughed with her.

Why? How can you be so hard? So uncaring? A fire started to burn in the pit of her stomach and began to grow. It felt like lava building inside, pushing itself to the point of erupting. "HOW COULD YOU BETRAY US AFTER WE RESCUED YOU!" Sky roared through the gag and a shockwave shot out of her in all directions, knocking everyone in the circle to the ground.

Sky stared in disbelief. *How did I do that?*

All eyes fell on her. Everyone wore a look of shock and amazement. The Roowk who had thrown her to the ground snapped his fingers, and Sky found herself immobilized once more.

"Ya won't be doin' that again." The massive Roowk climbed to his feet and hammered her across the face with his large hand. Blinding pain exploded in her already battered face, and she staggered as her vision momentarily failed before returning in time to keep her from falling.

"Put her in the wagon. We're leavin'." A different Roowk growled.

The other Dijinni used magic to transport Sky off the ground and into the back of a wagon a dozen yards away. For the first time, Sky's eyes met those of a male Dijinni who wore a very curious intensity on his face. It appeared to Sky as if he wanted to say something but decided against it. He released her from the invisible prison so she could move around once more.

Without the use of her hands she struggled to sit up. All the Roowks gathered around a couple of wagons. Sky's eyes met Feeleep's before the Roowks pulled out and he wore a look that confused her. He actually appeared frightened by something. *Maybe he didn't have a choice.*

The expression on Feeleep's face gave Sky a small amount of comfort. She couldn't blame Feeleep for wanting to protect his wife. *If that's what he was doing.*

The Roowks drove out of the farm and onto what Sky assumed was the same road she had traveled earlier in the day. They even turned left so they were heading in the same direction. There was only enough room in the wagons for a few of the Roowks. Sky counted out fourteen Roowks and two Dijinnis, both males. One of the Dijinnis walked on the side of

Sky's wagon, while the other slept in one of the other wagons. *Are they supposed to keep me in line?*

Sky recognized the secret road where her friends were still waiting, which indicated they were heading in the right direction. *What will happen to them? How long will they wait until they start looking for me?* The thought of them being captured by Rikits caused her great sorrow. She didn't have much in this world besides those with whom she had been traveling.

She tried to remember if they were going in the direction of the Black Fairy's kingdom, which it seemed they were. This thought gave her a little hope. *You need to find a way to escape. You also need to figure out what is the world's greatest magic. Even if you get away, you still have no idea how to defeat the Black Fairy.*

The Roowks traveled for several hours before stopping for a break. A large Roowk took her out of the wagon and set her on the ground. He removed Sky's gag and untied her hands so she could eat a small meal and drink some water.

"Now, ya be good and I'll see no cause ta be mean to ya," the Roowk spoke. "If ya get out of line, ya'll not eat."

They gave her water and some sort of animal flesh to eat, which she wanted to refuse, but the hunger pangs in her stomach won the battle.

"Where are we going?" Sky asked her captor.

"Well, I ain't holdin' much stock in this thar prophecy, but seems lots of others do." The Roowk sitting next to her took a bite of meat off a bone and started munching.

"The Dijinnis?" Sky questioned.

"It ain't jus' yer kind. Roowks put stake in it too." He chewed with an open mouth, took a swig of some strange gold colored liquid. "An' the real kicker is the Black Fairy herself believes it."

"The Black Fairy believes in the prophecy?" Sky questioned in surprise.

"Yep! So, that's where we're a headin." The Roowk took another enormous bite.

They're taking me to the Black Fairy? Why would they do that?

"Sorry, kid. I don' like involven' younguns in war. Ain't right. If ya ask me. But I got to be followin' orders." The Roowk eyed her curiously. "I can' figure how ya could destroy the Black Fairy. She be mighty powerful. I can' even figure how we Roowks are involved with her, but it seems she's on our side."

"What does she want with me?" Sky tried to meet the eyes of the Roowk but it didn't appear he wanted to look at her.

"You bes' not be worrin' about that now," he mumbled while gazing down at his food.

He actually feels bad or sad or something. Could there be good Roowks? Those who aren't power hungry? Sky struggled with these questions and more.

"Grawk, what ya talkin' to her fer," spat another Roowk toward the one who had been watching Sky.

"Ah, Narc, don' ya have a heart? She's only a little one," Grawk said. "How'd ya like if in it twas yer child bein' sent to…" He glanced at Sky out of the corner of his eyes quickly before turning back to Narc.

"Oh, life is so tuff." Narc chuckled. "If I could end this war for sure by sacrificin' one o me kids. I'd toss 'em in a river meself."

"Ya have no heart." Grawk waved a hand at Narc.

"Am I going to be drowned in a river?" Sky questioned in a panicked voice, a little louder than she would have liked, prompting everyone in the camp to look at her.

"That was jus' an expression. I'm sure yer fate 'll be much worse." Narc flashed a wicked grin. "The Black Fairy doesn' take too kindly to Dijinnis in general, but I hear she's got somethin' special planned for 'this one.'"

All of the Roowks except Grawk laughed while the other two Dijinnis fidgeted around nervously.

A sudden feeling of dread spread through Sky's body. It was as if someone had lowered a heavy weight on top of her and she was suffocating. *If only I had this magic the prophecy spoke of. They are going to deliver me to her. It would be perfect if I only had this weapon.*

"What ya thinkin?" Grawk asked after things settled down. "Ya look like yer tryin' to work things out?"

"What's the world's greatest magic?" Sky blurted out before deciding whether she should.

"I didn't know any type of magic was greater than another. Only skill levels," Grawk said.

He's never heard of the greatest magic. Who has? Sky finished her meal in silence. She spotted Grawk watching her when he thought she wasn't looking. He seemed curious about her and she couldn't figure out why.

After they finished their meal, they loaded up the wagons to leave.

"May I walk for a bit to stretch my legs?" Sky questioned before Grawk replaced the gag. "I've been sitting for two days." She rubbed her backside and then her wounded leg, wondering if she should rest her injured thigh or not. To get the circulation going might do it some good. "If I can't keep up, you can always put me back."

Sky's leg hurt but it felt good at the same time. She tried to slowly work her way closer to the Dijinni walking several yards behind her. Although she didn't know how she was going to ask a question with the gag in her mouth. *Use your magic. Slowly. You can do this - untie the knot. You may have to hide your magic from the other Dijinnis, if they are under orders to not let me use it.*

Very slowly, Sky reached out with two waves of magic. One to play with the knot and another to signal there was no magic present. It took her almost a half hour to finally feel the gag go slack in her mouth.

"How ya doin?" Grawk gazed at her. "Yer sweatin' up a storm. Are ya sure yer okay?"

Sky nodded. She didn't know why but she decided she liked Grawk. He didn't seem like the others. *What if he gets in trouble? Or you blow an opportunity for help later?* Sky changed her mind about betraying the little trust she had earned with Grawk in hopes she would be rewarded later, instead of possibly being punished now.

It was only a half an hour later when she caught his attention. She motioned with her head for the wagon. Grawk lifted her off the ground and set her in the back.

They traveled well into the night before finally making camp. The surroundings hadn't changed the entire day. They journeyed through what appeared to be the same forest she had entered earlier with Keal and the others.

The others. I hope nothing has happened to them.

"Ya best get some sleep," Grawk suggested.

The Roowks didn't build any fires. They set watches around the camp while those not on guard duty found positions on the ground to sleep. The Dijinni who had followed Sky during the day was sleeping already, and the other had taken up a position in the front of the wagon from which he could keep an eye on Sky and the camp.

Sky struggled to fall asleep. She continued to search her deepest memories of life with her sister for anything that might indicate what the world's strongest magic was. She stared up at the stars for a time, wishing she was with her friends, wanting more time to figure things out.

"I heard your question. The one you asked Grawk," the Dijinni in the driver's seat of the wagon whispered. "Grawk was wrong. It is true, people can develop greater skills than another, but there are also sources of magic greater than others."

Sky turned her head to better see the lone figure sitting there in the dark. The moon shone behind him, making his figure only a shadow. *If I didn't have this...* She remembered she had loosened the gag earlier in the day. She worked her jaw and tongue to push the gag onto her chin.

"Do you know what the greatest magic is?" Sky asked in a super soft whisper. The gag had stolen all the moisture from her mouth making it difficult to speak.

The Dijinni's eyes scanned the camp as if Sky's voice had surprised him. After a minute or two of silence he said, "I'm sorry. I don't know. I can't ever remember hearing that term used before."

"Do you think I'm the one?" Sky asked.

"I honestly don't know...but, you have something the others did not," he responded.

A Roowk grunted in his sleep, and the Dijinni jerked slightly.

Sky waited until the snoring and heavy breathing returned to normal. "What is that?"

"Free will. I have helped bring three others, but they were under the control of the dars. It was obvious they weren't the ones. I think the Roowks like to hand a Dijinni over every once in a while to make it appear they are hunting for the one."

"Why?"

"To keep the Black Fairy on their side."

"What does she do with the Dijinnis?" Sky questioned.

"I honestly don't know. Her servants take them to a designated area. We never see what happens to them after that, but I fear it is death," the Dijinni responded.

"What am I to do?"

"I don't know. But, if you are the one, which I sincerely hope you are, search your heart. Instincts usually provide the correct answer."

"How long until we get to the drop off point?"

"Tomorrow. I wish I could help you. You should try to get some sleep," the Dijinni said.

They sat in silence for a few moments. Insects and night calls from strange unseen animals mingled with the snores of the Roowks. An occasional breeze would rustle the leaves of the trees, all creating an eerie song.

"What is your name?" Sky asked after a time.

"Um...Seet."

"I'm Sky. Thank you, Seet."

"You're welcome, Sky."

Sky worked the gag back into her mouth before closing her eyes. Her dreams were unsettled, consisting of never ending mazes of tunnels and hedgerows.

"Wake up if ya want breakfast." Grawk nudged her awake.

The bright morning sunlight hurt her eyes when she tried to open them. Her head pounded from lack of sleep. She discovered Grawk had already untied her arms and removed the gag. She sat up and stretched with a wide yawn.

Grawk handed her a plate of some sort of morning stew and a cup full of water.

"Thank you." Sky accepted them.

She started to shovel the food into her mouth but paused, feeling Grawk staring at her curiously.

"What?" She met his gaze.

"Y—yer welcome. I ain' never heard a tank ya from a Dijinni. It surprised me." He turned suddenly and went and sat with the other Roowks around a small fire.

After breakfast the Roowks packed up and loaded the wagons. Grawk didn't speak to Sky again. In fact, he seemed to be avoiding eye contact with her all together. He just tied her hands and put the gag in place before putting her back in the wagon. Sky thought he actually looked sad. The other Roowks laughed and joked about the payment they were about to receive, but he didn't join in the merriment.

Sky wanted to receive some kind of signal from Seet that everything would be okay, but he was asleep in the other wagon. Her world was shrinking rapidly. Even the forest appeared thicker and darker with each new bend in the road. The air turned hot and humid, and Sky began to perspire. Continuing to draw a blank on what the world's greatest magic was only added to her discomfort.

After several hours of traveling, the forest started to change. Almost all the ground vegetation disappeared and the trees grew taller, with massive thick canopies which blocked out all sunlight. The forest floor turned to a dark brown dirt devoid of life. Only strange twisted rodents hurried about the ground and zipped up and down the massive tree trunks. Even sounds changed to a muffled version of themselves. The creaking of the wheels and the thudding of the teams pulling the wagons became hushed. The Roowks' voices sounded as if they were coming from a great distance.

The air, which had been stifling hot, turned chilly. Sky shivered several times in an attempt to adjust to the lower temperatures. Not only did it get colder, but Sky detected a change in the air, as if something unseen and evil watched them. Even the beasts pulling the carts fidgeted, throwing their heads and making noises at the dark presence.

About a half mile ahead Sky noticed the forest grew so dark she could hardly see anything. She thought she could discern darker objects within the blackness, scampering about. The figures were large and misshapen.

The wagons slowed to a crawl and the Roowks, who had been walking in a spread out formation, tightened in closer to the wagons. They held their weapons at the ready and glanced about uneasily as if expecting some unseen monster to spring on them out of nowhere.

Drawing nearer the darkest ahead, Sky could make out even less than before. Her heart started to thump harder within her chest, and her mouth was so dry the gag felt like sandpaper. She could feel evil things in the darkness, waiting, triggering uncontrollable trembling.

The Roowks brought the wagons to a halt. They acted as if they were waiting for something. They all faced the darkness for several minutes without moving. It felt as if everything had stopped. There was no sound, no movement. Then, in the darkness, small red and yellow objects appeared as if hovering above the ground.

Sky suddenly realized they were sets of eyes, glowing in the blackness. There were several dozen sets bouncing around and zipping back and forth inside the darkness.

"Bring her down." one of the Roowks ordered out of the side of his mouth.

Grawk lifted Sky out of the back of the wagon and set her on her feet. "So sorry, kid," he whispered out of the side of his mouth. "In a way I hope ya are the one."

Sky met his eyes for a brief moment and then turned her attention back to the blackness in front of them. She tried to swallow but the gag and the dryness of her mouth prevented it.

"You have another offering?" A deep penetrating voice sent stabbing sharp pains in everyone's ears, minds and hearts, making them wince from the dark speech.

Sky wished her hands weren't tied behind her back so she could cover her ears as she cringed and turned away. When she straightened around, she searched for the speaker among the many glowing eyes.

Several of the Roowks backed in behind the wagons in an effort to put something between them and the speaker.

"Y—yes," the Roowk in charge answered with a stutter.

"Bring them forward," the penetrating voice ordered.

This time Sky located the speaker. The creature had dark red eyes which floated a dozen feet off the ground. It was the only pair of eyes at this height, because all the others were around the normal height of creatures from the other races.

The head Roowk glanced at Grawk and gave him a nod in the direction of the blackness.

Grawk gently escorted Sky out of the pack of Roowks and started walking her slowly toward the barely penetrable shadow ahead. Sky's knees wobbled and she shook with fear. The dark speaker's presence grew more ominous as they approached the blackness. Even the other creatures hidden within seemed nervous, the way they kept back from the speaker.

"STOP!" the speaker commanded when Sky and Grawk had reached the halfway mark. "YOU BROUGHT US A CHILD!" The shockwave from the voice dropped everyone to the ground.

"The prophecy d—doesn't s—say it w—won't b—be a child," the Roowk back at the wagons offered.

"THIS BETTER NOT BE A TRICK," the creature roared.

"W—would n—never…"

"Okay, but since it is half the size we are only going to pay half the price," the speaker said and calmed a little.

Sky thought she could sense the Roowks fighting the urge to protest, but nothing was said.

Three twisted skinny dark-green and black life forms scurried out of the darkness. Their shiny yellow eyes bounced as they hustled toward Sky. They each had a tuft of black hair on the top of their heads. Their facial features were twisted and distorted, making them hideous to look upon. One carried a large heavy sack. They hissed excitedly when they reached Sky and Grawk.

"I'm so sorry," Grawk whispered again.

The creature with the sack dropped it at Grawk's feet. It created a jingling sound when it hit the ground. Then the crooked fingers of the small nightmares clamped on to Sky and carried her away into the darkness.

10

Sky struggled against the vice-like clawed hands carrying her into the darkness. She fought the urge to scream, not wanting to show any signs of weakness. Her heart leapt inside her chest as if it wanted to escape her body as much as she desired to free herself from the hideous life forms.

When they crossed the barrier into the shadow, it was like passing into a new world. The sounds changed from almost complete silence, to a chattering of excited creatures dancing around her with glee. She discovered her eyes could see once she was inside the darkness. Then she focused on the creature with the soul-piercing voice.

The thing appeared to be made of shadow. Dark mists swirled about it and its body shifted like smoke when it moved, taking time to catch up to the red eyes. Whenever it stopped, it formed a devil-like body with black wings folded behind it. The monster circled overhead in a mass of black smoke, wings, and eyes glaring down at Sky.

The smaller creatures set her on her feet in the center of a large stone circle. The monster above her flew around for a moment or two before landing in front of her, a massive shape of darkness which towered over all.

"Now, what am I to make of you?" His voice caused every nerve in Sky's body to burn.

A mist-like finger flicked and then evaporated. With that motion, Sky's bindings and gag disappeared.

"Take me to the Black Fairy," Sky said, trying to stand a little taller than she was, even though her stomach struggled to hold down her morning meal.

"Well, aren't you the brave one for someone so small. Do you know how much pain I can bring down on you?" The thing laughed, prompting Sky's knees to buckle.

With her hands now free, Sky clenched her teeth and put her hands over her ears to try to block the creature's powerful voice. Its laugh carried a note of madness and hunger as if it took great pleasure in torturing others. Sky noticed all the other twisted figures didn't seem to have as much of a problem with the monster's voice as she experienced. The torture continued, pushing Sky lower and lower to the ground.

Maybe it's better this way. Having the Roowks deliver me to this monster than having my friends follow me in this awful place, to be consumed. She felt a surge of happiness at the thought of her friends being safe from this torment.

The painful hot-iron-like laughter of the monster stopped. Its dark shadowy body actually retreated a ways before reforming again. Its eyes burned with a darker red fire as it glared at her. "Interesting."

"What is?" Sky climbed back to her feet.

"Bring her," the monster commanded.

The twisted creatures rushed her and their vice-like fingers clamped on to her body. Once more, they lifted her over their heads and carried her off the ground. They propelled her down a well-trodden path through the dark forest at a hurried pace. The monster swooped back and forth over her and the mass of tangled bodies following the road.

No sunlight penetrated this forest and a strange black moss-like substance covered almost everything. The deeper they penetrated the heart of the Black Fairy's domain, the more a strong decaying odor stung Sky's nose. Eventually she could actually taste the nasty smell on her tongue. She tried to tuck her chin into the top of her shirt to deaden the stench, but with her arms securely held by the strange creatures, she couldn't quite cover her mouth.

It wasn't until she attempted to bury her face in her shoulder that she noticed the source polluting the air. On both sides of the rough dirt road were rows of dead, decomposing bodies tied to crudely constructed wooden stands. The victim's bodies were stretched wide, their arms and legs pulled in a spread-eagle position. Many of the bodies were no more than skeletons covered in torn rags, while others appeared to be recent additions to the ranks. Strange black birds, small animals, flies, and other insects feasted on the rotting flesh still covering most of the deceased.

The gruesome sight forced Sky to stare up at the thick forest canopy and try to think of happier things. She tried to picture what Keal and the others were doing. This thought seemed to make her more miserable. *If they weren't caught by Mika or the Rikits, they are probably looking for me. That might lead them here.*

At this thought she glanced around her surroundings once more. Instead of just seeing the same forest with its rows of victims, torch light appeared, emanating from a massive black castle a ways ahead. It sat down in a deep valley so its high reaching towers didn't break through the canopy created by the massive trees. Sky could barely make out the shapes of small figures walking the high protective walls which encircled the fortress. Directly above the palace, dark clouds hovered where an occasional lightning strike gave the appearance it might rain on the structure at any moment.

The Black Fairy. Sky remembered she still had no idea what the most powerful magic in the world was. *Am I to wind up on one of those poles, to be devoured by birds?*

The black monster flying above them soared toward the castle and disappeared into one of the towers. His body turned into the shadowy smoke to fit through the smaller opening. His arrival triggered a wave of excitement among the creatures carrying Sky toward the castle, and those along its walls started to chant in unison with surprisingly deep voices.

What will happen to the chosen one?
She will fall like the others have done.
How will she scream when she's put to the test?
She'll be drawn and quartered just like the rest.
What will the Queen do to this nasty thing?
Crush her with magic until her ears ring.
How will she howl when she's cracked with the whip?
Wail like the prey of wolves whose flesh they did rip.
How will she cry when in the fire she's thrown?
Like villagers where the dragon's fire is blown.

The gruesome song continued with new ways in which Sky would yell to different forms of torture all the way through the castle gate and up to the giant wooden doors. The second the doors started to open the song ceased and everything grew deathly silent. The doors swung wide to reveal a long dark hall lit by the occasional torch on a wall bracket.

The Shadowy monster materialized in the doorway, almost taking up the entire entrance with his smoky body. The creatures carrying Sky set her down on the entrance steps and backed away.

"Welcome to your death, Odreshinik," the creatures spoke in malicious voices, causing Sky's nerve centers to feel as if they were on fire.

Sky's knees buckled again and she clamped her hands over her ears.

"So, it was a fluke," the monster chided.

"What was?" Sky questioned, rising to her feet.

"Follow me before I let the gurchins have their way with you." It was as like the creature's smoke turned itself inside out so its head pointed the other way and its large black wings sprouted out toward Sky.

Sky glanced at the creatures surrounding her and noticed a hunger in their eyes while they gnashed their pointy teeth and licked their lips eagerly. She suddenly felt colder than she had before and hurried up the steps. The doors to the castle slammed shut behind her with a loud echo and she jumped.

This was the largest building Sky had ever been in. The main hall seemed to stretch on forever. The soft taps of her boots on the stone floor created the only sound. Her escort floated ahead of her by several feet and didn't even appear to be breathing.

The other end of the hall was completely dark. There were no torches or any other light source. Sky tried to make out what waited in the darkness and could detect some object in the center of the room, but nothing moved. The fact all of the torches were now behind them made it even more difficult for Sky's eyes to penetrate the blackness ahead.

A loud crack rebounded off the stone walls and Sky saw the form of the creatures' misty fingers disappear into smoke. A wooden chair flew out of an unseen corner and landed in the center of the hall just at the edge of the blackness.

"Sit," the monster commanded, motioning to the chair with a shadowy hand.

Sky stepped forward and climbed onto the chair, which had been made for a much larger person. She could barely touch the floor with the tips of her toes. Her escort flew into the darkness a few short yards ahead of them and disappeared.

After Sky had pushed herself into the chair, several loud pops echoed through the castle as the rock floor around the chair broke apart. Several snake-like tentacles with long sharp thorns shot out of the ground and wrapped around the chair like a boa constrictor. The thorns pierced Sky's skin in several spots, and she cried out. The strange plant locked her into a very tight spot on the chair. If she attempted to change position, the thorns would stab another body part or the sharp objects already poking her skin pushed deeper into her flesh.

"Are we comfy, my dear?" a very soft, pleasant, female voice asked with a hint of sarcasm.

In the darkness, there was a faint rustling sound and a black shimmer moved in the center. It was as if a shiny piece of darkness created its own black light.

"What's the matter? Are you afraid?" the soft voice taunted.

Sky swallowed the lump in her throat and mustered all of her courage. "No!"

"NO!" the voice snapped, and the shimmer swirled around and stopped. "What's this? A child? Those *idiots* brought me a...*child*? I hope you didn't pay them for this." Her voice changed from a sweet, soothing sound to a high-pitched shriek.

"We paid half," the monster responded from somewhere in the darkness.

Sky wanted to flinch at the sound of his voice but the thorns held her in place.

"Half. Hmm," the pleasant female voice returned as if reflecting upon the amount. "So, those nasty half-breeds must be getting pretty desperate if they are turning to a child to save them." She spoke to herself.

The swishing noise and the shimmering resumed and moved back and forth through the darkness. Sky followed the figure with her eyes and slowly she began to make out more detail. It was a woman about a foot taller than herself, wearing a black shimmery dress. She appeared to be wearing a crown upon her head but Sky couldn't be certain. It was no more than a silhouette walking across the floor in the darkness.

"So, my dear." The pacing stopped. "You've come to destroy me? What great powers does a child possess that her elders do not."

"None!" Sky responded wanting to lower her head and stare at the floor, but the thorns prevented it.

"None. You are quite different from the others. They were so confident they could beat me in what they called a fair fight, *fools*." She chuckled in a sinister, mocking tone.

"And...what happened to them?" Sky swallowed with difficulty.

"You saw them. Didn't they say hello on your way in?" the voice sneered. "They line the road to my palace. Such welcoming decorations, don't you think?" The pacing started again. "I'm not sure what I am going to do with you. Would you be willing to do battle with me?"

"Yes." Sky's voice cracked slightly.

"Really?" The woman's speech held a note of skepticism.

"If I am going to...die. I'd rather go out fighting."

"What if I were willing to let you go? Have my servants drop you off at the edge of my kingdom?" She chuckled.

"I would be back."

"Why?"

"I have nowhere else to go," Sky muttered. The sudden realization she had nothing in her life almost brought tears to her eyes.

The walking picked up speed. The flashes from the dress and the wind-like sound increased with it. "Have you even heard the ridiculous prophecy, child? As if my daughter could do anything right." Anger rose with the woman's voice and became harder.

"Yes."

The walking stopped. "And you don't have this *most-powerful-magic-in-the-world?* As if something that great exists and I don't know about it myself."

"No."

"Then why are you here? Do you think you are this Odreshinik?"

"I'm not sure but others seem to think so." Sky paused. "Did the others think they were?"

"Some of them did...for a few brief moments." She chuckled again.

"Are you afraid of me, child?"

"Yes...and no."

"No." The laughter took on a much higher shrill that filled the entire hall. "Explain yourself." The edge returned.

"I've seen what you've done and it is terrifying, but then I can't see you so what's scary about a shimmering shadow."

The glistening began again, but instead of going back and forth, it headed straight for Sky's chair. Her heart started racing, realizing she couldn't protect herself because of the binding thorns.

At the edge of the dim light a woman appeared in a silky black dress with a dark glittering crown upon her head. She was both terrible and beautiful to behold. Her skin was whiter than a Dijinni's and her face was young and smooth in appearance. Her hair changed color with her movements from black to blond as if a shadow were constantly trying to claim and hide the natural color of her hair. Her lips were painted with a burgundy color and black circles surrounded her deep blue eyes. All the black surrounding her pale white face gave her a deathly appearance.

"Are you afraid now?"

"Wow, the Black Fairy," Sky muttered to herself.

"What's that child? Are you *not* terrified?"

"N—not really."

The shadow that constantly tried to hide the Black Fairy's hair color grew to cover her face.

"WHY?" the Black Fairy demanded.

"Well, I can see how you try to hide your true appearance…"

"AND?"

"You present the darkness and evil, but I can see Sarvina hiding in there and it isn't scary at all. You are actually…well…beautiful."

The Black Fairy jerked back into the darkness. "W—what? Why would you say that?" She acted stunned.

"It's true. I can see your face behind the shadows, and you're beautiful."

The Black Fairy spun around, her black gown shimmering behind her. She resumed pacing but at a frantic clip. She started muttering to herself as she walked to and fro. "Why did they send this child? Why is she here? How am I s—supposed to…She is a swe…" Suddenly the swishing sound and the flashing stopped.

There was another snap and the strange plant pulled away from Sky, retreating back into the ground and the stone floor sealed itself shut. Sky didn't know if it was a trick of her eyes, but it seemed as if a small amount of light began to pierce the darkened room.

Sky gently rubbed the small puncture wounds on her arms and wrists while eyeing the spot the Black Fairy occupied. She didn't know what to do so she decided to wait. She didn't possess the magic necessary to destroy the Black Fairy and didn't know if she had the will to do it.

"So, you've heard the prophecy?" The Black Fairy's voice was soft and pleasant once more.

"Yes."

"Did you understand it?"

"No. I only heard it once under hurried conditions. Who made the prophecy?"

The Black Fairy approached the light once more. She cocked her head slightly to the side as if seeing Sky for the first time. "My daughter."

"Your *daughter*?" Sky felt shocked. Sky tried to remember what she could about the prediction. "But, didn't the mother of the Dijinni's make it? I thought that's what it said." She repeated the words as if she were seeing them in front of her. "The queen had a beloved daughter, the fairest by far. A fairy princess, Lepotica, whose glory was greater than that of a star." She paused for a moment. "So, you are the queen and Lepotica, the mother of the Dijinnis, was your daughter?"

"Yes."

"May I stand now?" Sky felt confused and thought moving about would help her see things clearly.

The Black Fairy waved a hand out in front of her, still eyeing Sky suspiciously.

Sky hopped down out of the wooden chair. She felt sore all over from the wounds the thorns had created. She began to walk in circles around the chair, trying to remember everything she could about the prophecy.

The Black Fairy watched her, standing silently just inside the darkness. "Do you think you can destroy me, child?"

Sky stopped to look at her. "No!"

"But the prophecy says you must destroy me."

"I admit I was on my way here to do it but…" Sky paused.

"But what?"

"Well, one, I never found the world's most powerful magic. But, that's *not* the main reason," Sky said and stepped a little closer to the Black Fairy.

"What's the main reason?"

"I don't think I want to destroy you." Sky couldn't believe what she was saying but it was how she felt. There was something very familiar about the Black Fairy, as if they were connected somehow. "It's like I would be destroying something. I don't know, something important to me."

"Y—you think I—I'm important…to you?" The Black Fairy moved into the light and the shadow was no longer hiding her features. "Why would you say that?" Her voice quivered as if something had touched a nerve.

"I don't know." Sky looked at the ground as if she might find the answer. "I can't explain it. Maybe I wasn't sent to destroy you but help you. Like you're lost."

"Like I'm…lost?" The Black Fairy raised her eyebrows and a smirk crossed her face. "What makes you think I need help, child?"

"I don't know. Maybe I'm supposed to rescue you." Sky began pacing again.

"Rescue *me*? Why would you want to help a wicked woman like me?"

"It's like we need each other." Sky stopped and rubbed her temples.

"What makes you think *that*?"

Sky felt herself drawn to this dark woman. She wanted to look at her face again. "Wait. Wait. Wait. If your daughter is the mother of the Dijinnis…" Sky could see herself moving toward the Black Fairy. Her heart was racing. "Doesn't that make you…my great great…" Sky sprang forward and threw her arms around the Black Fairy in an embrace. "Grandmother."

11

Sky held the Black Fairy tightly after realizing she was the only family she had at the moment. Tears formed in her eyes and rolled down her cheeks.

The Black Fairy hovered her arms open in the air for several moments, looking down at the child wrapped around her. Slowly she lowered her arms and hugged the small girl back, stroking her hair. "My…gra—granddaughter." Her voice cracked.

With her arms locked around the Black Fairy, Sky could feel the woman starting to tremble. There was a warming sensation that started to grow as if the cold chill of early morning were vanishing with the rising of the sun.

Soon the ground started to shake and loud popping and cracking noises echoed around the chamber. Light began to fill the chamber.

"Master, no!" the shadowy monster wailed as it tried to avoid the light and a horrific scream drowned out all other sounds for a moment and then vanished.

Sky marveled at the light filling the hall. Through the windows lining the room, filters of light rained down from the sky. The lights chased away the shadows. Even the strange black mold retreated from the brightness, crawling away like a living thing as the sun consumed it.

When the quaking of the earth stopped, Sky glanced up into her grandmother's face, gone were the shadows covering her hair and skin. The dark circles around her eyes had almost completely faded and her lips changed to a dark red. Tears lined her pale white cheeks as she sobbed uncontrollably.

Sky felt a jerk as the Black Fairy's legs gave out and almost pulled Sky to the floor. Using all of her strength Sky helped the Black Fairy into a sitting position on the floor. Sky huddled close to her and held on tightly. They hugged each other for what seemed like hours. It wasn't until the front doors slowly creaked open that they released each other.

Several men, women, and children stepped cautiously into the entrance. They wore tattered clothing and appeared frightened and confused.

At first there were only a few, but soon several hundred had entered the castle and were slowly making their way down the long hall toward Sky and the Black Fairy. The soft sound of their whispers bounced off the stone walls.

"Who are they?" Sky questioned out of the side of her mouth.

"They were once my prisoners, but they are now free. Thanks to you, you wonderful child." She kissed Sky on the head.

"Are they...what was...your army?" Sky asked with wonder.

As a group of people got to within twenty yards of Sky and the Black Fairy, they stopped and eyed them for a moment.

"What happened to the Black Fairy?" an elderly man called.

"How was she defeated?" another asked.

Sarvina rose to her feet and Sky stood with her.

"The Black Fairy has been destroyed with the world's most powerful magic, *love*." Sarvina glanced at Sky with a smile.

A shock of adrenaline ran through Sky's veins as she realized what had happened. She had the magic all along. It just wasn't the magic she had expected. She hugged her great, great, great grandmother again.

"So who are you?" the people asked, not making the connection. They, like Sky and the others, didn't understand what was meant by destroyed.

"I am Sarvina. I was the Black Fairy. The Odreshinik from the prophecy has arrived and freed all of us from a dark prison," Sarvina announced.

This news seemed to shock and fill the people with awe as they chattered back and forth to each other. They appeared to be looking around for a great warrior who had helped release them from their pitiful state.

"Where is this Odreshinik?" a woman questioned as the crowd drew nearer and increased in size.

"My great, great, great...granddaughter." Sarvina put her hands on Sky's shoulder and moved her to the front. "What is your name, child?" Sarvina whispered in her ear.

"Er...Sky." Sky felt her cheeks redden.

"Sky," Sarvina called.

The crowd didn't act all that impressed with their deliverer, but eyed her curiously.

"What are we to do? Where are we to go?" another shouted. "You stole our *lives*! Now, we have *nothing* to go back to."

A rumble of agreement spread across the crowd. The air turned thick and tense as if they stood in a windowless room and more and more air pressure squeezed in.

"Wrong," Sarvina called. "I am the one who altered your lives. I must be the one to make amends. So, my lands *are* your lands. No harm will ever befall you if you live within my borders. My magic will protect you and assist you in rebuilding your lives."

The tone of the crowd and the feeling in the air changed with Sarvina's announcement. Smiles spread across people's faces and an excited rumble floated above the hall.

"Where will we get supplies?" someone called and a collective 'yes' responded.

"My store houses are your store houses."

A cheer erupted in the hall. People came forward to shake both Sky's and Sarvina's hands. Sarvina expressed deep regret for all she had done and pledged her help to everyone. They spent the better part of the day speaking with the people and addressing their needs. Sky wanted to find a place to rest. Her leg had stiffened up and her stomach rumbled with hunger. She had to constantly stifle yawns that were overpowering her.

When it looked like she was about to get some time alone with her grandmother, the hall filled with winks of light. After each flash of light disappeared a Fairy appeared. They wore elaborate bright shiny outfits that gave off the same shimmer as Sarvina's black dress. They were beautiful with pale skin and an air of magic hung around them. They spoke with melodic voices that seemed to warm Sky's whole body.

The Fairies gathered around Sarvina. They hugged and exchanged pleasantries. Sky was so tired. It wasn't that she didn't want to be part of the reunion, but weariness threatened to overtake her. She had just decided to find a nice corner to sit down when Sarvina motioned for Sky to come and join her.

Soon Fairies where hugging and thanking her. She felt like a dandelion seed being blown in the wind. Before she knew it, tables had appeared out of nowhere and all sorts of foods she'd never tasted were being passed to her. She ate so much she felt sick and her head swam with the need for sleep.

"You look exhausted," said a handsome male Fairy about her age with blond curly locks.

"I am." Sky managed a weak smile. She leaned on her hands supported by her elbows on the table. "How long will this thing go on?"

"Oh, this could go on for days." The boy laughed. "I'm Darn."

"Sky."

"Ah yes, I know. This party is in your honor." Darn motioned to the festivities.

"Too bad I couldn't sneak out and go to sleep." Even now everything in the room seemed skewed as Sky struggled to keep her eyes open. The room swayed back and forth.

"I can see the human side of you isn't prepared for a Fairy gathering. These kinds of celebrations can go on for weeks."

"*Weeks*? I'm not going to make a day." Sky yawned widely.

"Let me see what I can do." Darn smiled and hurried away.

Sky didn't have the energy to watch what Darn was doing. She pretended to be interested in the little bit of food left on her plate by stirring the contents around in a circle. The pattern increased her drowsiness.

Darn caught her just before her head hit the table as it fell forward. It felt like she watched the party through the end of a tunnel and she traveled in the opposite direction. Soon she was comfortable and warm and her eyes snapped shut.

Something wet and kind of rough rubbed Sky across the face again and again. Sky attempted to wipe her cheek when her hand collided with something hairy. She opened her eyes to see Feeleep's dog licking her on the face. *Feeleep!* She sprang backward in the soft bed until she hit the elaborate headboard with the back of her head. Rubbing the throbbing spot on her skull, she looked around for Feeleep.

"How did you get here?" She reached out and rubbed the dog behind the ears. The image of Feeleep and his wife accepting money from the Roowks played in the forefront of her mind. "Did they come with you?"

She slid out of bed to see she wore a shimmering sleeping gown. The dog bounced around her excitedly. *Who changed my clothes? Darn? That boy's going to get it.* She clenched her teeth and headed for the door.

She stepped into the hall and realized she didn't know where she wanted to go.

"It's about time you woke up," Darn said, leaning the chair he was sitting in against the wall behind her.

Sky jumped with surprise and then whirled around. "Did *you* undress me?"

"No. Sarvina did after you were asleep. I know better than to mess with the Odreshinik." Darn chuckled. "Anyway, your friends are waiting for you. It seems you have unfinished business."

Sky's mouth fell open and then she closed it again. With all that had happened in the previous day, she had forgotten her main purpose in coming in search of the Black Fairy. "The Roowks. My sister," she muttered.

"Yes. There is that little piece of the prophecy you haven't yet fulfilled." Darn hopped to his feet and motioned with his head the direction they needed to go.

"How many?"

"How many what?"

"Sorry, how many of my…friends are there." She gazed at Feeleep's dog circling them down the hallway.

"A…an old man and woman, a Dijinni missing a leg, a boy and a mother and her two daughters," Darn said.

"They came together?" Sky questioned.

"Yes, they arrived this morning. This dog lead them right here." Darn motioned to the animal.

Did Feeleep and his wife sell me on purpose? To get me here? Sky pictured the way Feeleep winked at her when she was being handed over to the Roowks. *If he did, that was genius.* "Weren't they questioned at the border? I mean, aren't Grandmother's lands secured?"

"Didn't you want your friends to come?" Darn arched one eyebrow.

"I did. But, I'm confused about two of them." As they turned a corner, she asked, "And did I walk this far last night?"

"Well, I wouldn't call what you did walking, but yes." Darn laughed. "What are you confused about? I can tell you, your grandmother knows everything that is happening inside her lands. Anyone posing a threat to her kingdom will not pass."

"That's good to know." *It must have been part of a plan.*

She followed Darn to a room where her friends sat around a long table, eating breakfast. They all looked much better than the last time she had seen them almost two days ago. They were the only ones in the room.

"I'll leave you alone. If you need anything, I'll be right outside." Darn closed the door behind her.

Everyone smiled at her as she entered the room and all but Sanya rose to their feet. Sariah scuttled forward on her spindly legs and gave her a big hug. "I'm sorry we had to put you through that, but we were being watched. Plus, we knew they would take you where you needed to go. I'm just so relieved it worked out like we planned."

"It's okay," Sky said and hugged her back. "I'm just relieved I had the world's most powerful magic after all."

The old woman released her and stared into her eyes. "And what was it?"

"Love. I destroyed the Black Fairy and saved my great, great, great grandmother at the same time."

"Of course you did." Sariah hugged her again and then led her over to the others.

After exchanging greetings, Sky helping herself to a large breakfast while they caught each other up on all that had happened since they'd parted. It turned out the others had barely avoided both Mika and the Ri-kits back in the valley.

"So, they are both still following us?" Sky questioned.

"Yes, but I don't think they will enter these lands," Feeleep commented.

"I wouldn't bet on it. We weren't going to either until it transformed right in front of us. They are a little more inviting now," Keal said.

"So, the change didn't just happen *here* at this castle?" Sky questioned.

"Nope, the forest flipped from dark and scary to warm and inviting," Sanya said.

All the while they chatted, Marga and her daughters fidgeted nervously.

"I'm sure my grandmother will help you. She is sorry for what she has done," Sky said to Marga.

"Speaking of your grandmother, did she tell you how to defeat the Roowks?" Keal asked eagerly.

"Um, no. I didn't ask. Everything happened so fast after she transformed. People were flooding into the castle and then the Fairies showed up to celebrate. I actually don't remember anything after that until Feeleep's dog woke me up this morning."

"Do you think *maybe* we should go and ask her? I mean, wasn't that the *point* of all this trouble?" Keal suggested.

Sky kind of liked the idea of putting off that part of her adventure. This was the most rest and the happiest she had been since Loov disappeared. "You don't have to go with me any farther. What if something bad happens to you if you do?"

"We've all agreed we're going with you until the end," Feeleep said. "We want to see the downfall of the Roowks as well and you are going to need help."

"Thank you. Well, let's go see what we have to do." Sky rose to her feet and went to the door. She nearly fell over when Sanya rose on two legs and walked to the door as well.

"Oh, a gift from the Fairies who escorted us in. It's a magical leg." Sanya smiled.

"They patched up all our wounds," Feeleep added.

"The perfect stop on our journey," Sky proclaimed.

Darn escorted them back to the great hall where the party from the night before continued as if it had just begun. The sound of beautiful voices singing reached their ears. Groups of Fairies sang ancient melodies up and down the long hall. The feast seemed to have no end and Fairies continued to appear and disappear in flashes of light. Groups of the humans set free by the queen's transformation joined in the celebration.

Sky and the others weaved their way through the crowd but Fairies and humans stopped them to greet them at every turn. They hugged them, shook their hands and kissed them on their cheeks. Holding Sky's friends in almost as high esteem as they did Sky.

When they approached the queen a loud voice rang out across the hall. "Hail Sky, the Odreshinik."

Everyone in the great hall repeated the words.

Sky felt her cheeks redden and wished there weren't so many people surrounding Sarvina. She didn't feel like she was anything special and didn't really desire all of these accolades. She just wanted to speak with her grandmother alone.

Sarvina sprang from her throne and embraced Sky tightly. She took Sky by the hand and pulled her back to the throne where another chair magically appeared for Sky to sit on. Another row of chairs appeared a little farther away for Sky's friends.

"How did you sleep?" Sarvina asked.

"Fine, thanks."

"You're here to ask how to defeat the Roowks," her grandmother said and frowned.

"Yes, and to ask if you can help my friends." Sky motioned to Marga and her daughters. "They were cursed while hunting for food on your lands. Can you free them from it?"

Sarvina motioned for Marga and her daughters to come forward. They hesitated, glancing around the hall nervously as everyone watched them. Slowly, they made their way forward where they bowed to the queen.

Sarvina stood and took Marga by the hand.

A sad smile crossed Sarvina's face. "I am so sorry for what I've done to you. You didn't deserve this. There is some bad news. Many of my curses are permanent. I made them so no one could reverse them, not even me. I am so sorry. Yours is such a curse."

Tears began to roll down Marga's face and she lowered her head.

Sarvina gently took Marga's chin in her hand and lifted it so their eyes met. "There is some good news. I may not be able to reverse the spell, but I might be able to…make it more tolerable."

"How?" Marga asked in almost a whisper.

"By making you know who you are when the transformation takes place and giving you control over your transformation. You will have the power. I wish I could do more. I'm sorry." A tear rolled down Sarvina's face. "You will also be welcomed in my kingdom and no one shall harm you, *ever*."

"*Control* would be great. I just don't want to hurt anyone. And I accept your offer to live under your reign," Marga said. "I do ask one more favor, if I may."

"Please?"

"That you watch over my daughters while I help Sky and the others." Marga put her hands on her daughters' heads and glanced down at them.

"They will stay with me until your return." The queen touched Marga and her daughters in the center of their foreheads. "You are now the masters of your curse."

"Thank you." Marga and her daughters returned to the others.

Sarvina returned to her throne and gave her attention to Sky. "I'm afraid your job will not get any easier, child. I have indeed thought of how you are to overthrow the Roowks. The path I am going to lay before you will not be simple, but I have the highest confidence you will be successful. I wouldn't put my trust in anyone else. You see the curse of the dar is also a curse I *cannot* undo."

"So, how am I to free my sister and the other Dijinnis?" Sky questioned.

"Remember, the prophecy may have a different interpretation than what is expected. I, too, thought to destroy the Black Fairy meant an end to my life, not just the end of my evil life. I feel there may yet be another explanation. I will only be able to give you advice as the strength of my powers remains in my kingdom. If I were to cross the border, I would still have magical powers but I would be vulnerable. As I said, I have thought about how best to help you and the solution will not be easy."

"What is it?" Sky gulped. She had hoped Sarvina would have just been able to break the curse so the Roowks would have no power over her people. This would have been the end of the Roowks rule and saved her sister. She didn't want to put her new friends in any more peril. This new road sounded treacherous and the thought of losing more friends pained her.

"Long ago, dark wizards from a distant world traveled here in search of magical mysteries yet untapped or discovered. They stole many secrets from our world and constructed a lair or base if you will. They thought their work went undetected but I kept an eye on them."

"Wait...wait. People from other...worlds?" Sky didn't understand what that meant.

"I can see where my curse really hurt my descendants in the lack of education. Yes, there are other worlds with life on them. At night when you look up at the sky and see the stars, some of those are worlds far, far away. Anyway, these wizards were extremely magical and had powerful weapons which aided them in their efforts. One such object, when invoked, allowed them to nullify all other magic except their own," Sarvina said.

"Nullify? What does that mean?"

Sarvina laughed a melodic sound. It wasn't a mocking laugh, but one of joy at learning things about her granddaughter. "I can see you will need to come stay with me so I can give you a proper education when this is over. It means, it will make it so no one but those ancient wizards would be able to use magic. This will even affect the power of the dars."

"So, with this thing the dars would lose their power?" Sky questioned.

"Only when this object's power is released and within a certain range. There are limits to all magic," Sarvina said.

"Wouldn't they be back under the influence of the dars once they weren't in the area of this magic?" Sky questioned.

"But if the owner of the dar is destroyed, so is the power of that dar. Freedom is never free. Your people, once temporally released from their bonds, must fight to secure true freedom from the Roowks," Sarvina said. "Anything worthwhile is worth fighting for."

"So, I would have to use it at the opportune moment."

"Yes. Some type of gathering or battle," Sarvina added.

"I was hoping to stay out of a war. I guess that's what you meant by the road may be even more dangerous." Sky frowned.

Sarvina took Sky's hand and patted it. "I wish that is what I had meant. I'm afraid war may be the easier part of this. To retrieve the thing you need is far more dangerous. Not only because of its location, but there are dangerous creatures guarding the lair of these dark wizards."

"And where is this lair?" Sky questioned.

"The Moors."

12

There was a collective gasp among the Fairies, followed by the steady buzz of murmuring, at the mention of the Moors. Sky, however, didn't understand the strange reaction. She glanced around for answers and noticed all the color had drained out of Feeleep's and his wife's faces.

"What's the Moors?" Sky questioned. "And what's this thing called?"

Sarvina cocked her head slightly to the side and eyed her granddaughter. "Of course, you wouldn't know any of the old tales. There are few left in the world who are as old as I, but it is believed the Moors are the origin of all dark magic in our world. Even at the depths of my descent into evil, I did not go there physically. I have, however, visited the Moors in visions. This knowledge I will share with you to aid you on your quest. And as for what this thing is called, I know not. I have seen it and its location in visions and will show it to you."

"How?" Sky swallowed. *I don't want to visit the source of evil! Not now, not ever.* A shiver ran down her spine and her palms started to sweat. Her friends had turned from pale to a slight greenish color.

"Like this." Sarvina put an index finger on the center of Sky's forehead.

Instantly, Sky found herself standing in a dark, mist covered swamp. She attempted to look at her physical body but it didn't appear to exist. It was as if only her conscious mind lived in this place. She observed the scene and suddenly sped forward through the marsh to a massive area of jungle, elevated several meters out of the swamp. A wall of thorns grew around the outer edge of this land mass to form a protective barrier.

The entire island spun counter clockwise until it stopped in front of an opening in the thorns with a stone archway. Once more Sky zipped forward, the jungle changing to a blur of green and black shapes until she stopped on the edge of a dilapidated fortress. The ancient structure had started to crumble in spots and the plant life began to reclaim the building.

The vision took Sky inside the walls and deep into the heart of the structure. She arrived in a large room with barely enough light to see by.

The entire floor was covered with a dark oily water except for a small walkway around the outer edge and a path leading to a small island in the middle. She flew over the water and hovered above the island. From this position she could see what looked like a large black diamond in the mouth of a serpent.

As soon as the vision came it disappeared, and she stared into her great- grandmother's eyes. She sat in that position for a few moments, trying to recollect every detail of what she had seen.

"How am I to use it?" Sky finally questioned.

"If my impressions are correct, I think you will need to activate it with your magic. How this is done exactly, I'm not sure. I have faith in you. You will figure it out."

"That isn't much to go on." Sky sighed. Just once she wanted something to be easy.

"Once more I need to caution you about the creatures who guard the keep. I did not show them to you in the vision, but they are there. They are very powerful and hunger for flesh. They also have the ability to change their skin. They can make themselves look like anyone in your party. You must be very careful. I also sense something in the water by the object."

"Is there anything else?" Sky swallowed.

"Yes, the Roowks will now know who you are by what has happened here. They delivered you so they know what you look like. They will be hunting you the moment you leave my kingdom. I have sent out spies and they have reported Roowk movements all around my borders. Armies are moving."

"And I thought the hard part was going to be defeating you." Sky grimaced.

Sarvina stood and pulled her into another tight embrace. "Look for help from me, when you are most desperate. I love you, child."

"I love you."

Sky and her companions stayed another two days in Sarvina's castle, recovering from injuries and the toils of their journeys. They spent their time packing supplies and weapons for their march to the Moors.

Sarvina supplied them with maps that would show them how to reach the Moors. "You will have to rely on what I've shown you once you actually arrive at the Moors."

It wasn't long until their wagon was loaded and they were saying their goodbyes. It seemed the entire kingdom showed up to send them off. Fairies and humans gathered around the castle to wish them luck.

Sarvina stood on the steps leading to the castle to wish them goodbye. She held Sky tightly for several minutes and kissed her on the forehead. "I have a present for you."

"I've never had a present before." Sky eyes misted.

Sarvina held out a beautiful blue crystal on a gold chain. "Turn around." Sky obeyed and Sarvina fastened the crystal around her neck. "If you ever need help, just hold the crystal tightly and think of me."

Sky spun around, embraced her great-grandmother, and then kissed her on the cheek.

"Come back to me, child."

"I will." Sky fought back the tears threating to overtake her. She turned quickly and joined her friends in the wagon.

Keal cracked the reins and the tall scaly beasts pulled the cart forward. Everyone in the kingdom waved a farewell. Many of the Fairies sang songs and tossed flower petals on them. Keal drove them down a road leading in the opposite direction from which they had entered. In their planning, under Sarvina's advisement, they had picked an exit on the southeast corner of her kingdom. For the Roowks to reach the road ahead of Sky and the others was almost impossible because of a jagged towering mountain range.

The transformation of her grandmother's kingdom astonished Sky. Where it had been a vile and lifeless place, sunlight breached the canopy and new flowers and green grasses had replaced the black moss. Birds and insects busied themselves about the new plant life. Deer and other animals nibbled on the grasses.

Sky wondered if there had been bodies lining this road like the one she had entered. She was sad to be leaving this beautiful place. It seemed to her, by the silence of her companions, they were struggling with the same thoughts.

They stopped for a quiet lunch. No one spoke and in a half hour they were back on their way. Shortly after noon, the road started to climb and a high mountain range appeared in the distance through the trees. The plant life changed from leafy forest to pines and tall mountain grasses.

"How much farther to the border?" Marga asked when the road turned upward at a sharper angle.

"According to the map it is at the top of the pass. So I'm guessing we should reach it by nightfall." Feeleep held the map out in front of him, gazing at it.

Everyone glanced at the towering peaks ahead. Dark rain clouds circled and started to collect around the mountain range.

"I'm glad we packed blankets. We could be in for a long cold night," Sariah said.

"We could build a fire?" Keal suggested.

"No, we can't," Sky cautioned. "That would indicate to unwanted eyes there are travelers on the road."

"Do you really think the Roowks are in these mountains?" Keal questioned, lowering his voice slightly.

"I'm not sure but we better act like they are."

"I think we should camp on this side of the border of Sarvina's land and maybe do a little scouting on foot before crossing over," Sanya suggested.

The higher they climbed the cooler the air temperature grew. The clouds now covered the sky and lightning began to flash in the distance. The wind, which had been still all day, began to whip them in the face, announcing the arrival of the storm.

As they continued to climb, the wind increased in intensity, carrying the smell of rain. Booms of thunder now reached them and lightning danced all around them. The road became more treacherous and narrow while the right side became a steep drop off.

"We should look for some place to camp," Feeleep called over the wind as the rain started to fall.

Rain poured down on them and the wind howled, penetrating their clothing, soaking them to the skin in a matter of minutes. The wind pounded their faces, affecting the beasts' ability to pull the wagon forward. The hard dirt road became a muddy mess. The beasts' hooves began to lose their footing in the ever deepening mud and the cart slid around each corner.

"There." Sanya pointed to a small overhang against the side of the cliff on the corner where they would be blocked from the wind.

Keal parked the wagon as tightly as he could against the cliff face so the beasts pulling would also be sheltered from the wind and their heads protected from the rain. They all helped empty the supplies and then huddled under the small overhang.

They all sat with their backs against the cold stone, watching the heavy rain fall. Their breath rose in steady mists into the cold night air. They leaned against each other in an effort to keep warm as all of the blankets and clothing were now wet. The meager meal of cheese and berries helped to ease some of their discomfort.

"We may be stuck here for a few days," Feeleep commented from the end closest to the corner. "There is a regular river running down the road now."

"Well, the storm won't be helping the Roowks either," Keal added.

"I wish we knew where they are," Sanya said in a worried tone.

"Is something the matter?" Sky asked, trying to meet her eyes in the dark.

"I just hope they aren't carrying a spare dar. They could turn me against you. The only thing that gives me hope is the fact they never brought extra dars on military missions, but that isn't to say they won't."

"We'll worry about that if the time comes," Sariah said and put an arm around Sanya's shoulder.

"Well, I don't think we are going to discover anything tonight." Sky yawned.

Everyone tried to settle down and get some sleep.

Sky awoke to discover the rain had stopped and the moonlight now made its way through the thinning clouds. A shiver spread through her body and she wondered how long she had been asleep. Keal snored softly beside her and the others appeared to be out as well. She was just about to close her eyes again when she realized Marga was gone.

Her head snapped up and she tried to spot her. *The moon is up. Did she transform? Why didn't she attack us?* She made sure she could feel her sword handle lying on the ground next to her. Very slowly, she slid away from Keal and rose to her feet. She quietly picked up a sword, a bow, and a sheath full of arrows without disturbing the others and made her way out to the muddy road. Sky slung the bow and arrows over her shoulder so she could keep her sword at the ready.

The light of the moon made it easy to see up and down the road. Her boots sunk several inches into the saturated surface. A cool wind whipped her hair, not helping the discomfort from her damp clothing. The wind also made it difficult to hear anything. She stood gazing up the road in the distance when a dark shape moved on the road several bends ahead.

Sky's heart thumped against her chest and she rubbed her dry tongue against the top of her mouth. The dark shape vanished around a corner but appeared to be heading in her direction. She gripped the hilt of her sword and held it out in front. Her cold fingers hurt as she tightened them around the handle.

The animal moved at a quick pace, as it would appear and disappear around the road, heading straight for Sky. She positioned her legs a little wider and bent her knees slightly, ready for a possible attack. Cocking the sword back, she prepared to swing.

The black creature put on the brakes as it rounded the final bend and caught sight of her standing in the middle of the street. It glanced around as if checking that it wasn't about to be trapped. Then it approached Sky cautiously.

Sky recognized Marga in her transformed state. *Why isn't she attacking? She didn't have...control...last...time. Control, of course.* Sky remembered how Sarvina couldn't remove the curse but gave Marga control to know who she was when she changed. Sky relaxed and lowered her sword. Even though Marga seemed at ease, Sky's heart continued to race. The memory of her first encounter flashed in the back of her mind.

When Marga, in her black monstrous form, was within a few feet she stopped and looked up into Sky's eyes. She kept eye contact and then glanced back over her slick black body.

Sky only had to bend slightly so she was on the same level with Marga, whose night form was larger and heavier than her human self. Marga kept gazing into Sky's eyes and then throwing her head back over her shoulder.

"What?" Sky questioned, trying to peer into the darkness behind Marga. The wind continued to move the trees, making it difficult to see anything that wasn't out in the open.

Marga turned and trotted back up the road a few yards before stopping to look back at Sky.

"Do you want me to follow?"

Marga gave a distinct nod and then waited for Sky to follow. Sky stomped through the thick mud, which made travel slower than normal. Marga would venture ahead and turn to make sure Sky was still coming. The almost full moon gave enough light to help Sky avoid stumbling or stepping into huge puddles. Trying to move as quickly and quietly as possible helped her body to generate enough heat to chase away the cold.

Clouds of steam rose from Sky's breath, which began to increase with the strain of chasing Marga up the inclining road through the mud. When Sky caught up with Marga at the summit, she stood like a statue peering ahead.

Sky traced Marga's position to an area to the left of the road where there was no longer a cliff face shooting up into the air. Watching closely, Sky thought she saw a small flicker of light. It would appear every few seconds and was very faint.

"What is that?" Sky whispered. "Can we get closer?"

With this question, Marga crept forward once more at a slower pace. Sky was able to stay right behind Marga at her new tempo. Marga stayed on the road for another fifty yards and then turned into the trees. They climbed up a natural gap between the trees and Marga scaled the slope with ease while Sky had to use her hands to scramble over a rocky section. When they reached the top of the hill, they weaved through the trees heading parallel with the road.

The branches scratched and poked Sky as she pressed forward. The tall structures blocked the moonlight, making it more difficult to see. Sky wondered how much farther when Marga stopped and the flicker of firelight danced through the trees not more than fifty yards ahead of them.

The fire was small and from Sky and Marga's position, Sky couldn't make out who they were or how many of them there were. She stepped forward until she was even with Marga's head.

"I can't see much. Can we get closer?" Sky leaned in tight to Marga's ear.

Marga moved like a cat stalking its prey as she crept silently forward. Sky stayed right behind her, trying to put her feet down in Marga's footprints. The rain soaked ground muffled their footfalls over the fallen pine needles.

They worked their way behind a large tree about ten yards from the camp. Three creatures Sky had never seen before huddled around a small campfire, while several others slept nearby. They all wore clothes that matched the forest and would help them blend in with the trees and shrubs. Even their skin was brown and had an earthy look to it. Their eyes were like black marbles and their hair green like the grass. When they spoke, their voices sounded deep and rough. Each one had a sword at his belt and other weapons strapped across his body.

Two more joined the others at the fire.

"I don't know where it went or what it was, but I didn't like the look of it," one grumbled.

"Why didn't you track it?" a creature at the fire questioned.

"You didn't see the size of its claw marks in the mud. I didn't want to tangle with some black nightmare that might rip us to shreds when we ain't got a buyer and when we have other important business. We have a chance to make a lot of gold," said the other who had joined the fire.

"You could have used the volks. There ain't nothing in these mountains that could get away from them, nothing," a second at the fire said and chuckled.

"Yes, but they might have let our friends hiding under the rock shelf a ways back down the road know we are here," another said. "And it wouldn't do us any good to have them turn back into that witch's land with the border so close."

Sky felt stunned. *They know we're here. And what are volks?* No matter what side of the tree she peered around, she couldn't locate any strange animals. *How are we going to get past this small army and their pets?*

"When are the others supposed to get in behind them?" another asked.

Sky's knees started to tremble and her stomach twisted into such a tight knot that she felt the urge to vomit. She shot a glance back over her shoulders, visioning her friends hiding under the rock shelf. Her eyes met Marga's and Sky could tell she was thinking the same thing.

Sky thrust her head behind them to indicate they needed to get back to their friends.

Once more Marga took the lead and followed the same path which had brought them to the camp. When they reached the spot where they needed to turn back to the road, Sky put her hand on Marga's back to get her attention.

She moved next to Marga's ear. "Don't wait for me, I can find my way back. You're faster. Get back and wake the others. Try to make them understand. I'd hate for them to be caught while sleeping."

Marga held her gaze for a moment and then bounded away. Sky watched her move with cat-like ease among the rocks until she had disappeared from sight. *What are these things that could take Marga out in that monstrous form? And can I do anything to help us get past while they aren't aware I'm this close to their camp?*

Sky knew she should return to the others but something told her this might be the best way to survive. *If I can find their weakness, we might be able to escape.* She snuck back down to the tree where she and Marga had hidden before. The strange men continued to discuss their future gains and how they would spend it.

The firelight still only revealed the five members of the group and the few sleeping close by she had seen earlier. She decided she would have to move about the camp to get a more accurate count of the enemy and a possible glimpse of the volks they talked about.

She proceeded slowly, triple checking to make sure she wasn't missing a guard or unseen danger. When she had managed to make it to the back side of the camp, off to her left savage growls and snarls reached her ears, mingled with what sounded like cheering. *What the heck is that? It doesn't appear to be coming from the camp.* The more Sky crept in the direction of the strange sounds, the more distinct it became.

There were people laughing and cheering amid roars and growls. Another light appeared ahead and down a slope into a small bowl-like clearing. Fires burned all around the clearing, lighting a wooden constructed arena where two horrible looking creatures fought a terrible battle. A walkway lined the top of the fence and a drunken crowd of these earthy men egged the combatants on. They swilled from bottles and mugs, cheering as if the only thing that mattered in the world was the fight.

We're in trouble. Sky counted well over thirty of these weird men, including the group back by the fire. *And with guards, we are probably talking closer to forty-five.* She inched her way forward and spotted a few strange men on the ground level, poking the creatures with spears to spur them to fight. *Fifty.* Each new discovery brought her spirts lower at the desperation of their situation.

She circled the small valley where she came across about a dozen of the strange monsters, shackled to trees with heavy chains. They resembled mutated wolves and stood taller than Sky, on muscular legs. Their skin appeared as if they had been dipped in boiling water. Large red and yellow bumps the size of Sky's fist covered over their skin. Their faces were a mass of teeth, with large bulbous eyes. The only hair on their bodies grew on their tails and a Mohawk like strip on their heads.

These nightmarish things cowered and whimpered at the sounds coming from the small arena, sensing something they didn't like. Every time the crowd roared with excitement, the creatures tucked their tails farther between their legs and tried to make their chains extend farther in the opposite directions.

Sky ventured a little closer when one of the beasts spotted her. It raced forward, howling wildly, until it hit the end of its chain, which yanked it off of its feet. Sky quickly ducked for cover when one of the earthy-men rushed out of nowhere, screaming for the beast to settle down.

"What are you yapping at? You'll shut it or you'll be next in the arena." The man cracked a whip at the animal, beating it back.

Sky watched in horror as the man continued to hammer the beast and any of the others who looked at him with the whip. The monsters tried to retreat and cried in pain under their master's brutality. A fire ignited in Sky's gut, which drove her out of her hiding place. She rushed forward with sword raised. The strange man didn't even know what happened when he fell.

Sky's rage turned to fear as every monster's eyes locked on to her.

13

There was a long uncomfortable moment of silence and time seemed to slow down.

Sky held her sword in one hand and put out the palm of her other toward the creatures staring at her. "Easy. I just want to leave," she spoke softly while taking a cautious step backward.

The monsters watched her curiously, tilting their heads to the side while their large pointed ears twitched back and forth. Their attention jumped from Sky to the fallen man, but they acted unsure of what they should do.

"He's all yours," Sky whispered softly adding a little magic to her voice in an effort to draw their attention away from her as she took another step backward.

After what seemed like an eternity, one of the creatures moved toward the corpse. It sniffed it before taking a huge bite and picking up the man while thrashing its head back and forth. The others quickly followed the first's lead. Sky tried not to watch the horrific scene as she continued to make her getaway.

"What's going on here?" Another of the strange men rushed forward. "What have you monsters done?" His presence startled the volks, but they didn't retreat. They exposed their teeth and snapped at him as beasts do to protect a meal.

The newcomer snatched a whip from his belt and began swinging it around, trying to restore order. He didn't appear to notice Sky standing only a short distance away when she attacked again.

This time the volks went to work on the fallen man without giving Sky a chance to back away. They appeared to accept her as one of their own, moving around her, sniffing her and rubbing against her.

Sky probably wouldn't have minded touching the beasts if they hadn't been so hideous, but she put her hand out so they could take in her scent. She used her magic to sooth and communicate that she wasn't a threat to them. Sky's final act to gain their trust caused her great anxiety, as she didn't know how well she could keep the pack from attacking her friends, should they meet. She found the key among the remains of the victims and released the volks from their chains.

They continued to circle her and followed her to the edge of the hill overlooking the arena. They seemed to sense she was going to rid them of their captors, waiting and watching.

Sky studied the arena, searching for a weakness. *They are drunk. All I need to do is get them on the ground. I wonder what would happen if I could get one of the walls to collapse? Would the others come down?*

"Wait," Sky whispered and used her magic when a couple of the monsters started forward. "I don't want you to get hurt. Let me even the odds."

The creatures seemed to comprehend what the magic was telling them, and they remained on the top of the hill while Sky hurried down the slope. Her eyes scanned every one of the strange men on this side of the arena. She paused once while one of the men poking the animals through gaps between the walls worked his way around to jab a creature on Sky's side of the cage.

Sky waited for him to move away before taking a closer look at the arena. The structure appeared to be fairly well constructed, which indicated they used it often. Torches propped up in brackets every few feet and on the second level illuminated the entire area. The spectators continued to cheer and spur the fight on. The scent of sweat and ale hung heavily around the entire valley. *I need to get them on the ground.* She followed the man around the enclosure, searching for a weakness in the stadium.

The man stopped and began cussing and stabbing the animal through the cage with a spear. "You'll fight or I'll stick you good," the man roared, almost shoving his whole arm through a crack between two poles.

The rage Sky had felt up on the hill when the guard beat the creatures returned in full force. She swung the bow off her shoulder and fitted an arrow in one fluid motion. Seconds before she let her arrow fly, the man prodding the other beast rounded the corner behind the first man and his eyes met Sky's. Before he could cry out, Sky's arrow silenced him. He fell into the other man, knocking him to the ground.

"What..."

The shocked earthy-man, didn't finish his sentence before Sky's next arrow silenced him.

Protest immediately rose from the spectators as the combatants, without the constant prodding, stopped fighting. Sky raced around the arena, pulling the torches out of their brackets with one hand and dropping them at the base of the wooden structure. She held her sword in her other hand and destroyed the ladders leading to the second level at the same time.

When she reached the door, she slashed the ropes with her sword and released the creatures trapped inside.

Cries of panic from the drunken crowd rose with the flames as they scrambled for a way off of the raised walkway above. As the fire spread, men started to leap off the higher level to land hard upon the ground.

With a call of magic, Sky set her new friends in motion. The terrible creatures launched themselves down the hill and attacked their former masters. The scene which played out before Sky's eyes was both horrifying and incredible at the same time. The monsters laid waste to their former jailers in an act of vengeance and a fight for freedom.

The nine or so earthy-men who were on guard and clustered around the fire raced to the scene and were quickly consumed by the monsters. Sky used her bow to aid her new friends from the sober watch, when they arrived on the scene. After she disposed of the first couple of men they tried to retreat instead of fight, but the speed of the four-legged monsters quickly overtook them.

In the early morning light of the predawn hours, Sky and her new companions found their way back to the road. A mist hung over the trees in the cool morning hours, a remnant from the heavy rains. The newly freed creatures pranced around Sky in an animalistic dance of delight as they followed her down the road.

The road felt surprisingly hard in the cool morning air. Sky's feet didn't sink in as deeply as the night before. She walked the road with the pack roaming around her, keeping her safe but also taking comfort in her presence.

Sky sang softly to them, with her magic calming and soothing them in an effort to keep them under control for when she reached her friends. She wasn't sure how these wild animals would react to her companions. *They've probably been used to hunting all sorts of life forms, including Dijinnis and humans.* She was having trouble recognizing any landmarks because it was night when she followed Marga on this section of the road. She slowed her pace and tried to listen. *Nothing! I would prefer to have a little distance between us instead of arriving on top of them with these creatures.*

To Sky's relief, the others were heading her way and she caught sight of them about a hundred yards away while they were rounding a corner. The creatures seemed to sense their presence before Sky spotted them. They bristled and snarled, sniffing the air while pointing in that direction. Sky stopped and reached out with her magic, calling the animals to her.

They responded and gathered close. She could feel them, they were relaxed and at ease. "Good boys," she whispered to them, touching them as they came within her reach.

Keal drove the wagon slowly along the muddy road. The beasts pulling the wagon sunk into the mud with each step, making the going slower than normal. Everyone in the wagon stared at Sky in disbelief. Keal kept a hand on the reins and one on the hilt of his sword, while the others appeared on guard as well. When they were within twenty yards, Keal pulled the wagon to a halt.

"Are you okay?" Sanya questioned.

"Yes," Sky responded, and she could sense an eagerness among the pack. It wasn't an aggressive urge but an inquisitiveness, as if they wanted to make new friends.

"Those are some lovely pets you got there," Keal commented with a worried look. "Aren't you afraid you might catch something?"

"Well, if that's what you are worried about. Start panicking. They want to meet you," Sky said and chuckled, then with her magic told the monsters to go to her friends.

Everyone nearly jumped into a huddle in the back of the wagon at once, prompting Sky to break out into a fit of laughter. She doubled over and tears formed in her eyes.

"T—they won't hurt you. In fact...they saved all of our lives. With their help, I wiped out a small army waiting for us just up the road," Sky said while laughing and struggling for air.

Slowly everyone relaxed and reached out of the wagon to let the animals sniff and lick their hands. Eventually, Sanya was the first to climb down into their midst. Sky joined them at the wagon and coxed everyone else down.

"They aren't very pretty are they?" Sariah said, still looking very uncomfortable standing next to a couple of the monsters.

"How many were there?" Marga questioned after everyone relaxed among their new friends.

"At least forty. And they were going to use these things to hunt us." Sky motioned to the animals, moving about them excitedly.

"So, I see you are keeping up your role of deliverer," Feeleep commented. "Or did you do something different to get these creatures on your side?"

"We should probably get going. I will tell you what happened while we are moving. I'm sure Marga already told you, there is another army coming up behind us."

Everyone climbed back into the wagon except Sky and Marga. They chose to walk to avoid weighing the wagon down in the mud and to keep their new friends close.

Sky relayed to them what had happened after Marga went back to get them. They in turn explained how they were worried sick, not being able to understand Marga until the moon disappeared.

"That's when they really started to panic. I was back well over an hour by the time I transformed. You should have returned by then," Marga added.

"Yes, that was not very smart," Feeleep added and his wife nodded.

"I just figured I was there and the enemy didn't know, so why not try to find a weakness," Sky shrugged.

"I think you were using your head…for once." Keal smiled.

A beautiful day greeted them. As the sun climbed higher in the sky, the mists disappeared and spread warmth across the high mountain pass. They reached the summit before noon and started on the way down. The sunshine dried the mud, making the road less treacherous and easier work for the beasts pulling it.

Their new four-legged friends moved off the road and into the trees. They continued to keep even with Sky and the others. Sky wondered why they were no longer dancing around her and kept watching for them in the trees.

"It's the sun," Sanya said while watching her. "I think it hurts their skin. It may be the cause of their boils. I was wondering if those weird men kept them in the sun during the day."

"Huh, now I wonder if their skin will heal if the sun was the cause of those sores," Sky said.

"Possibly," Marga added.

"I want to know what they are going to eat," Keal said with an edge of nervousness in his voice. "I mean, that's an awful lot of mouths to feed."

"I figure as a last resort we can offer them you." Sky chuckled and the others laughed.

They reached the low hills on the backside of the mountain range toward late afternoon. Feeleep constantly studied the map, trying to figure out the quickest and safest possible route to the Moors.

When the sun started to set, they stopped for the night. As soon as the sun sank behind the horizon, the strange creatures emerged from the shadows of the trees. Everyone noticed immediately the difference in their

skin. While they still had sores all over their bodies, the sores had decreased in size and number.

"It looks like Sanya was correct," Sariah commented.

"It's kind of nice having our own vicious escort. I'm sure they would
scare off almost anything taking an interest in us," Sky said.

"Yes, but I'm afraid we may lose them tomorrow. We are going to
move out of the forest and there won't be any cover for them," Feeleep
added.

"How long do you think it will take us to reach the Moors?" Keal
questioned as they ate a cold dinner.

They decided it was still safer not to build a fire. If the Roowks had
sent these strange men after them, there would be others.

"At least three more days. And that's if we don't run into any trouble
along the way. I figure once the Roowks know we slipped through their
net, they will send everything they can after us. I'm sure they are already
edgy, realizing a change has come over the Black Fairy. That will tell
them the prophecy is about to be fulfilled," Feeleep said.

"The fact Sky wiped out half of an army should buy us some time,
right?" Keal asked. "I mean, they might not even realize we came this
way for a while, at least."

"I hope you're right," Sanya murmured.

The next morning they left before the sun was up. It was midmorning
when they reached the end of the forest, and the rolling hills stretched out
in front of them with tall swaying grasses. Sky used her magic to try to let
the pack know they needed to stay behind to avoid the sun. They whimpered and their eyes dropped, conveying their sadness at the parting.

The next two days went by without incident. The road grew steadily
rougher and less traveled. Although they passed a few travelers on the
road, most of which kept their heads down as they went by, that was only
on the first day. Now even animals and birds were scarce. Instead of tall
lush grasses, the land appeared parched and dry brown stalks covered the
dusty soil. A tree grew here or there, with only a smattering of leaves
hanging from their branches.

Soon a nasty boggy smell permeated the air, making it so they didn't
want to breathe through their noses. Feeleep and his wife wore scarves
tied about their faces to lessen the effect of the stench. Sky and the others
pulled their shirts up over their noses to breath into their clothes. They
had been steadily climbing for the better part of an hour, blocking their
vision of what lay ahead.

"I sure hope we get away from this smell soon," Keal complained.

"Well, I hate to disappoint you, but that smell is where we're heading. This lovely aroma is coming from the Moors," Feeleep said.

"I was afraid of that," Sanya said and moaned.

"Let's get in and out of here as fast as we can," Keal pleaded. "I'm starting to taste this stuff in my mouth."

"I don't think it is going to be a short stop. We have to find an island in the middle of a swamp. And not only that, but we can only enter the island from a certain side," Sky informed them.

"How big is this island?" Sanya asked.

"I'm not entirely sure," Sky responded.

The wagon crested the top of a hill and a massive sunken valley spread out before their eyes. A swamp spread everywhere and stretched all the way to the horizon. Instead of the dry grass and dying trees which had greeted them for the last two days, a thick tangle of swampy plants and misshapen trees sprang from the water.

"STOP," Sky shouted, a little louder than she would have liked. She glanced around and everyone else followed her lead.

Keal immediately brought the wagon to a halt. "What?"

"This may be the best vantage point we get." Sky stood up on the seat of the wagon to get a better view of the Moors.

The others rose to their feet, hoping they could get a better view as well. Even with the sun high in the sky, a thin layer of mist hovered over the Moors, making it difficult to make out specific details.

"I'm betting the island is there." Keal pointed to an area of the swamp about a mile away from the edge of the valley.

"I can't see anything. What makes you think that?" Marga questioned.

"See how the mist sits higher there than anywhere else. There is a sizeable section where the mist is a lot higher than the rest of the swamp." Keal drew the area in the air with his finger for the others to follow.

"You know something, I think you're right…for once," Sanya razzed Keal and everyone chuckled.

"Hey, I'm bound to get something right once in a while," Keal responded.

"Should we go down for a closer look?" Sky eyed the area Keal had found.

"Wait a minute. Everyone move so I can see better," Feeleep said. He dropped down to the bed of the wagon. He flipped the map over and spread it across the wooden planks. Then with a small piece of charcoal, he used the parchment to sketch out what they guessed was the location of the island. "We may not recognize the different layer when we are on the same level as the bog. I want to give us a general direction to head for."

Everyone added comments about details they could see, to make Feeleep's picture as accurate as possible. Soon he had a drawing with a few prominent landmarks on it that they hoped they would recognize when they were right on top of it.

Keal coaxed the Falaps down the hill. They found a spot under some trees where they could hide the wagon and the beasts could find plenty to eat.

"Either the stench isn't as bad or I'm getting used to it," Marga commented as they set up camp.

"I'm sure it's the latter," Sariah commented.

"I think we should split up into two groups and go around the swamp in opposite directions to try to find the best way in. We could meet back here by sundown and then try to enter tomorrow morning," Sanya suggested.

"That's a good idea." Keal smiled. "Nice to see you *finally* get one. I noticed it came after mine."

Everyone chuckled again. It was decided that Sky and Keal would go westward around the edge of the swamp, while Sanya and Marga would travel an eastward direction. Feeleep and his wife would remain at the camp to keep an eye on things.

"Just don't do anything stupid," Sariah warned, while eyeing Sky and Keal as they went to depart.

"We won't," Sky promised, and the two of them took off along the shore.

Walking along the bank of the swamp and getting a decent view of what may lay just a little ways out into the water was more difficult than Sky and Keal would have liked. Thick reeds and willows grew everywhere and the shoreline was a muddy mess. After trying to fight their way through the thickets to see what was just beyond the shore, they decided that climbing the massive trees a short distance from the shore proved more fruitful. Some of the larger trees' heavy branches extended out over the water, giving them a better view than if they had just stood on the shore. They observed they could still make out the section where the mists rose higher than the rest of the swamp.

"There are also trees growing above the mists. That means we should be able to climb trees here and there to keep us heading in the right direction," Keal pointed out.

"Yes. Now all we need is an easy way out there," Sky commented as they descended a tree.

"Well, since we know how to find the place we think is the island, let's move a little quicker and see if we can just find a good spot to enter the swamp from."

"I think this swamp is making you smarter. It smells so bad that your ideas today don't stink." Sky smirked.

"Nice."

They continued to search for another hour without any luck. The edge of the swamp remained inaccessible, from what they could tell, and didn't show any signs of an entrance.

"I hope they found something." Sky glanced at the sun while shielding her eyes. "We should probably start heading back…"

The sound of a deep bell gonging caught their attention. A second later the first breeze they had felt all day swirled around them and disappeared. They froze, straining their ears for the sound again.

"Okay, you heard that too?" Keal asked.

"Yes. And I think it came from not too much farther ahead." Sky motioned toward the west.

For the first time all day, they drew their swords and started forward. They hurried from one place of cover to the next, always checking for any sign of life before advancing again. When they were about a dozen yards beyond the trees they spotted a clearing. They hid behind a large trunk to scope out the area.

It wasn't a natural clearing but appeared to be constructed by someone. A triangle-shaped cobblestone floor covered the ground, with one of the points extended under an archway out into the swamp. The archway stood taller than the trees, with a tower on each side. A bell hung on a smooth wooden poll next to the archway.

"I think we found the entrance to the swamp," Sky commented in a hushed voice.

"What is it?" Keal questioned.

"I'm not sure." Sky shook her head while focusing on the structure.

They remained in the trees while watching the strange area for almost a half hour.

"What do you want to do? If we are going to check it out, we need to do it now. The others will expect us back in a little while," Keal said.

"Do you think it's safe?"

"I don't know. And what rang the bell?"

Sky inhaled a deep breath and then released it. "Let's do it." She left their cover and moved out onto the cobblestone triangle, with Keal right behind her.

They held their weapons at the ready and constantly checked everywhere as they scoped out the strange structure. There were unrecognizable characters painted all over the cobblestone floor that appeared to be laid out in a pattern. In the very center of the floor was a pit filled with ashes.

Spiral staircases led to the pinnacle of each tower, where the tops were places for lookouts. They tried to spot their camp from the top of one of the towers but were unsuccessful. The mists from the swamp actually swirled around them, making it difficult to see the land behind them.

"No wonder we didn't see this from the hill." Sky motioned to the foggy substance floating around them.

"Well, let's check out the 'dock.'" Keal pointed to the section of the floor which extended under the archway and out onto the swamp.

They bounded down the stairs and headed for the archway. When they tried to pass under it, an invisible force lifted them off the floor and tossed them backward. They landed hard on their backsides, skidding several feet.

"What was that?" Keal got to his feet, rubbing his backside.

"It was dark magic. I could feel it." Sky collected her sword, which had flown out of her hand. "Ah." Sky winced as she grabbed the hilt of her sword. She noticed several cuts where her hands had slid across the rough stones. She gently wiped the blood on her pants.

They approached the archway again but didn't try to cross the threshold.

While holding her sword in one hand, Sky held the palm of her other hand up and slowly pressed it forward. Her hand actually went a few inches into the archway before she stopped. Her body trembled as she touched the magic protecting the archway.

"What do you feel?" Keal watched her closely.

"Darkness, like I've never felt before. It is terrifying. It is kind of like that monster on the battlefield which put images into our minds. While its images were of what it was doing and what it saw, these are of torment and suffering beyond imagination. Souls trapped in service to evil."

Keal glanced all around them. "Let's get back. It's starting to get dark."

"There is something else." Sky closed her eyes. "This is how we get to the island. The only way in. If we enter the swamp any other way, the swamp itself will deliver us to the protectors."

"Protectors?"

"Changelings. They can take the shape of anyone or anything. They will feast on our flesh." Sky pulled her hand away.

"Let's get out of here." Keal's face appeared as if he had seen a ghost.

"We have to come back."

"Yeah, but with the others." Keal took off in the direction they had come.

The sun set and the moon had risen into the night sky. The sound of movement had brought them to a halt when Marga, in her monstrous form, approached them. Marga led them back to the camp quicker than it would have taken them stumbling in the dark.

A small fire and a hot meal greeted them when they reached the others.

"I hoped you had just underestimated what time it was when you decided to turn back," Feeleep said.

"And I hope your search was better than ours. We didn't find any way to approach the swamp, let alone a way across it," Sanya added.

Sky and Keal explained what they had discovered, and Sky told them what she could discern from the magic protecting the structure.

"That's the way we have to go, I know it. I just don't understand…" Sky pondered.

"What?" Sanya asked.

"In my grandmother's vision, I didn't see the arch. She only showed me the island and where to find what we need. Why didn't she know about the arch?"

"She visited the island in her spirit form. She didn't need to travel across the swamp as we will. She was able to bypass the water. She wouldn't have known about the archway," Sanya answered.

"I guess that makes sense." Sky started to dig into a stew Sariah had prepared.

"So, you think it's safe enough to have a fire?" Keal questioned.

"Well, I'm using my magic." Feeleep smiled. "Unless the Rikits are around, no one else should see us."

They finished their meal and started making plans for the next day.

At first light they moved the camp closer to the archway. Feeleep and his wife agreed to accompany them to the archway but then return and watch the camp. The others packed some supplies in case they had to spend the night on the island, not wanting to be caught without food or water again.

"I don't think we will survive if we have to stay the night," Sky said. She didn't agree with the others' idea of taking supplies. The extra weight could slow them down, but she relented to make them feel better and prepared for the unexpected.

The sun had just risen above the horizon when Sky and Keal led the others to the strange archway. They explored everything Sky and Keal had the previous day. Sariah hovered over the strange writing on the ground. She wore a grave expression on her face the entire time.

"Can you read it?" Sanya asked. "I can't make out a single word."

"I wouldn't call it reading, but I'm getting impressions from it," Sariah commented.

"And what are they saying?" Feeleep asked as everyone's attention turned to his wife.

"That death awaits you."

14

"What do you mean, *death* awaits us?" Keal questioned.

"This place is very evil. Many times darker than the Black Fairy's lands at the height of her wickedness," Sariah explained. "Your task will not be easy."

"Can you tell us how to get through the archway?" Sky questioned.

"Yes, you must ring the bell for each person wishing to pass, and then leave some blood in the small dish beneath." Sariah pointed at the stone basin carved into the archway beneath the bell.

"Blood," everyone said in surprise, and then followed Sariah's finger to the bowl.

"How much blood?" Keal gulped.

"I'm not sure." Sariah shook her head.

"Is there any more?" Marga questioned Sariah.

"Something about the guardians waiting for their masters' return. The impressions are centuries old, so I don't think the masters have visited their keep for a very long time. I don't know what the guardians are or if they still live."

"I'm pretty sure they do and they will be the changelings my grand-mother warned me about." Sky eyed the basin below the bell.

"We don't have all the time in the world. Let's see how this thing works." Keal walked over to the bell and stared at it.

Sanya approached the archway the same as Sky had the day before. She held both palms against the invisible force field. "I can't see any way past it, except Sariah's directions."

"Well then, what are we waiting for." Keal pulled a knife out of his belt and sliced a cut across the palm of his hand. While bleeding into the basin with one hand, he used the other to ring the bell with the hammer.

The gong vibrated through the structure and jarred their bodies. Keal inhaled a deep breath and then walked through the archway. He passed through and stepped out on the portion of the triangle which extended out into the swamp. He suddenly spun back to give the others a do-you-see-that look. He spoke but his voice was silent.

The others all shook their heads and pointed to their ears to indicate they could not hear him.

Keal pointed toward the water behind him and then made a drawing with his hands.

"Is he trying to say there is a boat?" Marga asked.

"There's one way to find out." Sky followed Keal's example and then crossed through the invisible barrier. Her mouth fell open when a boat with a cloaked figure waited for them next to the point of the triangle. "Was it just waiting there?"

"No, it actually materialized out of the mists after I stepped through," Keal said. "Do you think we can trust it?"

"I'm not sure, but it might be our only way across this thing." Sky motioned to the swamp beyond the boat with its dark-robed driver.

A few moments later both Sanya and Marga exited the force field and wore equally surprised expressions.

After debating for a short duration, they all piled into the small boat. As soon as they took their seats the figure pushed off from the shore with his long stick, and started out into the swamp. The mist made visibility difficult. They couldn't tell if they were traveling in a straight line or if the driver followed an unseen route through the trees.

The swamp was alive with all sorts of unusual life and the air was full of a variety of calls. Most were from things Sky and the others had never heard. Many were ominous and threatening. The boatman appeared unconcerned with anything happening around them. His face remained hidden beneath his hood and it didn't budge in the least. The only parts of him that moved were his arms and gloved hands, which continued to push the boat forward with a long scull.

Every now and then they would catch sight of something large passing in the mist, but nothing approached the boat. A few lizards and snakes climbed the closest trees, with the occasional strange bird swooping past, heading to some unknown location.

Time seemed to slow down and Sky had to adjust her body position to alleviate the soreness starting to set in on her backside. *How much longer?* She tried to picture the distance in her mind from what they had seen on the hill before they descended down to the swamp.

Just when Sky was about to voice her discomfort, the fog lessened and the island appeared about fifty yards ahead. The driver had brought them to the entrance Sarvina had shown Sky in her vision. From this level, a smaller triangle and an archway appeared dead ahead.

"I hope we don't have to offer more blood to get onto the island," Keal murmured.

"I have a feeling it's only payment to call the driver for the trips between," Sanya commented.

"Let's hope we aren't in a rush to leave," Marga said with a worried tone.

After the driver parked the boat next to the smaller triangle, they all climbed out and stared at the archway. They studied the land on the other side for several minutes. The island looked similar to the border of the swamp where they had set up camp.

"So, should we get started?" Marga questioned.

"Okay, but I have a feeling the minute we pass through this archway, the guardians will know we *are* here." Sky searched for any movement.

"I feel it too," Sanya added.

"Then let's move quickly." Keal drew his sword and Sky followed his example.

They passed through the archway with only a slight static electric sensation, making the hair on their heads rise slightly. Once through, Sanya spun and held her palms out toward the archway.

"There is a barrier," Sanya said.

"There's a bell and basin as well." Marga pointed at the items on her right.

"Which wa..." Keal started, but a high-pitched guttural wail echoed across the island, followed by several others responding to the first cry.

"They know we are here." Sky glanced about, looking for any sign of activity.

"Which way?" Sanya asked.

"Straight ahead. My grandmother's vision took me straight on from here." Sky pointed with the tip of her sword directly into the jungle from where they stood on the smaller triangle.

"We should go at a quick pace. Just keep your eyes open." Sanya suggested.

They took off at a brisk walk, traveling in a straight line. They marched down an old road, which the swamp had slowly started to reclaim. Grasses grew up to everyone's waist and tree branches hung low forcing them to duck and stoop.

The disturbing calls grew in number and drew closer with each passing minute. Everyone's head moved as if it were on a swivel, seeking out the source of the calls. The intensity of the situation prompted them to quicken their stride. Soon the small group was jogging across the island.

After twenty minutes of hurrying through the jungle, the spires of the ancient keep appeared ahead of them. With each footfall, more and more of the dilapidated structure came into view. The main gate sagged on its hinges and the outer walls were cracked and broken down in many places. Like the road, the swamp had started to devour the old black keep. Most of the stone had moss or vines covering it and one of the towers had collapsed.

"That doesn't look any safer than what might happen to us out here," Marga commented as they continued hurrying toward the keep amidst the constant calls of the guardians.

"I don't know. I somehow have the impression they *want* us to enter that place," Keal said.

"So *do* I, but it's where we need to go," Sky responded.

They had to cut through some thick vines that had grown across the entrance. Once free, the main door completely fell away, and they all jumped back in order to avoid being crushed by the massive wooden gate. It hit the ground and cracked into several pieces.

"This place is *really* old." Keal whistled.

"Centuries old," Sanya said. "It's as if the whole place is still alive. I can feel it."

"Me too. And I think it knows why we're here," Sky added.

They made their way into the main entrance where they found several old torches, which they lit to give them light. Contrary to all the strange calls on the outside of the keep, the inside was quiet. Only the occasional drip of water falling from some crack onto the stone floor disturbed the silence.

"We need to go into the deepest parts of this castle. That's where my grandmother's vision took me to show us what we need," Sky's voice echoed off the stone walls.

"I don't think we are going to be able to surprise anything in here," Keal commented.

"Well, *try* to be as quiet as possible. Who knows what else lives here? There may be worse things than the guardians. If Sarvina only visited in spirit, she might not have aroused other things hiding inside," Sanya pointed out.

Even though they tried to be quiet, their footsteps reverberated off the walls, and clouds of dust followed in their wake. They found a set of stairs behind some wooden doors leading down a hall off to the left of the main chamber. The temperature grew colder the deeper they descended the stairs, and an even mustier smell filled the already putrid air. Their torches seemed to have trouble staying lit, as if the oxygen levels had dropped the lower they descended.

Sky noticed it took more effort to make her legs work and she breathed heavily. While the torchlight allowed her to see within a certain range, it didn't illuminate the entire area as if magic kept the light back. *Anything could be lurking in the dark.*

They reached the bottom of the stairs and entered a long straight hall-way. On the upper level, windows allowed a little light to enter, but down at this level it was pitch black. The smoke from the torches collected in the air above them with no current to move the fumes out. The tighter quarters of the hall made their movements even louder than they were above.

"The room should be at the end of this hall." Sky's whisper seemed like a yell in the silence.

They hurried to the end of the hall and into the room with the walkway surrounding the large pond. The doorway into the room allowed only a single person pass and the walkway was even narrower. They had to spread out along the wall to let everyone in to see. Once more, the dark-ness seemed to repel their torchlight. Visibility was only a few yards out onto the water.

Sky tried unsuccessfully to spot the island in the center of the room or the walkway leading to it. Her heart thumped inside her chest in antic-ipation. Something told her the minute she seized the item, something in the dark would be on them.

"There is magic here," Sanya whispered.

"Is it the item or…something protecting it?" Marga questioned.

"I'm not sure. It could be both," Sanya answered.

"Well, where is it?" Keal questioned.

"There is an island in the center of this room with a narrow path lead-ing to it, but I can't remember from what direction," Sky responded.

"Do you think you could light up the room for a second with magic? That way we can get a better picture of what we need to do," Keal ques-tioned.

"I have a feeling I shouldn't do that. Look at the way the darkness tries to overcome the torches. If I use magic, it might unleash something terrible on us," Sanya declared.

"I'm glad I wasn't the only one who thought it looked like the dark-ness was smothering the light," Sky commented. "Come on. Let's just work our way around the room. We're bound to hit the path sooner or later."

"I don't know why, but I'm getting a strong impression we shouldn't touch the water, either," Sanya said.

"Do you think I want to go for a swim?" Keal asked sarcastically.

Sky felt the corners of her mouth turn up in a smile. She was grateful Keal was still with her. His presence gave her comfort and lightened the situation.

They worked their way around the room. The farther into the chamber they went, the narrower the walkway became. It was only about ten yards before they were sidling sideways with their backs against the stone wall.

"Does this room have any corners?" Marga asked, when the path began to have missing sections.

"No, it's a round room," Sky said.

The gaps in the walkway forced them to take wide steps or jump from section to section. Sky went first and then helped the others. Sanya, with her magical leg, seemed to have the hardest time as she had yet to master all of her normal motor functions.

"Oh no," Sky gasped as the stone path had grown wide and easily manageable again.

"What?" the others asked behind her.

"We missed it. We're *back* at the door," Sky said. "We passed the path somewhere."

"How can that be? If your grandmother *showed* it to you?" Keal questioned.

"She might have visited it long ago and the water level has risen since or it sits just beyond our torchlight," Sanya suggested.

"You might have to use magic so we can see what we're dealing with," Keal said.

"That could be dangerous," Sanya cautioned.

"I wish I had the vision I have when I'm transformed," Marga added. "It is like ten times better night vision than I have as a human."

"*Hey*, didn't my grandmother give you control over your curse?" Sky wondered aloud more than asked.

"Yes," Marga said with a hint of I-understand-what-you're-suggesting. "You think maybe I can change when I want to?"

"That would be the definition of control," Sanya interjected. "Maybe you don't have to change because of the *moon* anymore. Perhaps you have just transformed every night because that is built into your memory."

"I'll give it a try." Marga handed her torch to Sanya.

Marga closed her eyes and put her hands on the wall behind her for support. She slid slowly down to the floor and black fur emerged all over her body. Several loud pops echoed through the chamber when her bones restructured and changed shape. Muscles stretched and grew while her face and hands changed shape. In a matter of minutes, the monster Marga became stood on all fours next to them.

As soon as her metamorphosis was complete, Marga slid ahead of Sky and headed along the path with cat-like precision. Her shiny black coat reflected the torch light, making it easy for the others to follow her. When they reached the area with the broken sections of the path, Marga sprang from one area to the next. The soft pads on her feet let her move about without making a sound.

After leading them for several minutes, Marga stopped and stared out over the water. The others crowded close to her and tried to see what she was looking at, but the darkness refused to let the torchlight extend beyond a couple of yards. Marga would glance at them and then back over the water.

"Is the walkway out there?" Sky asked. "We can't see it? How far?"

Marga coiled lower to the ground and then sprang out over the water. Everyone followed her until her leap took her into the black barrier where she disappeared.

"She didn't hit water," Keal observed after a moment.

"So the path..." Sky started but stopped when a strange scraping noise filled the air.

"Is that her?" Sanya whispered.

The sound continued for a moment and then stopped. They strained their senses in an attempt to get an idea of what was happening.

"It's all right, I'm here," Marga called. "There's a plank but I couldn't maneuver it with my clawed hands. You don't realize how much your thumbs come in handy until you don't have them."

Out of the dark a quick movement started Sky's heart racing and she flinched a little. A thick two-foot wide plank swung down out of the air and landed on the walkway from which Marga had leapt. It hit the stone with a loud crack that echoed through the chamber.

Sky was just about to jump to the section of walkway where the wooden bridge now extended to the path Marga waited on, when a strange bubbling noise caught everyone's attention. They stood motionless, listening for several moments.

"We're wasting time. Go!" Sanya snapped them out of their frozen state.

They all hustled across the small make-shift bridge to join Margo on the other path. Except for the wooden plank, this path was wide enough for them to walk two abreast. Instead of being built with concrete and black stone, it was smooth white stones just piled on top of each other. They rushed forward as the water started to boil all around them.

"Something's *not* happy!" Keal called.

There at the end of the walkway stood an altar built out of skulls, with what looked like a large black diamond placed in the open mouth of a coiled serpent statue. The sight actually caused them to pause a few feet away.

"We're standing on skulls as well." Keal pointed out.

"Go on, take it," Marga almost shouted to be heard above the loud churning water sound filling the chamber.

Sky stretched forth a shaky hand to take the black jewel, when a massive shape erupted out of the water. It appeared as if the devil himself had entered the chamber. A massive black muscular form with wings and horns pointing out of its head dripped water down on them as it towered over them and the altar. Hints of reddish fire flashed from its mouth, nostrils, and eyes. The blackness, which had been pressing on Sky and the others, gathered around this horrific monster.

The thing placed two large clawed hands on the ground on opposite sides of the altar and leaned lower over Sky and her friends. "Who enters my domain and attempts to remove my star?" a deep menacing voice thundered, casting a wave of hot air over the group.

Sky wanted to glance to her friends for help but her neck muscles refused to work. She didn't have an answer nor did she dare to speak.

"Well." The monster leaned closer so his face was only a few feet above them.

"T—the Odreshinik," Sky squeaked. Her voice sounded weak and small in her ears.

"And what does an Odreshinik need with *my* power?"

Sky swallowed in an attempt to add more strength to her voice. "To free my people, my sister."

"What, someone wishes to use my powers for noble deeds?" The creature's eyes burned a brighter red. "Interesting. And what would become of my stone when you are finished?"

The question shocked Sky. She hadn't considered what would become of the stone after the Roowks were defeated. "I'll bring it back." She heard herself say and couldn't figure out why she would ever come this way again.

There was a deep rumble which soon turned to laughter. A red light shone as the beast roared with madness. "Do you think me a *fool?*"

"N—no."

"I will give you a chance. One chance to take the stone. You must answer me a riddle. If you succeed, you may *borrow* the stone," the dark monster spoke.

"What if we fail?" Keal asked in a hushed voice.

"You will be fed alive to my pets and when your flesh is gone, others will come and they will walk over your skulls for a chance to capture the stone."

Sky and the others glanced down at the skulls beneath them that seemed to hold the ghostly faces of those they once belonged to.

"There will also be no escape for your souls as they will be *mine* forever." The creature's pupils flashed wider with anticipation.

"What are your pets?" Keal questioned.

"Look," the demon spoke, and the entire room filled with red lights as seemingly millions of eyes stared hungrily at them from the walls. Small flying reptiles with razor sharp teeth, like miniature dragons, flew about the room.

"Where did..." Keal started.

"They have been here the entire time. Watching you. Waiting for my command to devour you," the demon spoke with a hint of wicked delight.

"May my friends walk away before I hear the question?" Sky asked, amid protests from the others.

"No one may leave unless the correct answer is given. My pets would be on you before you crossed into the outer hall." The demon's nostrils flared.

"How much time do we have to answer?" Sanya spoke.

"All the time in the world." The monster chuckled.

"Well, then let's hear it," Keal squeeked.

The devil straightened up to his full height.

"I can maintain life or steal it away. I help villages thrive or I can make them my prey. I have the strength to move mountains or land, but can be soft and gentle when held in your hand. I can be pure and clean to make one's existence extend, or polluted and deadly and speed one to their end."

As soon as the monster finished his riddle, the small flying reptiles began to dive bomb Sky and the others. They didn't attack, but flashed their sharp teeth and claws to convey their hunger.

"Do take your time, I would hate for you to be *wrong*. My pets haven't gotten to feed in a very long time," the devil taunted.

"May we talk about it together?" Sanya used the torch to chase away the little flying nightmares.

Drops of water sizzled on the torches with each pass of the strange little reptiles, making the torch light dimmer and dimmer. It felt as if they stood under a small rain cloud just starting to sprinkle.

"As you wish." The demon's hand waved with a go-ahead motion.

While huddled together, they all held their torches high in the air so they could keep the swarm back. The creatures didn't act like they were in full attack mode, just harassing them.

"What do you think?" Marga questioned.

"I don't know about the riddle, but I have the impression he isn't going to let us go even if we answer correctly," Keal whispered.

"Even if he is going to honor his word, we need to plan for if he doesn't," Sanya said.

"What gives life but can snatch it away?" Sky questioned.

"It didn't give but maintain," Sanya pointed out.

Keal appeared to be the most annoyed by the little pests zooming past them. He turned and chased them with the torch, trying to burn them with the fire.

Sky, Sanya, and Marga speaking softly, debated several possibilities.

"I don't care, but let's hurry. I'm soaked. These things must be drenched in water," Keal spat.

"Hey," Sky almost shouted. She stared off at nothing in particular. "What was the entire riddle again? I think I know the answer."

"I think these things are coming out of the water," Keal continued, not listening to what Sky and the others were discussing. "They may even be made of water."

"What?" Sky asked as Keal's comments registered.

Keal repeated what he had said and Sky noticed all the drops of water falling on them like rain. She held out her hand and caught several drops in her palm. Her eyes met Marga's and Sanya's and they all smiled.

Sky spun toward the demon and said very loudly. "The answer to your riddle is *water*."

15

Time seemed to stand still. The little dive bombing razor blades stopped while the demon stood staring at them with red flames burning behind his eyes. His nostrils flared in displeasure as if someone had cheated him.

"Are we correct?" Sky stepped toward the black jewel.

"You are correct. Water is the answer. The jewel is yours…," the demon snarled while motioning Sky toward the item.

Sky kept her eyes on the monster as she approached the stand. She paused, then reached out and took the black jewel from the serpent's mouth. Finally, breaking her gaze away from the monster, she glanced at the stone which felt warm in her hand.

"Now, if you can only make it to the door." The creature laughed a deep menacing sound.

Sky spun to meet the others' eyes a second before a roar of a million wings and shrieks filled the air. She sprang to the others.

Sky and her friends huddled together while Sanya sent up a wall of fire a second before the attack reached them. The flying demons slammed into the fire, turning back into the dark water, dousing the flames and creating a wave of hissing steam.

"Up the path," Sky screamed.

Before Sanya could create another wall of fire, several of the little demons breached their defenses. They bit and scratched Sky's group everywhere. Whenever they would squash or hit the creatures, the things would just turn to water. Wave after wave of them continued to rise out of the lake and swarm the fleeing group.

The demon continued to roar with laughter, which was louder than the flapping wings and shrieks of the small attackers. Each time Sanya used the fire spell, the strength of her fire was less than the time before. Soon they had cuts all over their exposed skin and the beasts ripped their clothes.

"We're not going to make it," Keal warned.

"How can water transform into such terrible monsters?" Marga screamed, trying to swat them with a long knife.

"How can we get rid of the water?" Sky wondered. "It's too vast."

"We need something to dry it up." Keal swung his sword back and forth, only liquefying a third of his assailants.

"Or better yet, make it a solid," Sky mumbled. "ICE! Sanya we need ice."

Both Sanya and Sky cast spells that sent freezing cold temperature into the air. The bitter blast transformed the winged creatures into small figurines which dropped out of the air. Many shattered on the skull path or splashed into the black lake.

"Freeze the lake." Sanya turned her magic on the black liquid. Sanya used every ounce of energy she had to blast the lake into a solid sheet of ice. It even stretched up the main demon's smoky body and locked him in place.

Marga snagged Sanya before she dropped to the path.

"Over the ice." Sky leapt off the trail and onto the frozen lake.

Marga passed the weakened Sanya to Sky before she and Keal bounded down onto the frozen surface. Their feet slipped and slid as they scrambled across the ice. They were ten yards from the door when the ice encasing the large devil burst apart, sending ice flying in all directions.

"NO!" roared the devil, and fire erupted from his hands into the lake.

The ice began to crack and spread toward Sky and the others. They reached the door when the last of the ice melted and a new wave of the little beasts rose up out of the lake.

They rushed through the door and into the hallway. Once through the opening, Sky spun on her heels and created another wall of cold air immediately against the door. The desperation of the situation gave her power and she held the spell until the constant wave of attackers formed a solid door of ice blocking the exit.

Sky dropped onto her backside, feeling lightheaded and weak.

Keal looped an arm through Sky's and lifted her to her feet. "We can't wait. The head monster will melt that in short order."

They sprinted as fast as their tired and injured bodies would carry them. Halfway down the hall the icy door burst and the winged devils flooded the hall.

This time is was Sanya's turn. She summed up what little strength she had regained and sent a blast of cold air down the hall. The lower temperatures froze the first wave but wasn't enough to create a blockade.

"Run for the doors above," Keal shouted.

Sky and Sanya continued to take turns keeping the watery demons off them. They completely exhausted their strength but managed to protect their friends until they reached the main level and sealed the doors.

They hadn't caught their breath when the strange calls of what they assumed were the guardians penetrated the keep. The cries pushed their already frayed nerves to an even more fragile state.

Huffing and puffing for air, they scanned the darkened castle for any sign of another attack.

"I don't think they are in the castle," Marga whispered.

Keal dug jerky from his pack and passed some to everyone. "*Eat.* We are going to need our strength. I have a feeling we will have to fight all the way to the boat."

"At least we are all ready to give an offering." Sky smiled weakly, eyeing her cuts, many of which appeared rather nasty.

"Well, patch up what you can quickly. Let's get off this island as fast as possible. I know we are soaked but drink plenty of water as well. We've lost blood and energy." Sanya took out some clean clothes and passed them to everyone.

"Wait here, I will be back." Marga downed a water skin and turned to leave.

Sky snagged Marga by the arm. "Where are you going?"

"To find us the best route out of this place. I'm much faster by myself." Marga winked and transformed into the black nightmare right in front of them.

They watched her spring up to a high broken window and exit the castle. The calls from the strange beasts didn't change, giving them hope that Marga had left the building without being detected.

"I hope she finds us a way out." Sanya continued to stare at the window while dabbing at a cut on her forearm.

"Yeah, one where we don't have to fight several hundred monsters," Keal added.

"We should hurry to find a ladder or something to get up to that window. If they didn't notice her leaving that way, we might have to take the same route," Sky mused.

"Good thinking," Keal added.

"That was impressive by the way," Sanya said to Sky.

"What was?"

"The magic you performed down there. I wouldn't have expected a youngling to execute such difficult spells under those circumstances," Sanya said.

"Oh…thanks." Sky felt her cheeks redden and was happy they were waiting in poor light.

They quickly dressed their more serious wounds, drank some water and ate some food. Then they began searching for something that would help them reach the high window with ease.

"Why didn't we pack some rope?" Keal complained. "Remind me next chance we get, to grab some."

"There may be some in here," Sky offered.

"Would you trust a rope that is a *hundred* years old?" Keal worked his way around the main hall.

"We're about to climb on a hundred-year-old whatever to reach the window." Sky caught his attention and then gave him a smirk.

"Right."

"Hey, over here," Sanya called from out of the darkness.

Sky and Keal found her in a small alcove where there was a wooden table.

"I think we can use this. Help me carry it over."

They were just about to the window when Marga appeared out of the darkness and asked what they were doing.

"You scared me to death," Keal said, resting his hands on his knees to recover from the shock.

"We thought we would get ready to leave," Sanya said.

"I found a better way. Besides, they know I went out that way and will be watching it." Marga waved them to follow her deeper into the castle.

The calls of the creatures continued to penetrate the structure as Marga took them through a section where the roof was completely missing. They crouched low and circled a pile of bricks to avoid being seen by anything on the outside of the castle. Through the openings, it appeared the mists had grown thicker and a light drizzle began to fall.

Their eyes had to adjust to the changes from dim to darkness. They were in an area where they could barely make out each other's shadows when Marga brought them to a halt. A little light filtered onto the floor from the wall in front of them.

"You *will* have to crawl through the opening." There was a swooshing noise and a small opening in the wall appeared on the floor. "I'm going to transform as I'm more equipped to lead you and help fight if needed. Just follow me. If you lose me, wait where you are and I will come back for you."

"Do *not* try to take on an army all by yourself either," Sanya advised.

Marga managed a weak smile and then transformed. They all followed her through the small opening, crawling on their hands and knees. The hole went into an almost tunnel-like tube created by thick jungle plants. The chute went on for thirty yards where Marga paused before stepping out into the open. The calls of the guardians continued to ring across the island but sounded farther away than before.

I wonder what uses this as its home. Whatever it is, it isn't small. Sky thought.

Marga acted like a big cat on the prowl. She eased her way out into the open where the rain fell in a steady drizzle. Eventually, she moved far enough out in the open for the others to follow. She shot a glance back at the others and then started forward at a trot, forcing the others to hurry to keep up.

The cries of the guardians grew in strength and frequency. *Do they know we are not in the castle anymore? Or are we just moving closer to them where they are waiting for us by the boat?* Sky gripped her sword a little tighter and her focus jumped to every opening in the jungle, expecting to see some strange monster standing there.

They ducked a little to pass under a group of tightly knit trees where Marga brought them to a halt once more.

"They've left the castle, find them," a snake-like voice hissed and what sounded like several responses hissed back.

"The rain is hiding their scent," another snake-like voice complained.

"No excuses. Catch them. We must feast on their flesh," replied the first.

"Yes. Feast," came a collective response, followed by the sound of movement through the jungle.

To Sky's horror, she spotted one of the creatures when it passed near their location. It appeared to be a tall walking lizard. It stood well over six feet tall and ran upright on its hind legs. It had gray scaly skin with a long tail. Its head resembled a lizard with razor sharp teeth. A fork tongue flicked out to test the air.

A few moments later, only the one giving the orders remained behind. He paced around the small area out in front of where Marga had Sky and the others were waiting.

Marga lowered herself closer to the ground and when the creature had its back to them, she pounced. With lightning speed, she closed the gap between her and the lizard-like man. She hit him from behind and sunk her large fangs into the back of his neck. The attack was over in seconds as the lifeless body of the thing crumpled to the ground.

Without letting go of her prey, Marga dragged the dead guardian into the underbrush and returned to her friends to lead them out once more. She glanced at Sky and the others and then in the direction ahead of them. After performing this motion a few times, she started forward once more, with the others keeping in her wake.

The rain made everything wet, creating a slippery surface to scramble over. Marga continued to lead them in stops and starts. She disposed of another guardian the same as she had done before.

They had traveled long enough—Sky began to wonder how close they were to the boat. Maybe we'll get out of this easier than we thought. While they waited in another thick stand of trees, the calls of the guardians rang out closer and had a different pitch.

They found the dead or are on our trail. Sky's eyes met the others and she could tell they were all thinking the same thing.

There was a rush of loud splashing as a half dozen lizard men zipped past them. Some ran on two legs while others sprinted on all fours. They were a blur of gray, hissing and making their strange calls as they went.

Marga did something they hadn't seen yet. Only her head changed into her human self. "I think they are setting up in front of the arch. Wait here, I will check things out." Her head returned to the monster and she slunk off into the rain.

"I'm glad she's on our side," Keal whispered.

"And that she knows what she's doing," Sky added.

"What are we going to do if there is an army of these things blocking the boat?" Sanya asked.

"We need to get everyone through the barrier as fast as possible," Sky said.

"That means each of us has to put blood in the basin and ring the bell. That's going to take time and we'll be vulnerable. Either we have to kill all of these things or come up with an idea to get each of us through in a weird manner. Not that you aren't as scared as I am, but I'm the one without any special powers here." Keal's eyes reflected his concern.

"He's right. How can we get blood in the bowl and ring the bell while fighting these things. I'm sure fire would help us but this rain isn't going to help with fire." Sanya gazed up at the rain falling.

"Maybe Marga can take them all out." Keal smiled weakly.

"I don't think she's going to be able to sneak up on all of them," Sky remarked right as Marga returned.

Once more, Marga only altered her head so she could speak to them. "We're going to have to fight to get out of here. They are waiting at the triangle."

"How many?" Keal asked.

"Are they hiding or out in the open?" Sky questioned.

"There were about twenty, now there's only fifteen. There were some that were hidden but…"

"You took care of that," Sanya finished.

"Yes, they are pretty much out in the open now. I made sure of that. I'm just not sure how we should proceed," Marga continued.

"Maybe we can lead a few others out into the trees," Sanya suggested.

"That could get tricky. I don't think they will enter one at a time. It will probably be an all or nothing attack, which would give them the advantage," Marga said.

"Is there a safe place where we can get a better look?" Sanya asked.

"Follow me, but be ready. They are restless and may have already started searching again." Marga spun around while fully transforming again and led them forward.

This time Margo changed directions and turned to the left after proceeding forward only a short distance. The rain continued to fall on them and didn't show any signs of quitting. Instead of taking them to some underbrush, Marga sprang up a tree and worked her way out onto a large branch. Sky and the others managed to climb the tree without much difficulty, but it took them several minutes to reach the branch where Marga waited.

Using the main branch to step on, Sky and the others held on to the smaller branches for support. A small opening in the trees' thick green leaves created a window with a view of the triangle and the archway. They watched quietly in the rain.

Sky counted out the number of guardians she could see from this vantage point. She only managed to locate twelve of them, which meant either the three others were hiding or just not visible from where she sat.

"Do you think you can out run them?" Sanya asked Marga, whose head had changed again.

"I think so, but I don't know if I can lead them all away. They know there are more than one of us out here."

"I wasn't thinking of you leading them all away, but if you get a handful to follow, maybe we can hide in the bushes and take out one or two in the back of the group," Sanya said.

"That's a good idea but it will probably only work once, unless we get them all," Sky added.

"Then let's make sure we get them *all*," Keal said with a worried expression.

"These things aren't going to be easy to kill," Marga cautioned. "I had to take them by surprise. They've obviously ruled this island for a long time. Although, I doubt many things venture here."

"Well, let's give it a shot. We won't know until we try and we are wasting time. I don't want to spend the night. I feel the dark would give them the advantage," Sanya said.

They retreated farther back into the forest and found a spot from which to make their attack. Sky and Keal would use bows and arrows, while Sanya would rely on her magic. They found places of concealment in different trees and watched as Marga left to try to draw out their first victims.

Sky tried to listen but the pounding of her heart thumped inside her ears. She caught a little rain water on her hand and put it in her mouth.

The cries of the guardians rang out louder, indicating the chase was on.

Sky fit an arrow in her bow and got ready. *How will I know which one to shoot? Take number three. What if there are only two? Two would be easy to pick off.* She had a steady debate going back in forth in her mind. *What if we don't kill them quickly enough and they alert the others to our position?*

A black blur of Marga zipped past them, splashing mud and dirty water with her massive clawed feet. Sky pulled the string back to her ear and picked the best area to take a shot. One lizard-like man flew by, racing on all fours, and then a second. Judging by the speed of the first two, she released her arrow when the third crossed her chosen threshold. The arrow stuck the guardian right in the center of its spine.

Sky's arrow caused it to lose control of its lower extremities. As it tried to claw its way forward, Keal finished it with another shot.

"Ahh," Sky cried out as sharp claws raked her calf and almost knocked her out of the tree.

The creature managed to dig into the tree branch and hang on after injuring Sky. Sky pulled out a dagger from her belt and stabbed it through the lizard-man's hand, which stuck him to the tree. The creature screamed a high-pitched cry of pain and struggled to hold on.

Sky shot an arrow down into the creature, releasing it from its pain.

A ball of fire with another hair-raising cry caught Sky's attention. It took her a minute to realize Sanya had eliminated another guardian. Sky wanted to check her leg but maintained her focus on the area below them. She held another arrow at the ready when Marga returned.

"I got rid of the other two. How many did you get?" She asked in her strange half human half monster state.

"Three," Keal said.

"Let's try it once more. I don't think we will have the same luck, but one less is still better than none." Marga headed back toward the archway.

Sky grimaced as she first pulled her arrow out of the creature and then her knife, letting it drop to the island floor. "Disgusting," she muttered. She took a quick moment to check her leg to see that is was bleeding from two large gashes.

Fumbling in her pack, she found a piece of cloth and quickly wrapped her leg. She had just tied it off when several different calls rang out in the direction of the triangle. Then everything went silent.

What was that? Did they get Marga? Sky's heart raced faster than it had all day. She wanted to ask the others. *Do we wait here? What if she needs our help?*

The splashing of running feet filled the air and Marga flew past once more.

Sky didn't wait for a third and shot the first guardian to appear. Sanya killed a second with her fire, with Keal helping.

"Whew." Sky exhaled at the relief of knowing Marga was all right.

Pain shot through Sky's leg as she climbed out of the tree to meet the others below.

Marga had already returned.

"What was with those strange new calls? I thought maybe they caught you," Sanya said.

"Oh, I had to be a little more persuasive. I got one more right in front of them. With these two we are down to seven," Marga said. "I don't think we are going to be able to draw any more out."

Sky retrieved all the arrows that hadn't been burned and held them up in the air. "Well, we can do some damage from a distance."

"Let's go back to that tree and check things out," Sanya suggested.

They crept back toward the trees. Marga stopped several times to listen. Her head swiveled back and forth, prompting the others to do the same. Her uneasiness put the others on high alert. She shot them a quick glance and then took a sharp turn to the left. They finally stopped in a stand of trees where they could barely see the triangle through all the thick foliage.

"They knew we had watched them from that branch and were waiting," Marga whispered, answering everyone's question about why they had moved to this location.

"So, how do we want to do this?" Keal asked.

"How long can you hold a wall of fire?" Sky asked Sanya.

"I was thinking the same thing. We go for it. Stay in a tight group while I hold them off," Sanya said.

"I don't think they will be expecting that." Sky added. "We could work our way a little closer and then make a run for it."

"We will have to fight. Be prepared," Marga warned.

Everyone agreed and Marga got them to within twenty yards of the smaller triangle.

Sky's breathing echoed loudly in her ears as rain continued to fall on them. She debated whether she should use her bow or sword. *They will be close. Use your sword.*

They all exchanged looks with several short nods.

"Now," Sanya barked and they bolted from their hiding place.

They raced out onto the triangle and the guardians acted surprised by the sudden change in tactics. Everyone paused for a brief moment to stare at each other. The creatures tensed as if ready to pounce.

"*Wait*! We have your friends," one of the guardians hissed and then snapped his fingers.

Two scaly lizard-like men escorted Feeleep and Sariah out of the jungle.

16

There was a collective gasp from Sky and the others as they stared into the terrified faces of their friends.

Feeleep and his wife appeared to be a little battered but otherwise in good condition. Their hands were behind their backs, so they almost fell when their captors shoved them to their knees. Tears rolled down Sariah's face and they were both pale as ghosts.

"No," Sanya screamed.

"How?" Sky wondered.

"It's a trick. Keep moving toward the archway," Marga whispered.

"What?" Keal questioned out of the side of his mouth.

"Please, don't leave us." Sariah wailed, the tears flowing faster. "They're going to kill us."

"Yes, do what they say," Feeleep added, meeting everyone's gaze.

"Did we pass any prisons with captives?" Marga hissed in a low voice. "They *will* kill and eat us, just like we overheard them say in the jungle."

Something echoed in the back of Sky's mind. She couldn't tell if it was her grandmother's vision or something she had heard elsewhere. *They are changelings!* Without hesitation, Sky pulled out an arrow and shot Feeleep right in the chest.

The world stopped for one brief moment and everyone wore a horrified expression of disbelief. Then Feeleep transformed into a lizard-man and fell forward onto the cobblestones.

The rest of the guardians flew across the space between them. Sanya threw up a wall of fire to keep them back but it didn't even slow their attack. They sprang through the flames with a vicious hunger.

Sky barely got her sword up as the first guardian in front of her impaled itself on the weapon. The force of the attack and its body weight almost pried the sword from Sky's grip.

Marga's roar grew louder and fiercer while Keal screamed in horror. Sky didn't have time to worry about the others as another guardian was already on top of her. This new attacker didn't charge into Sky's sword but used its quickness to attack and retreat. Sky received several cuts from the creature's long sharp claws.

Sky managed to get in several of her own strikes to make the lizard beast use more caution. The constant assault of the foe began to drain Sky's energy.

Use all your talents! Sky's grandmother's voice spoke into her mind.

Sarvina's voice was so strong in Sky's thoughts she almost expected to see her come to their rescue. "Grandma?" she mouthed. The pendant hanging around her neck had a warm calming feeling against her chest.

Use your magic.

The creature lunged and Sky blocked the attack with the sword. As it went to retreat, she snagged its leg with a spell. The guardian, using its strength to retreat and avoid Sky's weapon, tripped over her spell then fell flat on its back. Sky hurtled forward and disposed of the attacker.

Sky spun to find her friends when a wave of the guardians' calls rang out from the direction of the castle. "There's *more* of them." Sky swallowed. She spotted Keal struggling for his life with one of the guardians on top of him.

In one fluid motion, Sky sheathed her sword and loaded her bow with an arrow. Letting it fly, she destroyed the guardian attacking Keal. Sky raced to his side to see what she could do.

He was in pretty bad shape, with several severe gashes.

"We need to get out of here. More are coming," Sanya shouted.

"Behind you," Keal shouted, giving Sky enough time to load another arrow which wounded another changeling.

"He needs help," Sky screamed. "We need to get him…to…" Sky loaded a new arrow and rolled the tip in some of Keal's blood pooling on the cobblestone floor. She then sent the arrow into the basin. With another shot she range the bell.

"Marga, can you get him through the barrier?" Sky loaded another arrow.

Marga showed up and dragged Keal away.

Sky sprang to where Sanya used spell after spell to keep a couple of guardians back. She appeared exhausted but otherwise didn't have any serious wounds. Sky glanced back to see Marga had pushed Keal through the barrier and was racing back to their aid.

"I'm going to cut you so don't panic," Sky said, moving closer to Sanya.

Sky used a knife to draw Sanya's blood from her forearm, which she collected on the tip of the next arrow. With two pulls of her bow, she had the barrier ready for Sanya to go through. "Get through the barrier, *now*."

Sky swung the bow over her shoulder and drew her sword once more. She, Marga and Sanya backed toward the barrier until Sanya dashed through.

Sanya stood straight behind the barrier, watching the action, when a guardian raced toward her at full speed. Sky sidestepped the creature to let it pass. It hit the force field with a massive impact which launched it backward at an incredible speed. Sky swung her sword and used the creature's rebounding momentum to separate it from its head.

Sanya discovered she could send magic back through the barrier. She drove the single remaining guardian back far enough to allow Marga and Sky to use the basin and make it through the archway as a swarm of guardians arrived from the keep.

Not wanting to chance that they might be able to get through the force field, they piled into the boat. A few guardians slammed into the force field trying to get through but were blasted backward. The cloaked driver pushed off from the shore and began to take them back through the swamp.

They immediately went to work on Keal. He had several deep cuts, along with multiple bite marks. The rain wasn't making it easy to stop the bleeding in several spots. Sanya used magic to help with some of the more severe injuries.

The farther away from the island they traveled, the lighter the rain became. It was now more of a heavy mist than a drizzle. The trip back seemed to take longer than the one in, but Sky assumed it had to do with the fact they needed to get Keal back to camp.

Keal was awake but kept his eyes closed. The expression on his face displayed a great deal of pain.

"How are you feeling?" Sky asked sympathetically.

"I've been better." Keal's voice was barely a whisper.

"We're almost back to camp. You can rest more comfortably there," Sanya said.

"How did you know?" Marga questioned Sky after things had settled down a little.

"Know what?"

"That those things weren't Feeleep and Sariah," Marga said.

"I remembered they were changelings. That's not the only weird thing." Sky took out her grandmother's jewel hanging on a chain around her neck to look at it. "I thought I heard my grandmother's voice speaking to me during the battle. Helping me."

"Maybe she was." Sanya smiled.

As soon as they landed, Sky ran to the camp to get Feeleep and his wife. They constructed another make-shift cot to carry Keal back to camp. Sariah took a look at Keal's wounds and applied some ointments she had brought with her. They got him into dry clothes and set him close to the fire to keep warm.

After they had Keal all settled, Sky, Marga, and Sanya related all the events of the day to Feeleep and his wife. They all took a turn holding and examining the black jewel they had taken from the keep.

"I am just going to say after that thing didn't keep his word, I will not be returning his treasure," Sky grumbled.

"So, the question is, how do we use it to defeat the Roowks?" Feeleep weighed the jewel in his hand. "I mean, if it can cancel out all magical powers around it, what is its range?"

"That's a good question. How close do we need to be to a wielder of magic to make the jewel take effect?" Sanya mused.

"And if it does have a range, how do we get everyone into it?" Sky questioned.

"A battle," Keal's weak voice spoke so quietly, they had trouble hearing it.

"What?" Sariah questioned.

"We need to start a war. A huge battle to get them all into an area with their Dijinnis," Keal said as loudly as he could.

"A *war*," they all muttered at once.

"Gee what is that, like, two good ideas in the past couple of days? You better pace yourself because you're physically injured. Don't hurt your brain too," Sky teased, and Keal and the others chuckled.

"Okay, but how do we start a war?" Marga questioned.

"Can you create a big enough illusion to lure the Roowks out?" Sanya asked Feeleep.

"I can but that isn't the only answer. I think we may have to play that card to draw the majority of the Roowks out, but we will need a real army to fight. As you yourself know, your people aren't trained to fight with regular weapons. They will be vulnerable," Feeleep said.

"This creates another dilemma. Who do we trust to fight the Roowks without wiping out the Dijinnis? They aren't the real enemy but a lot of races hold grudges against them because they are the tool which brought the Roowks to power," Sariah explained.

"Yeah, just look at my people," Keal added weakly, but he was paying close attention to the conversation.

"You know this could mean the Roowks would also be easy pickings. They haven't actually been fighting their own battles for so long they would really be caught off guard. Do they even train to fight for themselves anymore?" Sky glanced at Sanya.

"We need to get more than one army there. I think other races would love to help bring about the downfall of the Roowks," Marga offered.

"How are we supposed to do that?" Keal questioned. "There are only six of us here. I may be able to help with my people but, as Sky knows, that is a tricky situation."

"You are forgetting what Sariah and I used to be." Feeleep smiled. "We have a lot of connections and can spread the word. Whether people believe it or not will be another story."

"I'm sure news of the Black Fairy's transformation may have already circulated to help make our story more believable," Sariah added.

"So, what are we talking about here? Are we going to have to split up? Where are we going to meet again? Where should the battle be?" Marga questioned.

"Those are all excellent questions and things we need to decide in a hurry," Feeleep responded.

"We should probably stay here a day or two for Keal to recover." Sky motioned to Keal.

"I don't think we can. Remember, the Roowks are looking for us. I worry, they may be onto us already. We might have to fight our way through them just to get out of here." Feeleep frowned and waved his hand at the area around them.

At this comment, everyone glanced in all directions, trying to see what lay just beyond the borders of the firelight in the dark.

"Maybe I will go do some scouting." Marga transformed into her monstrous form and trotted off into the night.

"Her ability to change at will has been a great asset," Sanya commented.

"She saved our butts out on that island," Keal agreed.

"Yes, she did," Sky added.

They all quieted and stared at the small fire. Keal's eyes closed and his breathing grew heavier. Sky watched the flames do their slow rhythmic dance and her eyes became heavy. She found herself yawning every few minutes and unable to keep her head upright.

###

"Sky. Wake up. We have to leave." Sanya nudged her gently.

"Wha…what?" Her head pounded and she had trouble focusing in the semidarkness. "What's going on? How long have I been asleep?"

"Only about an hour. Marga returned. The Roowks are coming. We have to leave," Sanya ordered.

This statement snapped Sky out of her drowsy state. She got out of some blankets, wondering who had put her there, and helped the others pack the wagon. "How far away are they?"

"They're camped about ten miles back up the road. They are on a hill where they can see for miles in every direction. If we weren't down in the trees, in this valley, they may have spotted our fire. We are going to have to go cross country at night to avoid them," Sanya reported.

"I only hope we can get far enough. The ride won't be easy and it won't be good for Keal," Feeleep murmured.

It took them a half an hour to clean up the camp. They placed Keal on every blanket they had in the back of the wagon. Sanya used magic to make it difficult to tell anyone was ever there. Then they hitched up the team and started out into the night.

Sanya sat in the driver's seat while Sky and Marga walked out front of the wagon, scouting the smoothest route. They swung south and east, staying inside the rim of the valley. Feeleep and Sariah rode in the back with Keal, trying to keep him as comfortable as possible. Marga changed into her hideous self often to scurry ahead and scope out the path with her night vision. The course was rough and they traveled at a much slower pace than when they used the road.

"We are going to have to turn north in a little while. There is a canyon ahead that will take us within the Roowks line of sight for several miles. This is going to be close," Marga advised everyone.

"Well, if they think we are still down at the swamp, perhaps they won't be looking in this direction," Sanya suggested.

"After we make the turn, I will go off for one last look before the sun comes up." Marga created mock clawed hands to indicate she would travel as the monster.

It was another half hour before they made the turn, the color of the night sky turning a dark blue. Marga transformed and raced off toward the east.

The lighter the sky grew with morning's approach, the sleepier Sky became. It was as if her mind finally registered she had been up all night. Her feet weighed a ton and she was having trouble lifting them off the ground. *Keep moving. You can rest when we are behind the Roowks.* The need to find the best path for the wagon was the only thing that kept her awake.

As the light of early morning continued to grow, Sky shot constant glances in the direction of the hill Marga mentioned. Eventually the lay of the land became visible. She could make out the slope of the terrain to her right and thought she could make out the best location for the Roowks' camp, but couldn't distinguish any details.

The sun had just crested the horizon when Marga returned. "We need to hurry. They are up but not really paying attention. We should get behind them without them noticing."

"That's good." Sanya breathed a sigh of relief.

"Yes, but we will need to find a road in a hurry. I heard them speaking. A squad is preparing to go down to the swamp. They may figure out where we went and give chase," Marga added.

Feeleep got out the maps he had acquired from Sarvina's palace and began scanning them.

"You two should get in the wagon and try and get some rest. You've been walking all night," Sanya offered. "I can see well enough to drive the team now."

"There isn't another road for at least a day's journey," Feeleep said, as Sky and Marga climbed into the back of the wagon. "Probably longer, going cross country."

"How's Keal doing?" Sky asked Sariah, watching Keal's body jiggle with each bump that shook the wagon.

"He's sleeping, but I don't how. I've tried to doze but I can't sleep with this rough ride," Sariah answered.

"Seems like we take turns being injured," Feeleep said over his shoulder.

"Do the Roowks have ways of sending messages?" Sky stared in the direction of the Roowk camp.

"Oh *no!*" Sanya gasped. "I forgot, but yes, they have dark birds that carry messages and...spy?" Sanya glanced up at the sky uneasily. "I would be willing to bet this group is using birds for both. They are a long way from their homeland and hunting the Odreshinik."

"So, we need to put as much distance between us and that camp as possible," Feeleep said, casting a gaze skyward.

"We may want to be spotted," Sky said.

"What? Why?" the others questioned.

"That would bring the entire Roowk army down on us," Feeleep said.

"Isn't that what we want? We need to determine a place to lead them. Then we may have to split up to try and recruit some armies to join the battle," Sky added.

"Yes, but we don't want them to get too close to soon. We want that jewel and what it does to be a secret until it is too late. That means we don't want to get close enough for the Dijinnis currently under their control to be able to use magic on us," Sanya added.

"That's a good point. Well, hopefully, we can get a good lead before they give chase," Sky said.

"So, first things first. Do we try to make it back to the road we came in on or do we head for this other road?" Feeleep questioned.

"You know if we can make it to this other road without being spotted, it would give us a chance to decide how best to go about starting a war," Sanya said. "It's not ideal to make plans on the run."

"I'm for the other road too," Marga agreed. "We all need some rest before we make this final push."

They continued to forge a new road for the remainder of the day. Sky did manage to get a little sleep before replacing Sanya, so she could get some rest as well. The day was sunny and warm without a cloud in the sky.

They stopped at the bottom of a ravine to rest the team, stretch their legs, and have something to eat. To everyone's relief, Keal appeared much better than the night before. He was able to sit up and eat.

"Well, we better finish this after the butt kicking I took to get that jewel," Keal joked. "I thought that thing was going to eat me alive."

"Oh, I'm sure it wouldn't have gotten that far. I mean, you probably taste nasty." Sky teased and everyone laughed.

"I've been thinking." Feeleep stared at the map. "After we hit this new road, there is a crossroads. I think that will be where we may need to split up."

"I've been doing some thinking as well. I think we need to have the battle where Keal and I found Sanya," Sky added.

"Where is that?" Marga, Feeleep, and Sariah questioned.

With the help of Sanya and the maps, they were able to pinpoint the exact location of the rolling hills. They all agreed that would be the perfect location because it was large enough and central to several of the races.

"Well, before we take off, I think I will do a little snooping to make sure we don't run into any surprises."

"You know, if I didn't know any better, I'd say you kind of like your curse these days," Keal commented.

"Let's just say, I find it a lot more beneficial now." Marga winked, transformed, and disappeared.

While waiting for Marga to return, their conversation drifted to who should go where and what they were going to say to convince others to join the war against the Roowks. No matter how they tried, it didn't appear they could be all that convincing.

"We're talking about races who have been crushed and scattered by the armies of the Roowks." Sanya frowned.

They continued to debate various ideas on how to talk people into going to war and how the outcome would be different this time. They agreed that if news of the Odreshinik had spread it would make the whole thing a lot easier. After a half hour of deep discussion, everyone quieted down to await Marga's return.

"Do you think something's wrong?" Feeleep stared off in the direction Marga had gone after they had been waiting for the better part of an hour.

"I hope not, but I didn't expect her to be gone this long," Sanya said.

"I want to go up on the rise to see if I can spot her, but what if there is something up there?" Sky said.

Feeleep checked the position of the sun steadily moving toward afternoon. "Let's give her some more time. I think we might have heard something if anything had happened to her. She may have found something and we need to keep quiet."

"Yes, but *not* knowing is killing me," Sky protested.

"Maybe some of us should try to get some sleep in case we have to travel by night," Sanya suggested.

"Who can sleep with this?" Sky motioned in the direction Marga had gone.

"All right, I'll try." Sanya went and found a spot in the shade to lie down.

To keep herself from going crazy, Sky had Feeleep show her how to read the maps. He taught her what the symbols meant and how to figure distances. Even this distraction didn't keep her from looking up, hoping to see Marga every few minutes.

By the time the second hour had passed, Sky was pacing around the wagon, muttering to herself.

"Okay, I think you should climb the rise and check things out. The Roowks may be on our trail and we can't waste time," Feeleep suggested.

"Be careful," Sanya said, resting on the ground with her eyes closed.

"I will."

Sky climbed the hill in a low crouch. She was just about out of the small ditch when she almost collided with Marga. All the tension which had been building in Sky released with a big exhale. She followed Marga back down to the others.

By the time they reached the wagon, Marga had turned back into her human self.

"There is a man out there. *Tracking* us and he knows what he's doing," Marga informed them.

17

"What?" the others asked.

"How?" Feeleep questioned.

"Who is he?" Keal queried.

"Could he be working with Mika?" Sky looked at Keal, who shrugged his shoulders.

"I don't know who he is, but he isn't with the Roowks. Oh, the good news on the Roowks, they don't know we have left, *yet*," Marga said.

"So, this man is alone?" Sariah questioned. "Could he be working for the Roowks?"

"I don't think he is helping the Roowks. His look and his mannerisms remind me of Keal." Marga glanced at Keal.

"And he's alone?" Keal questioned, as if he hadn't heard the answer already.

"Yes. And he appears to be very skilled," Marga added. "Not just at tracking, but surviving in the wild."

"What are we going to do about him?" Sanya asked.

"I could get rid of him. I just didn't think it was right. I'm not certain he is an enemy," Marga said.

"Well, of course *he's* an enemy. Who else is after us?" Feeleep stressed, hissing through his teeth. "Why would anyone risk all this stuff we have gone through to help us?"

"How far behind us is he?" Sky questioned.

"He's not. He's ahead of us," Marga said, drawing many confused looks.

"Ahead of us? How is *that* tracking us?" Sanya asked.

"Because he acts like he is waiting for us. I followed the trail he came in on. He did an excellent job of covering his tracks. Unfortunately for him and fortunately for us, in my hideous state I have an excellent sense of smell. While visible signs can be covered up or disguised, smells remain. It appears he had been following the Roowks but broke off their trail to take up the position ahead of us."

"How would he know we are coming this way?" Feeleep questioned.

"He's good. He is sitting in a spot where he is difficult to find but he would definitely see us going by," Marga said.

"So, what are we going to do about him? We need to take care of this as soon as possible. The longer we debate, the greater the chance the Roowks will figure out where we are and come for us," Sanya said.

"How are you feeling?" Sky questioned Keal.

"I hurt like crazy. What are you thinking?"

"If he is one of your people, perhaps you know him," Sky suggested.

"The only problem is, I'm not sure who we can or cannot trust. If he was sent to find us, it can't be good." Keal shook his head.

"How far ahead of us is he?" Sanya asked.

"About a mile. We could take the wagon about half way before he would see us, but there's no guarantee he won't hear us. The way the wagon is bouncing around on this terrain, it might give us away," Marga reported.

"I say we use the wagon and go super slow. If we feel it is making too much noise, we stop and proceed on foot," Feeleep suggested.

"I agree," Sariah said.

"Okay, but everyone be quiet. I'm going to keep an eye on him," Marga said.

"I know we don't want to be that kind of people, but if he makes a move you don't like, make sure he can't hurt us," Sanya said.

They loaded up the few items they had unpacked for lunch while Marga disappeared. Sky decided to walk out front once more in an effort to guide the wagon on the best possible route. She flinched every time one of the wagon wheels would make a loud thud or the entire vehicle would creak while being twisted at an angle in the uneven land. Her vision constantly jumped from the path the cart was to travel to the land around them. She wanted to ask Sanya or the others if they could see anything from their higher vantage point on top of the wagon, but stuck to their agreement for silence.

Marga returned after what seemed like hours and had them turn the wagon down a small hill where they brought it to a stop.

"He's still in the same spot, just watching. It's like…" Marga glanced in the direction she had returned form.

"What?" Keal asked.

"Like he knows I'm out there and he doesn't want to provoke me. I know that sounds weird but I feel it," Marga said.

"*That* may be a good thing. I mean, what's his game waiting for us. If he was here to hurt us why would he be by himself?" Sky said.

"Maybe to try and lead us somewhere we don't want to go," Feeleep answered.

"Well, I'm ready for a little walk," Keal said and rose to his feet but quickly put a hand on the wagon as the blood drained from his face.

"I don't think he is going too far." Sariah rushed to his side like a concerned mother and helped him sit back in the wagon.

"Why don't Marga and I go check it out? If we need your help we will come back for you, okay?" Sky said.

"Okay." Keal managed a weak smile.

"Just hurry, I don't want to wait here too long," Sanya urged.

Marga transformed as she headed back toward the man. Sky followed after her, crouching low. Marga led Sky along the back of a small hill, then they weaved in and out of the sparse vegetation. Sky tried to spot the location of the man but was unsuccessful.

They stopped when they reached a small cluster of rocks. Marga lay on her stomach and then transformed back to her human form. Sky took up a position next to her. Marga used a finger to point upward and the two of them peeked over the top of the rocks. Even from this position, Sky still couldn't see any sign of life out on the plains.

"There," Marga whispered while pointing with her finger toward a large cluster of desert plants which stood about three feet above the ground.

"I don't see anything." Sky squinted, trying to distinguish anything out of the ordinary.

"He's there in the center of those plants. He's dug out a small trench to sit lower in the bushes."

Sky surveyed the area and noticed the wagon would have to cross over an area right in line with the bushes. "Can we get closer?"

"You might have to crawl," Marga said.

"Let's do it."

Marga changed again and crept along the ground like a large cat, with Sky crawling on her hands and knees right on Marga's tail. Marga used angles and an area that appeared to be a small wash whenever large storms dumped rain. This time they stopped behind a section of tall weeds.

From this new location only about thirty yards from the man, he came into view. Besides the small ditch, the man had added more vegetation to his hiding place for better concealment. His head remained forward as if he were still waiting for the wagon he knew was out there to come into view.

Sky wondered how they should proceed. She couldn't see the man's face, only a small portion of the back of his head. *Make him move. Or at least want to move, but how?* She wanted to ask Marga a question but feared they might be overheard.

A gust of wind rattled the tops of the plant life around them and pelted them with a smattering of dirt particles that and Sky jumped. She had to wipe some dirt out of her eyes when the man moved. He turned his face toward them and Sky's heart jumped into her throat.

"Are you going to attack me or just watch me all day?" Loov asked.

Sky attempted to scream with excitement, but nothing would come out. She sprang to her feet recklessly and fell over the bush in front of her. "Loov," her voice cracked. Tears swelled in her eyes and trickled down her face.

"Loov," she called, scrambling to her feet and racing toward him.

"Sky," Loov said and crawled out of his hiding place. He snatched Sky off the ground in a big bear hug.

Marga, who had changed back to her human form, strolled up to them.

"I thought you were dead," Sky cried into his shoulder.

"Almost." He sat her back on the ground.

"Marga, this is Loov. Loov, Marga," Sky introduced them.

Loov shook her hand while glancing over her shoulder to the spot where she and Sky had hidden. "Where did it go?"

"What?" Sky exchanged a grin with Marga.

"That creature. I could have sworn it was with you. It came around before. I didn't dare test it so I just kept still. I could have sworn it was out there again when I noticed you."

"Oh, I'm sure it's still out there somewhere." Sky smiled. "So, what happened to you? I went to find you."

"I was wounded but managed to get away by going toward the Roowks. This meant I had to hide out for a while until they withdrew their troops. When I returned home, you were gone and so was Mika," Loov started.

"Ah, I hate to interrupt but should we join the others. We need to get out of here before the Roowks come for us," Marga said.

"Good point." Loov gathered up his things and they all headed back to the others.

While they walked back to the wagon, Sky filled Loov in on what had happened to her since he left for the battle. She told him how Keal had saved her life and finally got down to the Black Fairy and what had brought them here.

Loov explained how he found out Mika had a small group hunting her and he took off after them. "I bypassed them before you entered the Black Fairy's domain because I didn't think it would be a happy reunion. Those that Mika are with are thirsty for blood." He related how he had passed the Roowks who had delivered her to the Black Fairy. "I greatly feared for you and I didn't dare cross into her lands. She is powerful and would detect me instantly. Then her land changed before my eyes. Roowks came out of the woodwork. I kept myself concealed and learned who they thought you were. Anyway, it was through spying on them that I found my way here."

When they got back to the others, Sky introduced Loov to Sanya, Feeleep, and Sariah. They quickly started forward toward the road once more. Sky and the others told Loov their plans on starting a war and how they would need help to defeat the Roowks.

"Well, I can take Keal and go to our people. I still have enough sway that I should be able to get a small army together," Loov said. "But, there is one major problem."

"What's that," the others asked.

"There is a Roowk army waiting for you. They fear you now and are on an all-out hunt for you. Every crossroad is being watched by a large force. We may have to travel cross country the entire way back to that battlefield and at night," Loov suggested. "I'm not even sure any of us will be safe when we separate to recruit people to fight. They know you were here and will be suspicious of anyone coming out of these lands."

"That's not good," Keal acknowledged.

"Or, it could work to our advantage. If we can somehow get by the lines and then let the Roowks know we got past their army, it could draw them to the battlefield," Loov said.

"That is a good idea, just how do we do that?" Feeleep questioned.

"Well, we have about a day's journey to figure that out. Although we may have to ditch the wagon sooner than that. We will need to be able to hide at a moment's notice," Loov informed the group.

"It's a good thing we have the world's best scout on our side." Sky winked.

"Thanks, but I'm not that good," Loov said and blushed a little.

"You're right. I wasn't talking about you." Sky laughed and the others joined in.

Loov wore a confused look. "What's so funny?"

"Well, you know that creature you were worried about back there? Let's just say it is on our side, is an excellent scout, and deadly when it needs to be," Sky said.

Loov glanced around the area, expecting to see the strange creature keeping pace with them just a short distance away.

"I'm the creature," Marga said. "I transform into it."

"No." Loov started to shake his head but everyone else's nods stopped him.

"It's a curse but it has turned into a blessing," Sanya said. "She has saved our lives numerous times now."

"I'm sure she is going to have to do it again," Loov commented.

The sun had started to sink behind the western horizon when they finally reached the road. With a much smoother surface to travel over, they agreed to keep traveling into the night. They decided to sleep in shifts to try to keep everyone as fresh as possible. Since Loov and Marga were the best trackers and scouts, they took opposite turns with Loov taking the first watch.

Sanya drove the wagon at a slow pace to allow Loov to check the area ahead of them for any hidden dangers. It was close to midnight when they reached the edge of a forest and Loov brought them to a halt. He had Sanya drive the wagon up into the trees where it wouldn't be spotted easily. The sudden stoppage woke everyone up.

"There is a squad of Roowks up ahead and those we left behind are giving chase," Loov declared.

"So what are we going to do?" Keal asked.

"It's time to ditch the wagon," Loov said. "We also need to make some decisions how we want to proceed."

"Like where do we split up and who is going with whom?" Sanya said more than asked.

"Exactly," Loov agreed. "Keal and I will need to peel off sometime to try to bring at least one army."

"Feeleep and I can't really recruit an army but we can get the word out that may bring others," Sariah said.

"Especially if they believe this could be the end of the Roowk's rule," Feeleep added.

"*Again*, how are we going to do this?" Keal stressed.

"My suggestion…" Loov paused to make sure he had everyone's attention. "Keal, Feeleep, Sariah, and I go to find help, while Sky, Sanya, and Marga head for the battle zone."

"I agree," Feeleep added. "I think once we are away from you three we should be able to move about without raising too much suspicion. Plus, you three together make a pretty powerful group to contend with."

"So, we sneak through the Roowks' perimeter and then split up?" Sky questioned.

"No, if we still agree that once you are through, you can get them to give chase to lead them to the battlefield. It might be better if we wait until they follow you. We should then be able to move about without any hindrance," Loov said.

"So, we can keep the wagon?" Keal asked.

"Sorry, that might be too much of a giveaway. Your sore legs are going to have to tough it out," Loov said.

"How are we to let them know we're through their lines after we *are* through?" Sanya questioned.

"Oh, I think that is an easy one," Sky interjected. "If we quietly take out some of the line on our way through, they are bound to notice sooner or later."

"That's what I had in mind." Loov smiled sadly at Sky. "It's not a very nice thing to think about, but they *will* kill you if they catch you, so think of it as self-defense."

"We've had plenty of it already," Sanya said. "War is an ugly thing. Hopefully, we can make this the *last* one."

"There is one thing. They will have Dijinnis on the line. You might have to target them too," Loov said and frowned in the moonlight.

The thought of killing slaves, who were her people, saddened Sky. The look on Sanya's face told the same story. Sky gave a quick nod to indicate she understood but didn't know if she had the strength or will to do it.

"I know it's hard. But you are setting them free. If we don't succeed in overthrowing the Roowks, death is their only release from bondage," Loov pushed.

"Let's just find a spot without any Dijinnis," Sanya said.

Sky, Sanya, and Marga prepared light packs with a few supplies and weapons for their dash to the battlefield. After exchanging goodbyes and good lucks, Loov accompanied them into the forest to find a spot to cross the Roowk lines. Loov carried Marga's pack as she took off into the darkness to check on the situation.

Sky, Sanya, and Loov continued to creep forward, trying to make as little noise as possible. The calls of night time predators, insects and a river running nearby aided them in their efforts. The moon was almost full and filtered through the forest canopy, creating enough light to negotiate the terrain.

Marga returned after about a half hour absence. "There is a line of Roowks and Dijinnis about a half mile ahead," Marga whispered. "They mean business. They have trip lines and lookouts in the trees. They almost saw me. If one hadn't adjusted his position in a tree, I wouldn't have seen him."

"Did you find a good place to cross?" Loov questioned.

"Yes, but we're going to get wet."

"The river?" Sky questioned.

"Yes. It is deep enough and slow enough we may be able to swim upstream without having to fight our way through," Marga said. "It is a warm night and the water temperature isn't *that* bad."

"Okay, so how do we let the Roowks know we are through without getting caught?" Sanya questioned.

"I have my bow. Maybe if we are lucky. They will think we aren't through yet," Sky whispered.

"It may work, plus, it may take them a while to find your trail if you use the river," Loov added. "I can follow you to the river and aid you from there if there are any surprises."

"I guess." Sanya didn't sound too convinced of the plan.

"The bad news is, all our stuff is going to get wet and we will be going against the current," Marga explained.

"Might I suggest using some rope and tying it to each other so no one gets swept away," Loov suggested.

"Good idea, if we had some rope," Sky said.

"I have some. I never go anywhere without it." Loov patted her on the shoulder.

Marga transformed in front of Loov, and his eyes widened with shock. He shook his head in disbelief as she led them through the forest. She took them to a spot where they could easily get into the water. The large black river moved slowly along in the moonlight. The sound of rapids in the distance created a soft roar.

After changing only her head back to human, Marga whispered, "I'll stay like this as I *am* a stronger swimmer."

Loov secured the rope around Marga's shoulders before creating a little slack and tying Sky and Sanya onto the line. "Good luck," he whispered and the others nodded.

Marga entered the water first, wading out to where she could still touch the bottom. Sky followed as the next link in the chain, with Sanya bringing up the rear. The water's cold touch created goose pimples at first, but eventually they got used to it.

Sky noticed the slight pull of the current when the water reached over her waist. The rocky bottom of the river made her struggle to keep from falling all the way into the water. Eventually she picked her feet off the bottom of the river and started to swim upstream. Her water soaked clothing made the going difficult. If it hadn't been for Marga pulling them along with her powerful body, Sky guessed she and Sanya would have been carried downstream.

Very few trees extended their branches over the river, allowing the moonlight to illuminate the entire area around the river. Sky kept her hands and feet paddling while watching the shore for any sentries. It wasn't until she scanned the area behind them that she spotted the enemy.

There was one Dijinni and a Roowk on the side of the river where Sky and the others had entered, and a lone Roowk on the opposite side. They were using the trees to hide from anyone approaching from the other direction.

With the constant battle against the current, it seemed like they were barely making progress in getting behind the guards. Even after they had created some distance between them, Marga kept them out in the water. Sky's slight discomfort with the water temperature began to change rapidly. She struggled to keep her teeth from chattering while continuing to swim in Marga's wake. She wanted to ask Marga how much farther when another Roowk appeared ahead of them.

The Roowk stood on a large rock right next to the shore. Sky wondered if Marga had spied him when she changed direction, angling farther away from the shore.

We will have to fight if he spots us now. We are behind the lines. How can we keep him from raising the alarm? Sky put her foot down to feel that they were only in about three to four feet of water.

Suddenly, Marga stopped swimming and the current started to carry them away from the man.

What is she... The Roowk stared right at them, prompting Sky's heart rate to increase.

The Roowk climbed down off the rock and started walking along the shore. It appeared he was trying to figure out what they were.

Sky slipped the bow off her back and retrieved an arrow, forcing her to put her feet down to keep her head from sinking under the water. Marga floated past her and then the tug of her and Sanya's weight on the rope nearly pulled Sky backward off her feet. When the Roowk was almost in line with Sky on the shore, she rose up out of the water and let her arrow fly.

The Roowk fell forward into the water with a loud splash, prompting Sky and the others to glance back toward the other guards not too far behind them.

"Are there any more?" Sky whispered.

Marga had already started swimming toward the shore. Sky and Sanya followed her lead and they hurried to the bank. They had just stepped out of the water when another Roowk arrived and appeared to be checking on the disturbance.

Before Sky could silence him with another arrow, the Roowk rose the alarm.

"They're coming," Marga said, with just a human head.

18

Sky and the others began to sprint away from the Roowks when the forest behind them erupted with activity. A line of torches sprang to life, extending in a line as far as they could see in each direction. Horns rang out, announcing the breach in the Roowk lines.

"Follow the river," Marga's human head said from on top of the monster before it changed back. She then raced off into the trees.

Sky and Sanya dashed through the forest, dodging obstacles in the dark to best of their ability. Every so often a branch would scratch them across the face or arm, or a tree root would snag one of their feet, tripping them. Whenever one fell the other would help her up before racing forward again.

While trying to avoid any major collisions with trees or other objects, Sky continued to scan the area for Marga or anything else that might be moving around them in the darkness. Her and Sanya's heavy breathing and thudding footfalls blocked Sky from hearing any sound of pursuit. Despite the aching stitch in her side and the burning in her lungs, Sky pushed herself forward.

Attempting to glance over her shoulder, Sky almost smacked head-first into Marga, who had changed back into her human form.

"Whoa, slow down. They don't yet know what's happened, but let's keep moving." Marga spun on her heels and continued to follow the river.

Sky welcomed the change of pace and slowed to a brisk walk. "I thought...they would...have been...hot on...our tails." Sky puffed through gulps of air.

"Me too." Sanya panted. "It looked like we woke up an army back there."

"We did. An army facing the wrong direction. It looks like our idea worked, at least for the moment." Marga led them down a trail, one she had already traveled before.

"Do you know the way to the battlefield?" Sky questioned after catching her breath.

"Yes, I had Feeleep show me on the maps. The river will take us some of the way. It will branch out and form the smaller river where we'd caught fish before we reached Feeleep's house," Marga said.

"So, we find the road and make for the battlefield?" Sanya asked.

"I don't think we can cross those open plains on the road without being seen. At least in the daylight," Sky added.

"You're right. We are going to attempt it south of the road and at night," Marga continued.

"I've been thinking. You know a sure way we can set the Dijinnis free, at least for a while. Destroy the dars," Sanya said while they continued to march at a fast pace.

"And that won't hurt the Dijinnis?" Sky questioned.

"Nope. Look at me, I'm currently free because mine was destroyed. It will make sure they are free, at least for the duration of the battle. That could give us a great advantage. You would only have to use the magic of the dark jewel until we destroy the dars," Sanya explained.

"And the Roowks will have the dars there?" Sky asked.

"The Roowks always have each Dijinnis' dar wherever they take the Dijinnis. They fear they will lose control if it isn't in close proximity," Sanya said.

"Is that true?" Marga questioned.

"No, the magic of the dar can hold a Dijinni from opposite ends of the planet," Sanya said.

"Okay, do you know where they keep them when they travel?" Sky queried.

"Yes, there is a special wagon which will be heavily guarded. If we take out that wagon with the dars and you stop the using black jewel's magic, the Dijinnis will be able to use their magic against the Roowks," Sanya said.

"That sounds like a plan. We may need help to gain control of that the wagon though," Sky said. "Even without Dijinni magic to protect it, I'm sure it will have heavily armed guards."

"Yeah, we may need Loov's help on that one," Sanya admitted.

"I just don't know if we will get a chance to speak with him before the end," Sky added.

"So, the three of us might have to capture it by ourselves and that will be a huge task," Sanya said.

"I wish we would have thought of it before we separated." Sky ducked under some low hanging branches to avoid being hit in the face.

"Me too. I wish we could get a message to him." Sanya followed Sky under the same branch.

"Perhaps there is." Marga smiled. "Speaking of which, I think it's time I take a look around once more. I don't want to miss anything. Just keep following the river and I'll return."

"You're *not* going back to find them. What if you get into *trouble*? How will you let us know?" Sanya questioned.

"I might just check the options. Besides, I think the risk is greater if I'm not prowling than if I am. I will be careful. Just follow the river until you reach the plains. I should be back by then." With that Marga transformed and slinked back into the forest.

Sky and Sanya pushed on through the night. Fatigue started to overpower them with the rising of the sun. They struggled to lift their legs over rocks, tree roots and small bushes. They hadn't seen or heard any signs of pursuit and it had been several hours since Marga had left. The landscape had slowly changed for the last mile. The thick forest trees started to thin and instead of lush grasses and shrubs, smaller areas of prairie bushes and weeds popped up.

"There's the plains." Sky pointed through an opening in the sparse trees about a half mile ahead.

"I think we should take a short break before we try to cross it. If we aren't fresh, we won't be fully ready to fight or flee," Sanya suggested.

"I won't argue with that." Sky yawned widely.

They found a spot under a tree at the edge of the plains where they wouldn't be spotted easily from the ground or air. After drinking some water and eating a hurried meal, they decided to take a quick rest. Sky remembered feeling grateful that her clothes had dried out before she fell asleep.

Sky awoke to a loud constant noise in the distance. It took her a moment to remember where she was, then her heart sank. The sun shone directly in the center of a cloudless sky, telling her it was around noon. *Oh no.*

"We slept too long." Sanya sprang to her feet and began scanning the plains.

Sky joined her. "Do you see anything?"

The noise, which sounded like a combination of rattling chains, dogs barking, whistles and calls, continued to grow with each passing moment. The source of the racket was difficult to lock down because it seemed to be coming from multiple directions.

"What is it?" Sky searched in every direction to spot the source.

"Whatever it is, I don't think it's good. I think it's the Roowks. We need to move, *now*."

"Why would they want to make so much noise? We can hear them coming from miles away," Sky questioned.

"I think they want to drive us. They know we are past their lines and now they are going to push us into some kind of trap. Come on." Sanya picked up her pack and scurried out onto the plains.

Sky followed after her. "And where is Marga? I hope she is okay."

"Me too. We should probably keep a good distance from the road. I think that would be like waving a banner saying, here we are come and get us," Sanya said.

They raced out onto the open plains, running low to the ground. Their heads swiveled back and forth in an effort to spot the source of the increasing noise. They used the sparse vegetation as much as possible, zigzagging through rock structures and small ditches.

Out of the corner of her eye a strange sight caught Sky's eyes. "Birds." She pointed to the sky.

From out of the southern sky a black mass grew and extended toward them rapidly. In a matter of minutes the air directly above them was full of large black birds with red eyes. The flock circled them in a tornado-like fashion, squawking a harsh call. Every so many seconds, one or two birds would dive bomb Sky and Sanya, forcing them to duck.

"I don't think we are going to make it." Sanya shooed away a bird.

Sky had her sword out and managed to wound a couple of the flying pests so the others didn't dare get to close. "Just keep going. And try to think of something."

The calls from the birds had drowned out the racket meant to drive Sky and Sanya, still they raced forward. The ground all around them exploded, throwing dirt and rocks in every direction, filling the air with clouds of dust. The flying debris forced Sky and Sanya to cover their faces to protect themselves from the flying projectiles. The birds rose higher in the air to avoid the bombardment.

"What's happening?" Sky screamed as another explosion knocked her off her feet and sent her flying into Sanya, wiping them both out.

"The Dijinnis are attacking us. They are casting spells at us." Sanya sprang back up and helped Sky to her feet before they started fleeing again.

"What are we going to do?" Sky noticed all around them a massive army was closing in.

"I think we should surrender." Sanya breathed heavily.

"WHAT? I could try to *use* the stone."

"That won't help us. Our people wouldn't be able to do magic, but they would be defenseless and there would be no one to fight the Roowks." Sanya stopped running and raised her hands in the air.

Sky sprinted a few paces past her and then gave up as well. She sheathed her sword and walked back to Sanya. "I guess we will have to trust in the prophecy again."

"They will find out about the stone." Sanya gave Sky a sad look. "They will make me a prisoner once more and I will have to answer all their questions. I'm sorry." A tear rolled down her cheek.

Sky felt a chill spread through her body at the pitiful expression on Sanya's face. She looked totally defeated, like her life was ending. *What am I supposed to do?* An overwhelming sense of loneliness crept over Sky when she realized Sanya would soon be working for the Roowks.

The explosions stopped but the birds continued to circle them like a tornado, with their shrill squawking. The Roowk army closed the circle tighter until they were in a tight bunch about ten yards back from Sky and Sanya.

After a short pause where they all stopped and stared, a massive Roowk, at least two feet taller than the rest and double the width, stepped forward and raised his hand. The birds flying in their non-stop circle, separated and departed the scene. For a brief moment, silence reigned.

"Snar," the large Roowk barked after the birds vanished.

The sea of Roowks and Dijinnis began to part off to Sky and Sanya's left. A few seconds later, the head Roowk who had delivered her to the Black Fairy emerged from the crowd. His eyes locked onto Sky's.

"Yep, Klook, that's the one we're lookin' fer," Snar said.

"And who's that with ya? A Dijinni without a dar. We'll have to change that." Klook snapped his fingers and another ripple in the crowed started behind him. A Roowk carrying a box, like the one Sky had seen when they took her sister, stepped out into the circle. When he opened the lid Sanya gasped and staggered forward like a drunken man. Her hands shook as she put them on the dar, losing all her self-control.

"Now, tell me everythin'," Snar ordered and Sanya spilled all their plans to the Roowks.

Tears filled Sky's eyes and she dropped to her knees. "Sanya, no."

The Roowks seized Sky, stripped her of her weapons, and bound her tightly. When they found the dark jewel, the Roowk who snatched it held it away from him as if it might somehow infect him with a contagious disease.

"So, tis true. Put it with the dars." Snar wore a worried expression.

After the search they threw Sky on the ground, while several Roowks took a couple of hard kicks to her midsection. Sky cried out as pain erupted in her body. Then a serious debate started on how to deal with the golden opportunity given to them.

"I say we kill er now and end this nonsense," one said.

"Wait a minute. Why not use er an' the information to crush all opposition to our reign," another added, which brought several agreements.

To Sky's horror, she listened in as the Roowks planned a deadly trap for her friends in which she would be the bait. They would take her to the battlefield in order to give the other races hope, before they unleashed everything they had on her friends.

"Then we'll leave ta lile princess's head on a pike in the middle of ta battlefield," one laughed and the others joined in.

What am I to do? No matter how hard Sky tried, she couldn't see an option that would save herself or anyone else.

A Roowk picked her up off the ground like a sack of wheat and threw her over his shoulder none too gently. She bounced around on the Roowk's bony shoulder for what seemed like a half hour, before being tossed in the back of a wagon. Tears streamed down her cheeks and, although there seemed to be a lot of activity around her wagon, she refused to look at anyone.

She didn't lay there very long until the wagon started moving. The Roowks appeared to be in high spirits as if they were heading to their final battle where victory was certain.

Among the deep guttural speech, a familiar voice spoke to her, "So, yer the one?"

"Grawk." Sky sniffed and her voice cracked. It took her a moment to spot the Roowk striding along the side of her wagon.

"How are ya hangin' in thar, kid?" Grawk's voice carried a sad note.

"All of my friends are going to die." Sky cried softly.

"Easy. You've already done defeated the Black Fairy. You'll get out of this," Grawk said.

"They are going to kill me," Sky said and a long moment of silence followed. Grawk hadn't left but he was walking while staring at the ground. *He knows what they are planning to do and he feels bad.*

"Will you do me a favor?" Sky swallowed the lump in her throat.

"I can' get ya out of this."

"No. Stay with me...until...the end?"

"I don'" Grawk seemed to be having trouble speaking.

"Please. I don't want to go alone," Sky pleaded.

"All right," Grawk promised. "If I culd help, I wuld."

"Thank you."

"I have duties to perform, but I will be back before..." Grawk disappeared from view.

The wagon rolled along the plains all that day. It wasn't until late afternoon the first trees started to appear, indicating the end of the plains. No one checked on Sky's comfort all day. Her wrists and ankles were extremely sore and she had to keep adjusting her body to ease the cramps that kept invading her muscles. She resolved not to cry anymore, but to face her death with her head held high.

The Roowks continued to march even after the sun had set. By the position of the moon, Sky guessed it was somewhere around midnight when they reached the rolling hills of the battlefield. The smell of rotting carcasses permeated the air, turning Sky's stomach.

Instead of setting up a normal camp, the Roowks ran a cold base, hiding the majority of their forces and the Dijinnis back in the trees on the northern side of the battlefield.

It was difficult for Sky to figure out what was happening as the loose talk from earlier in the day had stopped. *How are they going to convince the other armies to attack? They have to make it look like I'm in control.* Sky continued to try to figure out how the Roowks were going to use her.

"Ya hungry?" Grawk whispered.

"Yes."

Grawk helped Sky into a sitting position and then fed her some strange meat and water. He didn't speak the entire time and wouldn't meet Sky's gaze.

"Are there others like you?" Sky questioned.

"Wha' ya meanun?" Grawk finally looked into her eyes.

"Good Roowks, not interested in war and power."

"More than ya know. Jus' wantin' peace."

They fell silent and Grawk fed her some more.

"Ya should get some sleep." Grawk said after she had finished eating. He helped her to lay down.

As much as she wanted to, Sky couldn't sleep. *Maybe death will be a welcome relief.* Her head pounded with lack of rest when several Roowks, including Grawk, showed up in the early predawn light. The group surrounded her and her bands were cut.

"Ya'll do what yer told. The results for yer disobedience will be severe," said Klook, the massive Roowk from the day before.

"You're already planning on killing me. What more could you *possibly* do," Sky said defiantly.

"Who says the punishment will be fer ya?" Klook laughed and snapped his fingers.

Another Roowk pushed a Dijinni into the circle and then shoved her to the ground. When Sky finally registered who it was her heart leapt for joy. There on the ground in front of her lay her sister, Masha.

"Masha." Sky sprang forward into her sister's arms.

"Sky." Masha hugged her back.

The two of them cried while they held each other. Asking each other how they've been.

"Very touching." Klook grabbed Sky by the arm and tossed her away from her sister.

"Noo!" Sky screamed.

"Now, pay close attention," the large Roowk said and turned his attention to Masha. He drew a knife out of his belt and threw it into the ground next to Masha. "Slave, cut yerself across the forearm."

To Sky's horror, her sister picked up the knife with a shaky hand and drew the blade across her forearm, creating a deep gash. Sky tried to rush to her sister's aid but received a brutal kick from Klook, knocking her back gasping in pain. Masha didn't stop at just one, but repeated the motion a second time before the Roowk told her to stop.

A tear rolled down Masha's face as she dropped the knife and clamped her hand over her injuries. Klook finally allowed Sky to go to her sister's aid. After tearing some cloth off the bottom of her shirt, she tied off her sister's wound.

"As ya can see. If ya fail to do as yer told, ya'll be forced ta watch yer sister carve herself ta pieces. Is that understood?"

Sky had to take a calming breath through gritted teeth. "Yes," she hissed. A rage started to turn inside her stomach like a pool of lava ready to explode. It took all of her self-control to not lash out at the hateful creature.

"So, yre goin' ta take this lile staff." The massive Roowk retrieved a long pole with a crystal that resembled the black jewel fastened to the top of it. He stabbed the staff into the ground next to Sky. "Out ta the middle of the battlefield and stand as if yer goin' ta bring some ancient magic ta life. See that hill which is slightly taller than the rest?" Klook pointed.

Sky followed his finger to the spot indicated. "Yes."

"That's where ya'll stand."

"For how long?"

"Until our enemies are defeated. A small group will escort yer sister so they will be standing just below ya. Any funny business and ya'll get ta watch yer sister's death." The Roowk then turned right to Grawk. "Before she climbs the hill, shackle hur legs together so she can' run."

"Yes, sir," Grawk responded.

"Get going."

Sky helped Masha to her feet as a small group of six Roowks, including Grawk, escorted them out onto the rolling hills. They traveled the base of the hills to keep out of sight, twisting and turning like a snake through the grass.

When they reached the bottom of the desired hill, four of the Roowks broke away to scout the area. Grawk came forward and stooped to put some shackles on Sky's legs. He wore a sad expression.

"I'm sorry, kid," Grawk spoke so softly only Sky could hear. "Wish I culd help ya out of this."

Sky put a hand on Grawk's shoulder. "Thank you for your kindness. I will never forget you."

"I would've thunk the Black Fairy would've given ya sum help. I mean, ain' she yer great-grandmother or sumthin'? That's all I'm sayin'." Grawk gave her a sad smile.

"My grandmother. The stone..." Sky's hand clutched at her chest to feel the present Sarvina had given to her.

19

"My grandmother's stone." She noticed the other Roowk eyeing her curiously, so she slowly released the stone and lowered her hand. She turned as best as she could with her feet chained together and crept up the hill. Her bindings kept her from taking big steps. She used the staff with the fake black jewel to help her climb without toppling over.

About halfway up the hill, Sky's free hand returned to the crystal hanging around her neck. *Grandmother, what am I to do?*

When she reached the top of the hill, a large army stretched across the border of the southern portion of the plains. Glancing over her shoulder, she noticed the top half was filled with Roowks and Dijinnis. Everyone seemed to be staring at her.

This is going to be a slaughter. What am I to do? The tension in the air was thick and oppressive, like fog trying to choke off the light.

You will be able to influence one item to aid you, Sarvina's voice sounded inside her mind.

"Grandmother?" Sky muttered to herself, and for a moment she felt at peace.

Yes.

What item? A person, animal, sword...

The item can be living or inanimate. It is your choice.

How long will I be able to influence this item and in what way? And how am I to know which item to choose? Sky questioned.

Suddenly it was as if Sky had been lifted off the ground by a giant bird and flown into the air. She could see the whole of the battlefield below her, including a small pale blond girl holding a staff in the middle of the rolling hills. *Is that me?*

Yes.

Are you showing me another vision?

Yes.

Sky surveyed all that lay before her. She could make out all her friends and Mika positioned among the army to the south. She also noticed the lines of Roowks and Dijinnis secreted behind her friends and surrounding the whole of the battlefield.

How am I to help them without the real stone? The Stone? Do you know where the stone is? And can I influence it from this far away?

Yes, I know where it is, but I cannot tell you how to work the stone. I am not its creator so I cannot control it.

Then how am I to use it?

Sky zoomed back toward the ground but not in the direction of her physical body. She flew into a group of trees where a large enclosed wagon made of steel sat surrounded by armed Roowks. The vision carried her through the exterior of the wagon so she could see its contents. Hundreds of small wooden boxes which contained dars filled most of the wagon, but there on a square red cushion rested the black jewel.

Only its keeper can work the stone. Anyone who tries to wield it will only call its master.

Wait. Wait. So I can't control it? And if I try I will...Can I control its master?

Yes...and no. You will be able to hold him here but not control him.

Sky was moving again. This time she shot back into her body. *What am I to do?*

Hold on to my crystal and project your voice. Sing child. Music is a powerful weapon. You must not release the beast too soon or the lives of your friends will be at risk.

But I don't know how to sing.

Sarvina's voice faded from her mind with a final soft, "Sing."

Sky's eyes snapped open to see the armies marching toward her. The ground vibrated to the pounding feet and a rumble rose across the hills. She glanced at her sister and then in the direction of the wagon.

The pounding in Sky's chest surpassed the thudding footfalls of the advancing armies. In her mind's eye she pictured the stone in the back of the wagon. Slowly and softly Sky started to hum. Her voice cracking from the strain. *Use your magic, dummy!* With her magic, her voice took strength and the humming became a melodic tune, spreading warmth through her body.

To Sky's horror, in the corners of her vision she saw that the battle had started. As if from a great distance away, she could hear the conflict. There were explosions, the clash of metal on metal and cries of distress and pain. Arrows and spells zipped past her in all directions.

The thought of her friends being caught in the Roowk's trap increased her drive to reach out to the black jewel. Her humming changed notes rapidly as if it followed a long forgotten song, one that someone had locked inside her. The music continued to increase, gaining strength, filling her whole body with power and light.

Her vision of the battle, which had been limited to flying objects and the occasional spell exploding here and there, was now raging all around. Dijinnis used their magic to hammer men with shields and swords, while Roowks finished off weakened pockets of resistance. Soldiers fought all around the base of the hill. Sky figured she was safe until she accomplished the task of calling the demon. Once the Dijinnis lost their power, the Roowks would be on her.

At the base of her hill, Masha protected Grawk and the other Roowks. She wasn't really launching attacks but simply blocking any incoming assaults. A flash of black sped past Sky and attacked an unsuspecting Roowk, killing him instantly.

Marga. My friends, sounded somewhere in the back of Sky's mind. The need to protect them surged through her, and she could no longer contain her song to just a hum. Her mouth opened and with the aid of magic, the melody spread rapidly over the battlefield, causing a momentary stoppage in the fight.

Sky's magic created a volume that cast her voice for miles in all directions. In her mind she could picture the dark jewel filling with magic, which radiated a dazzling purple light. The light shot out through the roof of the wagon in a purple pillar and arced southward.

The battle scene changed when Roowks ordered Dijinnis to the wagon. Several of the Roowks below charged up the hill toward Sky, while Masha took out a knife.

No, Sky's mind screamed when the cloudless day grew dark, like an early dusk.

The ground shook violently as the massive black demon from the underground lake landed next to the wagon. A swarm of his black flying minions filled the sky, casting shadows over the battlefield. With a swing of his massive fist, the creature smashed the wagon to pieces. It snatched up its black jewel and then its eyes locked on Sky.

A tug almost pulled Sky off her feet when the demon reclaimed its prize. The purple light, which had brought the monster, formed a link between Sky and the foe. A wave of horrible, graphic images flooded into her mind prompting a desire to pull away from the demon.

Keep singing. Sarvina's voice spoke softly to her.

Release me. The deep angry voice of the demon shot through her like a bolt of lightning, creating a painful burning sensation.

The jewel, which had created a purplish light, turned to a dark green. At the edges of Sky's vision the battle changed. All of the explosions stopped and no more spells whizzed by in any direction. The cessation of magic forced the Roowks to deal with their enemies in ways they weren't prepared. Decades of relying on the Dijinnis' magic had lessened their hand-to-hand combat skills. Roowks began to fall all around the battlefield.

To Sky's relief her sister dropped the knife and broke free of the Roowks below. She raced up the hill toward Sky with a shocked expression.

Not only were the other armies battling the Roowks, but the winged devils controlled by the demon attacked everyone around the destroyed wagon. They decimated the Roowks who had been protecting the dars and were creating an ever widening buffer zone around the demon.

RELEASE ME!

Sky's body began to tremble with pain. Her knees shook so violently, she was having trouble remaining upright.

You can hold on, Sarvina comforted.

RELEASE ME!

The song changed tone with Sky's pain level. The pitch reached an earsplitting level, forcing those around her to retreat. Masha paused a dozen feet away and clamped her hands over her ears while recoiling. Arrows rained down around Sky and her sister, who covered her head.

Loov sprang into her vision and contended with a small group of Roowks charging up the hill. His skills were superior to those of the Roowks and he cut them down with almost every swing of his sword.

RELEASE ME!

The heat from the demon grew so intense Sky thought she was going to burst into flames at any moment. On the opposite edge of her vision, Sky spotted Mika and other men cutting down fleeing Dijinnis. Targeting them with arrows and other weapons.

NO!

Don't let go, Sarvina encouraged.

Then Keal appeared, following in the same path Loov had taken. He carried a long bow, loaded and ready to shoot. He pulled back his bow and let his arrow fly. It struck Masha in the midsection, sending her backward down the hill.

Sky's heart stopped. And with disbelief, Keal fitted another arrow and shot Loov in the back, dropping him to the ground where the remaining Roowks finished him off.

Sky ripped her eyes away from the demon to Keal who wore an expression of evil delight. His eyes seemed darker than the demon's when he drew out another arrow and took aim at her.

"NOO!" Sky screamed as she stopped singing.

The green light vanished, along with the demon and his winged devils, with a roar of thunder that shook the ground. The pain caused by the demon was nothing compared to the heartache of Keal's betrayal and the deaths of Loov and her sister.

Keal released the string, launching the arrow directly at Sky.

Sky's rage and anguish released a power she didn't know she possessed. The arrow shattered against Sky's spell as it reached out and crushed Keal.

"What did you do?" A terrified Feeleep appeared out of nowhere, looking as white as a cloud.

Sky staggered forward. "He killed…he killed…he killed…my sister, Loov." She collapsed sobbing in Feeleep's arms.

"WHAT?" Feeleep screeched above the raging battle sounds.

"He shot them with arrows." Sky cried, pointing to the fallen.

Marga appeared with her monstrous body and human head. "We still *need* to destroy the dars. The Roowks are recovering." She glanced in the direction of the smashed wagon.

Feeleep set Sky on her feet. "No time for sorrow now. We still have a job to do."

All around them, the battle began to intensify among the survivors. The Roowks, who had been in retreat mode after suffering heavy casualties, regrouped with the restoration of the dar's magic and their Dijinnis. The Dijinnis, who had also suffered great loses while temporarily losing the use of their powers, succumbed to the will of their masters once more. All of the gains made by the armies opposing the Roowks, began to disappear.

You still have work to do, Sarvina's voice sounded in Sky's mind, giving her strength.

Sky cast one final glance in the direction of her sister and Loov. She swallowed the lump in her throat. "I have an idea. Feeleep, recreate the demon and his pets and me right where we were before the spell broke! Marga, you and I will have to destroy the dars."

A moment later, the demon and his winged devils appeared where they had been before, with a beam of green light connecting him to Sky on the hill. The illusion created the desired panic. The Roowks scattered away from the destroyed wagon in all directions. It also had a strange effect on other areas of the battle as well. Roowks appeared to think they had lost control of the Dijinnis again, giving up on their commands.

A surge of rage and deep sadness flashed through Sky as she raced to the lifeless body of Keal. She snatched up his bow and arrows, then raced after Marga. Surprised Roowks pointed their fingers at her and regained their composure after recognizing Sky from the hill.

When they were within fifty yards of the wagon, the attack came. Spells hammered them from all angles and armed Roowks rushed forward to finish them off.

Marga was a tornado of teeth and claws, ripping any Roowks in their path to shreds. Sky used her magic to try to deflect the incoming spells. A firestorm burned the tall grasses all around, filling the air with thick white smoke. The heavy plumes actually aided them by blocking the vision of the Dijinnis attacking them with magic. The spells came in wild and off the mark, but a wall of Roowks still continued to hinder their progress.

A spell caught Sky and tossed her into a patch of burning weeds. She cried out and sprang to her feet. Swatting frantically, she extinguished the flames that caught hold of her clothing and burned her leg. *Fire!*

Sky dashed to one of Marga's victims, tore off a strip of cloth, wrapped it around the tip of an arrow, and then stuck it in the fire. After the flames had caught hold of the cloth, Sky fitted the arrow and shot it into the smashed up wagon. She repeated the process several times until the wooden cases holding the dars turned into an inferno.

The Roowks, realizing the Demon was an illusion and the fire was about to consume their most prized possessions, raced toward the burning wooden boxes. Their efforts to regain control were too late as the heat of the blaze caused the dars to explode. At first it was only a few loud pops here and there, but the first couple of detonations started a chain reaction. The remnants of the wagon, boxes, and dars exploded in a blinding white light that shot a hundred feet in the air. The shockwave flattened everyone within a mile perimeter around the blast zone. Dust, dirt, and other bits of debris rained down on everyone.

The massive destruction brought an instant stop to all of the fighting. Everyone stood around covered in dust, staring at the massive crater where the wagon used to be. Moments later, the Roowks began fleeing into the forest.

Marga, in her human form, rushed to Sky and gave her a tight hug. "We did it."

Minutes later, Sanya appeared and all three stood in a tight embrace. Tears of joy and sorrow streamed down their faces.

When they released each other, Sanya and Marga beamed at Sky, who hung her head.

"What's the matter?" Sanya asked.

"K—keal be—betrayed us." Sky cried.

"WHAT?" they both questioned.

"H—he k—k—killed my sister and L—loov," She stammered and dropped to her knees and buried her face in her hands. "I helped so many but I couldn't save them."

"Why would Keal turn on us?" Sanya questioned as she and Marga picked Sky up off the ground and comforted her.

Everyone but the Roowks wandered around the battlefield, trying to piece together what had happened. Dijinnis with huge smiles passed, exchanging hugs and celebrating their freedom with excitement. A few skirmishes between Dijinnis and those who were trying to exterminate them came to a halt when the attackers realized the Dijinnis had their freedom and could strike back.

"Who saved us?" Some Dijinnis questioned.

"Did the Odreshinik come?" others asked.

"Where is the girl who was on the hill?"

"Please don't tell them," Sky requested. She didn't feel like celebrating. The deaths of Masha and Loov weighed heavily on her, squeezing her, making it difficult to breathe.

"Let's find Feeleep and Sariah," Marga suggested and they began walking back toward the hill.

Slowly, the questions began to change.

"Isn't she the one from the hill?"

"I think she's the Odreshinik," others exclaimed, and a small gathering started to follow Sky, Sanya and Marga.

By the time they reached the hill where Sky had stood, not only were the Dijinnis following them, but so were peoples of all races who had been involved in the battle. Sky felt empty inside and wished to find a secluded place where she could cry. The energy she had expended from the battle threatened to steal her ability to function properly.

Feeleep, wearing a large smile, met them at the base of the hill. "She's alive!"

"Who?" Marga asked.

Feeleep stared into Sky's eyes. "Your sister." He motioned with his hand to the side of the hill where Sariah and another Dijinni appeared to be assisting someone lying in the grass.

Sky's heart began to race, spreading life back to her limbs. She broke away from the others at a full sprint until she reached her sister. Tears of joy streamed down her face as she slid on her knees into an abrupt stop next to Masha.

Sky cradled her sister's head on her lap. "Oh, Masha, I thought you were dead." Tears of joy ran off her cheeks to splash on her sister's face.

"If the arrow had been a little higher, she would have been," Sariah said, as she finished tying off a bandage around Masha's midsection.

"I never would have thought my sister was the Odreshinik." Masha smiled.

"Well, I had to do something to save you."

20

"Maybe we should set up camp," Feeleep suggested after Sky had sat with Masha for a time. "We have supplies."

"Plus, I think you are going to have to address these people at some point." Sanya motioned to the large crowd which had encircled them.

Sky had forgotten about all the Dijinnis and the other armies who were watching them. *What do they want from me? Don't they know they are free?*

"I think you should go to them," Marga suggested.

"Only if you come with me." Sky nodded to all of her friends.

"I will stay with your sister," Sariah said and smiled, while the others agreed to join Sky so she could greet everyone.

Sky, joined by her friends, went to the people. She thanked all those who had helped defeat the Roowks, listened to those who had lost friends or loved ones, and shared in the joy of the freed Dijinnis.

By the time she had finished meeting with everyone, Sky felt wiped out. She wanted something to eat and a place to lie down and go to sleep. To her great relief, camp had been set up while she made the rounds, and a feast prepared.

Masha was doing a lot better. Sky sat with her and they shared all that had happened to each other since the day the Roowks took her. It saddened Sky to hear of her sister's enslavement, with the pain and humiliation she'd had to endure.

Masha wore a huge smile and constantly shook her head. "I still can't believe my sister was the chosen one." Masha confessed she hadn't even heard about the prophecy of an Odreshinik until after she had been taken by the Roowks.

Soon, Sky's exhaustion turned the feast into a blur. Her mind screamed for sleep and her eyes drooped heavily. She felt someone leading her away from the party and taking her into a tent.

###

The next morning Sky awoke to the sound of heated voices. Masha was already awake, sitting on her cot, listening to the discussion.

"What's going on?" Sky questioned with a wide yawn.

"I don't know. It sounds like someone has taken prisoners and they're trying to decide what to do with them." Masha met Sky's gaze.

"Roowks?" Sky questioned.

"I don't think so."

The door to their tent opened and Feeleep entered. "Some people wish to meet with you."

"Who?" Sky swung her feet out of her cot and began tying on her boots.

"Some prisoners have been captured and there is a debate on what to do with them," Feeleep said.

"And why would they care what I have to say?" Sky stood as did Masha.

"It seems one of the prisoners begged to see you." Feeleep turned and held the tent flap open for Sky and her sister.

"One of them knows *me*?"

"That's what he claims." Feeleep escorted them to an area just outside the camp, where a crowd had gathered and the heated discussion continued.

In the center of the crowd stood Mika and several other boys ranging from Mika's age to manhood. All of their clothing was torn and burned and they had multiple cuts and bruises wherever their skin was exposed.

Sky's emotions ran the gamut of feelings once more. Rage, sorrow, and pity all flooded through her, changing with each new thought. *They killed Loov. They're only boys. Maybe they're sorry.*

Before Sky reached the location a large excited pes almost knocked her down. Dek leapt about her, trying to lick her face.

"Hey, Dek." Sky petted the animal, scratching it behind the ears before making her way into the circle.

The argument seemed to be more about what they were going to do with these murderers who had been killing Dijinnis during that time when they didn't have the use of their magic. One group pushed for ending their lives while another wanted to show mercy.

Everyone fell silent when Sky entered the circle. All the other emotions Sky had been feeling disappeared and had settled on pity. Mika looked pathetic, his gaze still held a lot of hatred toward her.

"So, what am I supposed to do?" Sky whispered to Feeleep out of the side of her mouth.

"They wish you to pronounce judgment on their crimes," said one of the Dijinnis, keeping Mika and his group under control.

"They murdered our people," another shouted.

"And how many of our people has your kind slaughtered?" one of the boys sneered.

"But we didn't have a choice," a Dijinni claimed.

"And we were just trying to protect ourselves," a boy next to Mika yelled. "What if the Roowks would have won the war?"

"You killed my father with your plans." Mika stared hard into Sky's eyes.

Sky shook her head slowly and tears filled her eyes. "I'm sorry, but you killed your father with *your* plans and *your* schemes. You put your trust in the wrong person. Your friends here." Sky waved at the other boys. "They will only bring you misery and sorrow."

This statement seemed to anger Mika, "My friends have kept me alive. They would give their lives for me."

"Would they have saved your father if they could have?" Sky questioned.

"Yes." Most commented and nodded.

A tear rolled down Sky's check. "So, why did one of them shoot him in the back?" Sky's voice rose with agitation.

All of the boys and young men began proclaiming their innocence.

"What are you talking about?" Mika questioned.

"It took me a while to piece it together. You sent Keal to get me out of the house. I imagine Loov talked about the Odreshinik, so you sent Keal to find out. Then after we found Sanya, Keal dropped back to inform you. You weren't all that eager to overtake us, but drive us. Am I right?"

"Yes," Mika answered.

"It was your plan all along to use me to overthrow the Roowks. Then when Keal returned with Loov and Keal told you what would happen to the Dijinnis magic, you devised a plan to wipe us out," Sky said.

"Yes." Mika answered with defiance. "After he told us it would only temporarily detach you from the dars, we decided to not give the Roowks another chance of using you in the future."

"Well, it was Keal who killed Loov. I saw him shoot Loov in the back with an arrow, right before he tried to kill me," Sky shouted, tears rolling down her cheeks. "So, it was *your* man who killed your father. A member of *your* team."

"What? You're *crazy*." Mika appeared shocked. "Keal wouldn't do that."

"He would and he did. I think he knew Loov was good at discerning signs and understanding situations. He couldn't risk Loov figuring out who killed me. H—he shot him in the back while he was fighting with several Roowks. A—after he was shot, the Roowks easily overpowered him." Sky began to cry harder. Her knees shook and she clutched Masha to remain upright.

Mika tilted his head to the side slightly and then glanced at his friends faces. They had all turned pale but shook their heads and denied any knowledge of that part of the plan.

Mika's body began to tremble. "What have I done? It's true. M—my dad taught me how to discern things. Your sorrow and their expressions, I h—helped kill him."

Mika dropped to the ground and buried his head between his legs. He started to sob. Dek approached him cautiously and nuzzled him softly. Even the other boys acted stunned, suddenly realizing what they had done. They hung their heads and grew silent.

"What should we do with them?" asked one of the Dijinnis, who had been arguing before.

All of the boys, except Mika, stared at Sky with fearful looks. Mika continued to cry with his head down.

"Let them go," Sky replied.

This statement shocked the boys—they couldn't believe what they had just heard. Several protests rose from the crowd.

"But they murdered our friends and family."

"They must pay somehow."

"Are you leaving it up to me?" Sky shouted and wiped the tears from her eyes.

Immediate silence fell.

"It was war. They were thinking of helping their people. If they will swear never to attack us again, they may depart in peace. Besides, who would be their jailer and where would we keep them. Who wants to be their executioner? We will let them go if they promise to never declare war against us. If they break this promise, they will not receive mercy again. Besides, in their own way they played a part in the prophecy, which means they helped set you free." Sky swirled a hand in the air as if motioning toward all that had happened.

"Yes, let them come forth and swear it," several in the crowd shouted.

"Does everyone agree?" Sky called to the gathering which agreed with a positive response.

Mika finally lifted his tear-stained face. He looked bewildered by Sky's decision. His head swiveled back and forth as he watched, one by one, each boy make his way to Sky.

Each boy stepped forward and made an oath never to attack the Dijinnis again. After they had all finished, Mika climbed to his feet and, with Dek at his side, approached Sky.

He had trouble maintaining his gaze with Sky's. "I—I'm sorry. I promise I will never to attack your people again."

Sky put a hand on his shoulder. "Take care of yourself, Mika. You have Loov's legacy in your hands. Do him proud."

"I will. I promise. Thank you for your kindness. I wish I had shown it in return."

"We're young. You never know. Our paths may cross again."

"I hope so." Mika smiled weakly.

"Me too."

Everyone watched as the small group of boys departed southward toward their own lands.

###

They spent the next few days burying the dead and resting from their trials. All the Dijinnis were eager to meet Sky and thank her for setting them free. Sky warned them it was only a temporary release and they could still be imprisoned by another dar.

"We need to decide where we want to go," Masha said one day while she hung out with Sky, Marga, Sanya, Feeleep, and Sariah. "We can't stay here forever."

"No, we can't." Sky took out the crystal Sarvina had given her and stared at it. "I think we should go see Grandmother."

"Well, that's where I'm going no matter what. I want to be with my daughters again," Marga added.

"I think that is where Feeleep and I want to retire. The Rikits are still out there. That may be the only land where we would be safe," Sariah added.

They remained in the valley another two days, relaxing and recovering from injuries. Sky spent time with her sister, trying to talk through her grief of Loov, Keal's betrayal and death. She felt sorrow for their loss and regret for what she had been forced to do to Keal.

"You did what you needed to do to save us all," Masha repeated for the umpteenth time.

Sky announced to the camp where she, Masha, and her friends were heading. The majority of the Dijinnis decided to follow them. Small groups here and there decided to go in search of missing family members first, before proceeding to Sarvina's land.

Sky cautioned them to be careful because they would still have the curse of the dar and could fall under its influence once more. "This time I won't be able to help you. I doubt I could get anywhere near that demon's lair before his little winged devils mow me down."

A large procession followed Sky and her friends off the battlefield early on the morning of the third day, since Sky had made the announcement they were leaving. The journey to her grandmother's land took about five days traveling at an easy pace, stopping for breaks and at night.

The celebration that had taken place at the transformation of the Black Fairy's was nothing compared to the party that took place at the arrival of the Dijinnis into Sarvina's land.

Choirs of Fairies surrounded the wagon chain and sang ancient tunes to welcome them.

The journey in astounded Sky and her friends. The transformation of the land was spectacular. Light had come to the forest and people had begun to farm and small communities were already popping up here and there. Flowers and plant life grew everywhere and the highway in had been rebuilt with smooth white stones. The palace itself was a spectacular sight. It looked like a giant white jewel creating its own light.

Sarvina, with a crowd of Fairies and humans, welcomed them at the main entrance to her castle. As Sky had done after the battle, Sarvina went around and greeted all the Dijinnis. Sky was grateful to her for doing it but a little sad too. She wanted some alone time with her great-grandmother, but all the Dijinnis were her grandchildren. She desired to know what to do with her life now that she had freed the Dijinnis and thought her grandmother would be able to give her some direction.

Once more, the festivities lasted way longer than Sky cared for. She, Masha, and her friends spent a lot of time together outside in the sunshine. The activities with her friends kept her mind off her wish to speak with her grandmother alone. She felt frustrated at night from not getting any private time with Sarvina but understood the demand that a kingdom with so many guests put on her.

At the start of the second week, Sky stood alone in her room one night, staring up at the stars, thinking about the other worlds and life forms her grandmother had mentioned.

"I love looking at the stars as well," Sarvina spoke out of the darkness, making Sky jump.

"You startled me." Sky patted her chest as if to calm her racing heart.

Sarvina spread her arms open and Sky jumped into them and embraced her grandmother.

"You did well, child. I'm so proud of you. I knew you could do it." Sarvina stroked Sky's long hair.

"I'm just glad it's all over," Sky said with her face buried in her grandmother's shoulder.

"Oh, I wish it were." Sarvina continued to brush Sky's hair,

Sky pushed back to stare into her grandmother's face. "What do you mean? I freed the Dijinnis from the Roowks. What else is there? Are there more Dijinnis to deliver? I want to stay here with you."

"I wish you could remain with me as well. Out of all my grandchildren, you will always be my favorite, but you have more work to do. I see great accomplishments in your future. You are not meant to stay safely within my borders. You are needed by the world and worlds outside."

"So what am I to do? Where am I to go?"

"Your part as the Odreshinik to the Dijinnis is over but a greater danger looms on the horizon. A power greater than the Roowks will soon be upon us. The demon in the keep has alerted his masters about a threat to their dominance in the universe. Evil is coming. War approaches. And you may have to lead once more."

James Todd Cochrane was born in California in 1969. He received his BA from Utah State University, where he majored in Business Information Systems with a minor in German.

A writer since elementary school, he published his first novel, Max and the Gatekeeper, in 2007.

The author writes part-time while working as a computer programmer.

BOOKS

The Prophecy of Sky

Max and the Gatekeeper (Max and the Gatekeeper Book I)

The Hourglass of Souls (Max and the Gatekeeper Book II)

The Descendant and the Demon's Fork (Max and the Gatekeeper Book III)

The Dark Society (Max and the Gatekeeper Book IV)

The Reign of Hudich (Max and the Gatekeeper Book V) in progress

NOVELLA SERIES (EBOOKS ONLY)

Centalpha 6 Part I

Centalpha 6 Part II

Centalpha 6 Part III

Centalpha 6 Part IV

Centalpha 6 Part V

Centalpha 6 Part VI

Centalpha 6 Part VII

Centalpha 6 Part VIII

Centalpha 6 Part IX coming soon

Centalpha 6 Omnibus

www.ingramcontent.com/pod-product-compliance
Lightning Source LLC
Chambersburg PA
CBHW070822120626
46556CB00002B/622